RENEGADE
CRUEX

RENEGADE CRUEX

BOOK TWO

KRISTEN MARTIN

BLACK FALCON PRESS

For information contact :

Black Falcon Press, LLC

http://www.blackfalconpress.com

Library of Congress Control Number : 2018900246

ISBN: 978-0-9979092-2-7 (paperback)

Cover Illustration by Damonza © 2018

Map by Deven Rue © 2017

10 9 8 7 6 5 4 3 2 1

To my Dad – for your unwavering enthusiasm, for taking the time to read (and reread) my stories, and for the encouragement to keep going no matter what. I love you.

PRONUNCIATION GUIDE

CHARACTERS

Arden: Ar-den

Rydan: Ry-den

Darius: Dare-ee-us

Aldreda: Al-dray-duh

Cerylia: Sur-lee-uh

Braxton: Brax-ten

Xerin: Zer-in

OTHER

illusié: ill-oo-see-ayy

magick: ma-jik (magic)

Caldari: Kal-darr-ee

Cruex: Crew

PLACES

Trendalath: Tren-duh-loth

Sardoria: Sar-door-ee-uh

Vaekith: Vy-kith

Orihia: Or-eye-uh

Ipcea: Ip-see

Chialka: Key-all-kuh

Miraenia: Mur-ay-nee-uh

Lonia: Lone-ee-uh

Lirath: Leer-ath

Eadrios: Ay-dree-os

Vaekith
Mountains

Drakken
Isle

Roviel

Volkh.qm

Miraenia

Trendalath

Dectorath

Crostan Islands

Ipcea

THE LANDS

Athia

AERID

Sunngate

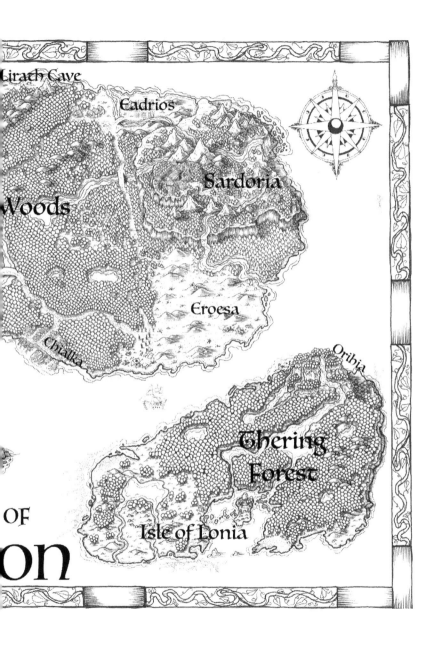

RENEGADE
CRUEX

ARDEN ELIRI

I KNOCK ON the door to Braxton's chambers, fully aware of the late hour. I don't expect him to answer, especially after the strenuous training Delwynn's put us through over the past week, but I have to tell *someone* about what just happened.

That Rydan's gone.

That he's gone because of *me*.

The torch in my left hand flickers and dances as a cool draft sweeps through the corridor. I realize I'm barefoot and shivering, with only my cloak and this pathetic fire to keep me warm.

Fire.

My mind draws back to what I'd just witnessed outside the castle doors. Rydan losing his temper. The sparks at his fingertips. A nearby tree bursting into flames. The shock and disgust on his face.

I squeeze my eyes shut to clear the image. When I finally open them again, I knock one more time.

I'm met with silence.

Just as I'm about to turn to leave, I hear faint footsteps on the other side of the door. *He's awake.* I wait somewhat impatiently as it creaks open and Braxton's platinum head pops out.

He rubs the sleep from his eyes with a yawn. "Is it time to train again already? I could have sworn I'd only fallen asleep an hour or so ago." He's about to yawn again until his eyes land on my grave expression.

"Can I come in?" I say under my breath.

He stiffens before nodding, then opens the door wider. I place the flickering torch in the wall sconce, moving slowly as I enter and approach the center of the room. I arrive just a few steps away from the hearth where I'm met with yet another reminder of Rydan. The fire dances to and fro.

Taunting me.

I turn away from the flames to face Braxton. No longer is he in his half-asleep state—he's now wide-awake, his eyes alight with curiosity and . . . something else.

Fear?

I realize that *I* must be the reason for his reaction, what with knocking at his door after-hours, all wide-eyed and disheveled. I'm surprised he still has his wits about him. Perhaps he assumes I'm bearing bad news regarding the king—his estranged father. I quickly reassure him that this isn't the case. "It's not about the Tymonds."

Braxton looses a breath, looking relieved, then closes the door quietly behind him before joining me in the center of the room. He stands directly in front of me, but doesn't speak. Neither do I. The sweet scent of cinnamon and nutmeg—from an abandoned mug on a nearby table—lingers between us. Eventually, his eyes lock on mine as he says, "I know."

I regard him with a puzzled expression, my heart thumping in my chest. "You know what, exactly?"

He averts his gaze as he takes a step back, his eyes dancing in time with the flames. "It's about Rydan, isn't it?"

"How—?"

"I saw him take off into the woods." He shakes his head, eyes still fixed on the fire. "It's a shame, really. I wonder where he plans to go. Certainly not back to Trendalath, what with your history and all."

My cheeks burn at the remark as I recall what started Tymond's tirade—our failed assassination attempt at the Soames' residence. I stroll over to an armchair and brush my fingers across its velvet-covered top. "Did you see anything else?" I ask gingerly, suddenly feeling the need to protect what little information I have left.

He raises an eyebrow. "That's an odd question. I saw him leave. I didn't know there was anything else to see."

"There wasn't," I say almost too quickly. "It's just that . . . Rydan and I sort of got into a heated argument."

What an ironic choice of words.

I try to play it off like it's nothing, but, given the amused expression on his face, I assume I'm failing. "As one would, I had hoped that our conversation was private."

Braxton shrugs before giving me a small smile. "Didn't hear a thing. Just saw the poor sap leave."

I try to keep a straight face. Originally, I'd planned to tell Braxton everything, including Rydan's newfound abilities, but our current conversation has me thinking otherwise. Something seems . . . off. It makes me want to keep my mouth shut.

My thoughts disperse when he asks, "Should we alert the queen?"

I consider this for a moment, weighing the different scenarios. On one hand, if we tell Cerylia about Rydan's fleeing, it may raise questions as to *why* he's left— questions I'm not willing to answer just yet. On the other, Cerylia seems to have an uncanny way of finding things out, and I want to build her trust, as do the rest of the Caldari.

The decision comes easier than I would have thought. "We need to tell her."

Braxton nods in confirmation. "Tomorrow then?"

Just as I'm about to reply, a clang sounds from the bell tower. We exchange perplexed expressions, then rush to the door. Braxton pokes his head out first before stepping into the dimly lit corridor. I grab the torch and follow him, closing the door gently behind me.

The bell sounds again.

The soft padding of our bare feet against the marble floors is the only audible sound as we head toward the front of the castle. The Grand Hall comes into view, and we realize we're the last ones to arrive. Queen Jareth, Opal, Estelle, Xerin, and Felix stand before us. I'm not at all surprised by Rydan's absence, but I quickly realize there's someone else missing.

Elvira.

My heart sinks.

I catch Felix's eye and he tilts his head to the empty space next to him. I fall into line. Braxton follows.

"Thank you all for coming. Given the late hour, I'll make this brief." Cerylia glances sideways at Delwynn, who seems to be hurrying to steep her tea. She sighs somewhat impatiently as he places the cup in her hands. I notice they're trembling as they fold around the fine china. "It has come to my attention that both Rydan and Elvira have fled Sardoria."

I shift my head slightly to steal a glance at Xerin. He doesn't look rattled at the news of his sister, but I notice a small tremor flicker just above his jawline—it's just enough to tell me that he's unsettled.

I turn my attention back to the queen.

"Does anyone have additional information as to *why* these two have suddenly fled the premises?" My stomach lurches as her gaze travels across the group and lands on me. "Arden?"

There's a hitch in my throat as I try to conjure up a dignified response. At first, I'm not sure why *I'm* specifically being called out, but then I realize that I'm the only one who has an actual relationship with Rydan. I'm the queen's best bet—and best source—for information.

Unfortunately for her, I don't feel like giving it up. So I lie. "This is the first I'm hearing of this, Your Greatness." Beside me, I can sense Braxton's discomfort. "This news is alarming. Would you suggest we send a search team?"

The queen regards me for a moment with narrowed eyes. I don't dare flinch for fear that she'll see right through my idiotic ploy. I immediately regret lying to her, but I know it's too late to take it back. What's done is done.

Traitor, my mind whispers.

"Xerin," she commands, "I'd like for you to go on the search alone. Based on your unique abilities, I believe you'll have better luck spotting our two refugees from the air than we would on foot."

Xerin nods. "Yes, Your Greatness."

"Then that's where we'll start," Cerylia says with a steadying breath. "As for the rest of you, I expect to see you just before dawn." She waves her hand in the air to dismiss us.

As I turn to head to my chambers, Felix shoots me a knowing look. I have an unyielding sense that this night is far from over.

I'm folding the sheets down from my bed when I get the uncanny sense that I'm being watched. I stop what I'm doing, purposely keeping very still. Although invisible, the presence surrounding me is undeniable. As it draws closer, I realize it's not a dark presence—lords know I've had my fair share of those—but rather one that is all too familiar. I'd know it anywhere.

"You don't have to hide, Estelle. I know it's you."

I glance over my shoulder, eyes focused on the doorway. First to appear is a head of wavy black hair, then a shaggy russet one. Estelle and Felix.

"What's the point of this ability if I can't go undetected?" she mutters as she finishes uncloaking the two of them. In the dim light, her violet eyes stand out even more against her mocha complexion.

A small laugh escapes me as I continue making down the bed. "You were going to reveal yourself anyway—plus, it should make you feel good that I can detect you. I assume it means our bond is growing stronger." Warmth rises to my cheeks as I accidentally shift my gaze to Felix.

With a coy smile, he raises his hands, palms facing me. "I'm not amplifying. Promise."

I turn away from them, throwing the last pillow on the floor, desperate for a distraction. Luckily, Juniper jumps off the seat of the armchair and hops up onto the edge of the sheets, circling multiple times, like a cat would do, before curling up into a perfectly symmetrical ball. She falls asleep almost instantly.

"So, to what do I owe this visit?" I ask casually as I crawl into the bed, setting the blankets around me. I remain upright out of respect, even though all I really want to do is lay down and drift into a deep, uninterrupted sleep.

Estelle approaches the bed and sits down on the edge of it. I expect Felix to follow, but he just leans against the bedpost. "Arden, we need to know what you know." Her voice comes out just above a whisper, but even so, it doesn't make her tone any less intimidating.

I do my best to ignore the mounting tension in my chest. "About what?" My voice comes out surprisingly steady.

"Don't play dumb, Arden. You're better than that."

My eyes flick to Felix. His words sting. What's worse is I don't have a response—not one they'd want to hear, anyway. Their relentless stares continue until I finally gather my thoughts and muster the courage to speak. I decide to tell them exactly what I'd told Braxton—nothing more, nothing less. "Truth is, I was there when Rydan left. We got into an argument before he ran off into the woods. I don't know where he was headed."

Felix looks at me pointedly. "What was your argument about?"

I can feel the heat in my cheeks rising again as a lump forms in my throat. *Braxton didn't ask me that.* I freeze mid-thought, fearing that my expression is going to give away everything I haven't yet said.

A shadow dances across his eyes—as if he already knows. Fortunately, Estelle eases my panic. "If I had to guess, I would say that your argument with Rydan had something to do with your failed attempt during the Soames' assassination?"

I thought with Estelle taking over, I'd breathe easier, but this day is turning out to be one colossal reminder of my many mistakes.

"Is that a fair assumption?"

I meet Felix's gaze before quickly nodding my head, afraid that if I speak, I'll turn to stone. I've told enough lies and omitted enough information for one day—hell, probably for one lifetime. I grasp the blankets and tighten them around me, hoping that they'll both get the hint and back off a little.

"Well, if it's any consolation, I'm sure he's just blowing off some steam. He'll be back soon enough." I force a smile as she pats the edge of the bed. "See you tomorrow morning, or I guess, technically, today." She angles her head at Felix. "Ready?"

But Felix doesn't move. Even as I pretend to focus on the threads holding the blanket together, I can feel his stare burning a hole in the side of my head. "You go ahead," he says softly. "I'll be right behind you."

I lift my head just enough to see Estelle shrug, then re-cloak herself as she leaves the room. Slowly, Felix circles the bed, running his hands along the knots in the wooden bedframe. He stops right in the center and places his hands on the edge of the comforter. The heat from his skin radiates through the covers to my feet . . . and up my legs. I curl up then, wishing he'd left with Estelle.

"You don't have to lie to us." His voice is gentle.

I avoid looking him in the eye, knowing that my undivided attention is the easiest way for him to amplify.

As if reading my thoughts, he says, "I'm not going to use my abilities, Arden. I just want to talk to you."

The way he says my name is so mild, so calm, that I can't help but look at him. "About what?"

He shrugs. "I just wanted you to know that I think it was really big of you to go back to Trendalath and free your friend, Rydan." His voice catches on the name. "You risked a lot—your freedom, your safety . . . you didn't owe him anything—and yet you still went. I know I've already apologized to you for how I behaved in the Thering Forest when we first met . . . but I want to reiterate how wrong I was."

The sentiment brings a smile to my face.

"You're a good person, Arden. I never should have doubted that."

My face begins to fall, but I force the smile to stay.

How can he say that? He doesn't even know me.

He pushes back from the bed and rakes both hands through his hair before putting them in his pockets. "Anyway, I was just hoping that maybe we could start over. Call a truce. Something like that." He casts his eyes toward the floor. "What do you think?"

My smile is no longer forced. "I'd like that."

He lifts his gaze, eyes twinkling. "Starting now?"

I study him for a moment, recalling the undeniable connection I'd felt when we'd first met on his ship on the way to Lonia. As soon as I'd learned of his illusié abilities—that he was an Amplifier—I'd essentially written off the connection, mistaking it for something that had unwillingly been forced upon me . . . but perhaps I'd been wrong. Looking at him now—the sincerity in his eyes, the kindness in his voice, the vulnerability in his words—I realize that our connection hadn't been due to an amplification of my feelings . . . or his.

It had been *real.*

He clears his throat, snapping me out of my daze. I realize I haven't said anything, and, by the look on his face, he's eagerly awaiting my response. "Yes, starting now."

He smiles, bows his head, then makes for the door.

I sit fully upright in bed, confused, then ask, "Do we have different definitions of *now*?"

With his hand on the door handle, he glances over his shoulder. "We've made a lot of progress for one night—wouldn't want to ruin it with my big mouth."

I'm disappointed, but I don't dare show it. "Tomorrow then?"

"Tomorrow then." He opens the door and winks at me before closing it behind him. I wait until his footsteps fade down the corridor before rolling onto my side. I pull the blankets up over my shoulders and close my eyes.

Our conversation replays in my head and, although it was good, only one phrase repeats itself over and over again. *You're a good person, Arden. I never should have doubted that.*

Without meaning to, I curl into my subconscious.

A good person doesn't lie. A good person doesn't betray or deceive those closest to them. A good person doesn't seek vengeance. A good person doesn't take innocent lives.

Try as I might to dispel these thoughts from my mind, they linger, just like the budding darkness around me. I pull the blankets up even tighter, but they don't provide much solace. How can they when I'm starting to become the very thing I hate?

RYDAN HELSTROM

"DO YOU KNOW where we are?"

Rydan stops in his tracks and turns to look at a shivering Elvira. He removes the pelt he'd managed to grab—steal—from a nearby campsite just outside Sardoria's castle walls. It's all he has for warmth, but poor Elvira, with her small, petite frame, needs it more than he does. He wraps the fur around her shoulders and tugs it tight. Her shaking begins to cease as a shiver cascades down his spine.

"No, I can't take this," she says through chattering teeth. "It's all you have left."

Rydan shakes his head in protest. "We're almost on the outskirts of Sardoria. Eventually, we'll make it to the Roviel Woods. It'll be warmer there, I promise." As the fallacy leaves his lips, he feels a twinge of guilt, but keeping their spirits high along this grim journey is likely the only thing that'll keep them alive. That, and warmth.

They've been trekking for at least a couple of hours now, and he's certain that shortly, at dawn, the queen and the rest of the Caldari will be alerted to both his and Vira's disappearance.

We need to move faster.

"Come on," he urges, grabbing Vira's hand. "If we hurry, we'll make it to the woods before sunup."

Vira coughs as she slowly removes her hand from his grasp. "I need to rest." Her voice is hoarse and strained, and Rydan immediately feels guilt-ridden for putting her through this—but, come to think of it, this actually wasn't *his* idea.

After storming away from Arden and the Queendom of Sardoria, Rydan had bumped into Elvira. She'd been in the process of saying good-bye to the dragon—about to set it free—when, out of his all-consuming anger, he'd accidentally let a spark fly from his hands. Fortunately, it had dissipated as the dragon spat in the line of fire— causing no one to be harmed—but it'd certainly gotten Elvira's attention. She hadn't seemed at all surprised by his . . . ability. She'd given the dragon one last pat before it'd flown off into the distance, then turned her gaze on him. "Are you leaving?" she'd asked.

He'd nodded, afraid that if he parted his lips to speak, he'd somehow manage to breathe fire.

"Will you take me to Chialka?"

The question that had led to this very moment.

Rydan eyes her hand and attempts to grab it again, but she promptly tucks it away. A pale, ghostly sheen cascades down her face, her lips turning an iridescent shade of blue. She begins to sway, but before she gains too much momentum, he manages to throw one arm around her shoulders, and the other underneath her legs, scooping her up in one swift motion. "I've got you," he whispers as she buries her face in his chest.

Within minutes, she's either asleep or unconscious—which one, he can't tell. The snowfall grows denser as he continues to trudge through it, growing more and more disoriented as the polar winds nip at his face. His legs tremble—eyes watering, lips quivering. He blinks a few times, although the frost on his lashes makes it difficult. They're all sticking together, making his eyes water even more. He tries to blink back the faux tears before attempting to focus on the vast expanse before him. Everything beyond his line of sight is blindingly white; the sky, the ground, the horizon. Even the tree branches are covered in inch after inch of icicles, making them almost invisible to the naked eye.

With another labored breath, he moves forward. Knees shaking, ankles twisting, he's almost certain his legs are about to give out, when he spots something in the near distance. It crosses his mind that, given his current state, it's probably just a mirage.

Please be real.

Somehow, he manages to take another step forward, followed by another, and another, until, *finally*, he's just a few feet away from what appears to be a cave.

A harsh wind knocks him to his knees, his arms quivering as he tries to keep Elvira's unconscious body above the snow. Just as he's about to surrender to the aching in his arms, the weight suddenly lifts. His eyes follow the upward motion of Vira's body as she continues to rise.

"Well, come on then. Stand up," a gruff voice says. "Let's get you two inside before you freeze to death."

Rydan doesn't get a good look at the man's face—what with his eyelashes being frozen together and all—but he decides he has no other choice but to trust him. With tremendous effort, he finds the strength to stand and follows the man into the cave.

It's dank and dark and doesn't feel much warmer than outside, but as they draw further in, a flickering light grabs his attention. He stops in his tracks as images of his last encounter with Arden flood through his mind. His gaze travels downward to his hands. He balls his fists so that his fingertips—the source of his wretched power—are hidden.

His focus diverts as the man carrying Vira begins to mumble something, but, fortunately, it isn't directed at Rydan. Shame burns his cheeks as potential reactions from the Cruex members finding out about his abilities pass through his mind. As much as he wants to go back to Trendalath—as much as he wants to pretend his abilities don't exist—he knows he can never go back. Tymond would most certainly have him exiled, if not killed. Lords, he'd probably send one of the Cruex—one of his own—to assassinate him.

Oh, the irony.

Rydan watches as the man lowers Vira and gently lays her by the fire. Her shivering ceases almost immediately. He covers her with a thick wool blanket before turning to face him.

As Rydan draws nearer, he can see that the man is not as old as he'd originally thought. His beard and deep-set emerald eyes are extremely misleading. No, this man is maybe five or so years his senior. He looks familiar, but Rydan can't seem to place where he's seen him before.

"What's your name, traveler?"

His brusque tone throws Rydan off a little. A brief moment of hesitation, and then, "Rydan. Rydan Helstrom." He chooses his next words carefully so as to not offend his gracious host. "May I have the privilege of asking yours?"

The man looks him straight in the eye as he says, "Haskell."

Intimidating name for an intimidating brute.

"It's a pleasure to meet you. Thank you for your generosity and for taking us in—"

"Right," he interrupts, "Well, I prefer to be alone, but I'm not going to leave two of my own out in the cold to suffer and perish." A small smile breaks through his dense expression. "It's the least I can do."

Rydan's ears burn at the insult, but he's more interested in what Haskell means by *two of his own*. He attempts to probe a little further, again using caution with his words. "Did you also flee from one of the kingdoms?"

17

His smile vanishes, and Rydan immediately wishes he could take his question back.

"As I just said, I prefer to be alone, which means my business is my own. I'm not here to share stories of my past with you, and you're not here to ask about them."

Rydan swallows the lump that's formed in his throat, then slowly nods his head. "Understood. Please accept my sincerest apologies."

His response appears to satisfy Haskell because he suddenly turns around and grabs two loaves of bread from a makeshift table. "Here, eat this. You look famished."

Rydan greedily takes the bread, tearing his teeth into it. It's dry, almost to the point of being stale, but he doesn't care. With each bite, he can feel his body becoming stable again.

"Shall I wake your friend?" Haskell asks. "She should probably eat something, too."

With a mouth full of bread, Rydan averts his gaze to Vira, then shakes his head. He swallows each morsel, running his tongue over the grit on his teeth. "She needs her rest. I'm sure she'll wake soon. She can eat then."

Haskell appears to weigh the pros and cons of his response, but ultimately agrees with Rydan's reasoning.

Good.

"So, whereabouts are ya headed?" Haskell asks. He grabs a canteen and guzzles some water before handing it to Rydan.

Rydan takes a swig. The cool liquid feels refreshing and utterly satisfying as it hits all the right places. He takes one more drink before saying, "Chialka."

Haskell lets out a boisterous howl, then, in a fit of laughter, slaps his knee—which is quite uncharacteristic given his unruly, gruff demeanour.

Rydan's face falls. "I don't understand. What's so funny?"

Haskell tries to catch his breath, wiping tears from his eyes, before pulling something else from the makeshift table.

A map.

"Well, I hate to be the one to break it to you," he says through a couple clearings of his throat, "but I'm afraid you've been traveling in the wrong direction."

DARIUS TYMOND

"I KNOW THERE'S something you're not telling me."

Darius braves a look at his wife, who's been following the same routine every morning. As of late, she's opted to sleep in the guest chambers, where she then wakes, dresses, and makes her way to the Great Room, seats herself on the throne, and waits, with predetermined disappointment, for him to arrive. And every day, he dreads pushing those giant doors open, knowing he has to face her.

"You may as well just get it over with," she continues, her tone sharp enough to slice through the mounting tension between them. "You and I both know it's just a matter of time before I find out anyway."

Darius regards her with a grim disposition. For over a week now, he's been weighing whether or not to tell Aldreda about the incident—or rather, *incidents*—that had taken place in the town square. Given her fragile state, combined with the emotional turbulence of her pregnancy, it's no wonder he hasn't broken the news yet.

Not yesterday, not today, and likely not tomorrow.

Best to keep that catastrophic day to himself.

But in reality, how long can he *really* keep it from her? If he's not the one to break the news, someone else will be . . .

All bets are on Clive Ridley.

The thought makes him shudder. No, Clive doesn't deserve any additional praise from his wife, and Darius will be damned if he's the one to give it to the bastard.

Just tell her the truth. The full truth.

"About a week or so ago, in the town square, the executions didn't quite go as planned. There were unexpected . . . complications."

At this, Aldreda rises from her throne, her hands resting atop her protruding abdomen. "Such as?"

Darius can't help his roving eyes. Even this far along in her pregnancy, Aldreda looks stunning. He doesn't recall her carrying Braxton so well . . .

The gut-wrenching memory of seeing his son for the first time in ten years flashes across his mind. Seeing him appear amongst the crowd—it'd been the moment he'd both waited for and dreaded. The unruly display of disrespect for his kingdom had been just cause for him to sic his guards on his own flesh and blood.

21

And what good that had done.

The resurgence of recent events sends his mind spiralling into a storm of rage and contempt. As if being yanked from the past back into the present, an unnerving feeling takes root. *I can't put her through this again. Not in her current state.*

Aldreda seems to notice his distress because she swiftly walks down the steps until she arrives at his side. Eyes alight with concern, she sets a hand on his shoulder. "What is it, my love?" Her tone has softened, as if treading lightly on an ice-ridden pond in the dead of winter.

Darius sighs before placing his right hand on her stomach. Even through her robes, it's warm to the touch. He waits a few moments, hoping to feel some sort of movement from their unborn child, but there's nothing. He presses harder, waiting for something—*anything*—but there's only stillness.

Unprecedented anger consumes him. He flings himself away from his wife, almost knocking her off balance. And then, without a second thought, he murmurs, "Children are a mistake. All of them. Just a giant waste of space and a huge disappointment."

As soon as the words leave his mouth, he knows the damage cannot be repaired. Even so, he whirls around to apologize for his unwarranted outburst, but it's too late.

With her back to him, Aldreda slowly climbs the steps to the throne. She intentionally stalls, taking more time than necessary to get comfortable before finally meeting his gaze.

"Get out," she mutters under her breath. "Now."

Chest constricting, panic seizes him from head to toe. "My Queen—"

His last attempt is futile.

"I said get out!" she screams hysterically. "Get out now!"

He can see the tears forming at the corners of her eyes, her mouth twitching with rage. Emotions are high, but the stakes are higher. One false move and their unborn heir could cease to exist. He knows better than to try to reason with her, especially right now. Without another word, he leaves. The Great Room doors slam shut behind him, the echo following his every step down the empty hall.

CERYLIA JARETH

"WHERE DO YOU imagine they went, Your Greatness?" Delwynn finishes polishing a glass before setting it down and looking his queen right in the eye.

Cerylia slumps in her seat, fiddling with the place setting before her. It's a question that's been nagging at her, one she's been too afraid to ask aloud. A wave of disappointment washes over her as she breaks his unwavering gaze. "I suppose far away from here."

He doesn't hesitate. "And why do you think that?'

Cerylia lets out a long sigh as she tugs at a stray thread. "Sometimes people do things for the sole purpose of causing chaos and upset. And, oftentimes, we'll never understand why."

"But, Your Greatness, you must realize that you've given them everything . . . *everything* they ever could have wanted," he stammers, "and so much more."

"Ungrateful," Cerylia mutters under her breath.

Her loyal advisor nods in agreement. "Speaking of the Caldari, shouldn't Xerin be back with some news by now?"

One glance out the window tells her it's nearly dusk. Delwynn is right. Xerin should have returned by now. Either he'd found Rydan and Elvira and decided to go with them, or he'd been taken hostage by Trendalath.

Or . . .

She pleads internally with herself not to think that final, persistent thought.

"Should we send someone after him? I'd be happy to go. I may not move as quickly as one of the guards," he clinks his staff against the ground, "but what I lack in speed, I make up for in efficiency."

"Hmm," Cerylia murmurs absently, tracing her finger around a blemish in the marble table. "That's precisely what we *shouldn't* do. You, nor anyone else, should go gallivanting off right now."

Delwynn clamps his mouth shut, his face twisting in confusion.

"We need to keep the remaining Caldari occupied," she explains. "We must appear *calm*—like everything is going according to plan."

"But it's not."

Somehow, she manages to repress the need to lash out at him. "Delwynn," she says coolly, "I need you to

25

keep the Caldari busy. Ramp up their training schedules. Make the assignments twice as difficult. For the time being, I want them exhausted and useless, until you hear otherwise from me. Understood?"

"Your Greatness, I must insist that you reconsider—"

Cerylia shakes her head, immediately silencing him. "That'll be all, Delwynn." She angles her head toward the door.

He seems to get the hint, and, albeit begrudgingly, exits the White Room without another word.

Cerylia waits until the door clicks securely in place before resting her forehead on the table. She closes her eyes for a few moments, saying a quick prayer to return her refugees safely to her. She remains hunched over for a while, completely engrossed in thought.

Completely unaware of her surroundings, she finally lifts her head and opens her eyes. The sight of Opal suddenly standing before her is enough to make her jump out of her own skin.

"Please forgive the interruption, Your Greatness," Opal says, swiftly taking the seat across from her. "It wasn't my intention to startle you."

Cerylia regards her with genuine curiosity. "It's quite all right, Opal. I was just," she gazes at the table, "resting."

"On the dining room table?"

A forced smile. "I assure you, everything is just fine."

Opal narrows her eyes in what is clearly disbelief. "Your Greatness, we both know that that isn't true. I was hoping, what with our past and the experiences we've shared, that you'd at least be somewhat honest with me."

The blunt hostility in her voice takes the queen aback. Whatever she *hadn't* been about to share with this audacious girl suddenly becomes irrelevant.

"It's okay to have concerns, Your Greatness. We all do." A small twinkle flashes across her jade eyes. "I promise, you can tell me."

Cerylia's irritation dissipates, leaving her to wonder exactly what Opal means.

All of the Caldari have concerns?

About what?

Is it possible they could be planning a mass exodus?

Her thoughts scatter as Opal says, "I think you're forgetting that I could be of great assistance to you." A smile tugs at the corner of her mouth. "Or have you forgotten our last rendezvous?"

Cerylia swiftly catches on. "I haven't forgotten. But, in the scenario of which you speak, we require someone who can look into the future, not the past."

Opal angles her head in contest. "Suit yourself." She pushes herself up from the table and marches toward the door. "I just thought perhaps you'd be interested to see why Rydan left Sardoria in the first place."

This catches Cerylia's attention. She quickly rises from her seat. "Tell me what you know."

"I'll do you one better." Opal extends her arm, palm up, directing it straight at the queen. "I'll show you."

BRAXTON HORNSBY

BRAXTON'S FASTENING HIS winter training coat when a hurried knock sounds at his door.

"Are you still in there? We're going to be late!"

He smiles at the sound of Arden's voice, and at her persistent timeliness. He secures the latch on his armoire, pulling on the handles to make sure it's shut. He makes for the door, fumbling with the last button on his coat, before flinging it open. Arden stands before him in black leather boots and a navy blue coat, an exact replica of the one he's wearing. "Cerylia or Delwynn?"

She looks him up and down. "Cerylia. I doubt Delwynn would care what we wear. When I woke up this morning, it was hanging outside my door."

"As one unified Caldari, I suppose it makes sense."

Arden grins before linking her arm in his. "Ready for today?"

"Against you?" he teases, walking in step with her down the marble corridor. "I've never felt more ready."

She pulls her arm from his, stopping in the middle of the hall. "I'll have you know, I'm somewhat merciless when it comes to training."

"Is that so?"

"Are you mocking me?" Arden asks, clicking her tongue in disapproval. "I'd be careful if I were you. I've done a lot of damage with these babies." She pats at the holsters on her hips, the chakrams invisible in their sheathes. "I wouldn't want our first training session to end poorly . . . for you."

Braxton flashes a toothy grin. "I'm not worried."

"And why is that?"

"It's a level playing field. We're both learning how to use our illusié abilities."

Arden punches him playfully in the shoulder. "Seems like you're forgetting one thing."

"What's that?"

"I have Cruex training under my belt."

"Were you always this confident in front of your opponents? Did you also let Rydan in on . . ." His voice tapers off as the mention of her friend stuns them both into silence.

"I'm sorry, I didn't mean—"

"It's okay," she says quietly. "Don't worry about it."

"I didn't mean it like that."

She forces a small smile. "I know."

It doesn't do much to comfort him, and he suddenly feels the need to reassure her. He lowers his voice to a whisper. "I haven't told anybody about . . . well, you know."

She lifts her gaze to meet his. "Has anyone asked?"

The question strikes him as odd, but he answers nonetheless. "No. I don't think anyone suspects that you know."

Her shoulders loosen as she exhales. "Good."

Braxton considers what he wants to ask next. "Have you told anyone else? You know, besides me?"

"No. Just you."

A flush warms his cheeks. "I'm happy that you trust me enough to tell me."

Her lips curl into a sincere smile. "Me too."

Happy to have that past them, Braxton extends his arm for her to take. "We'd better get moving. If I recall, Delwynn doesn't particularly like when his trainees show up late."

She rolls her eyes before taking his arm. "If anything, *you're* the one who made us late. Not me."

"But seeing as we're partners today . . ."

As if she'd read his mind, she breaks away from him in a full-out sprint. "See you in the courtyard!"

Braxton shakes his head, laughing, as he takes off behind her.

After a hasty reprimand from Delwynn, Braxton takes his position in the middle of the courtyard, regarding his opponent with narrowed eyes. He doesn't so much as flinch as Arden takes another calculated step toward him. Her chakrams, two menacingly sharp weapons, now rise above her head, gleaming in the white winter sky. From afar, he hears Delwynn shout a string of sentences—probably another rebuke—but most of it is indecipherable.

Snowflakes fall onto his eyelids, nose, and mouth, making it even more difficult to concentrate on his training partner. Braxton blinks through the unrelenting cold, determined to maintain his focus. He crouches, like a panther ready to pounce, watching intently as she smirks, then suddenly twirls around and releases the chakrams.

He doesn't dare blink as the blades come sailing toward him. He can see the results almost too clearly—and what a painful end it would be. Spinning, spinning, spinning. Slicing, slicing, slicing. Severed limbs. Gushing blood. He, the target, just a pile of bones.

It only takes him a split second to realize his fear is stronger than usual—amplified—which means Felix must be nearby. *Damn him.*

"Deviate!" he hears a distant voice shout. "Now!"

From his peripheral, he can see that the blades are just inches from his face—but his focus remains on Arden. The look on her face is one of complete and utter horror.

"Deviate!" she screams, but it's just another echo of their trainer's desperate plea.

The amplification of fear is too strong. Instead of using his illusié abilities, he ducks and falls to his knees, covering the top of his head with his hands. The chakram slices his skin from his wrists to his knuckles, and an unmistakeable chill infiltrates his bloodstream as if his hands themselves were responsible for creating the impending snowstorm. He expels an agonizing wail.

Merely reactionary, he plunges his hands into the snow, watching as feathery stains of crimson appear. He yelps again, but doesn't dare look up, even as he hears Arden shouting in the background. He's not sure who she's yelling at—him or Delwynn or . . . Felix?

Is Felix even here?

Within seconds, she approaches him, but he remains still—crouched and shivering. Even though his hands are numb, he's almost certain they're trembling beneath the blanket of powder. Thankfully, the pain seems to have subsided—but, for some unnerving reason, the fear is still there. Somehow, he finds the strength to shout, "Command Felix to stop amplifying this second!"

No response.

The silence is enough to answer his question.

Felix isn't here. Felix was never here.

A roar of agony escapes him as Arden attempts to lift his arms from the snow, her hands now hovering over his own. The sight of his own blood-clotted skin is enough to make him queasy, but the pain . . . it's the worst pain he's ever experienced in his life. As Arden attempts to heal him, her hands moving closer to his own, the pain only grows stronger. He shoves her as far away as possible as he scoots onto his heels, backing himself into a corner that doesn't exist.

Arden gapes at him before looking down at her hands. Her gaze then follows the bloody trail of snow that leads to her fallen comrade. She takes a few steps forward, reaching for him. "Braxton, I am so sorry." Her voice is shaking. "I can heal you." She holds up her hands. "That's what I'm here for."

He meets her request with an outstretched arm, fingers splayed. "Don't come any closer."

She desperately turns to Delwynn for help, but their trainer's eyes are fixed on Braxton. Like a fawn separated from its mother, she tentatively takes yet another step forward.

"Did you not hear me?" he growls. She stops in her tracks, face falling. "Do *not* come near me."

Arden just stands there in shock. Snowflake after snowflake sticks to her strands of chestnut hair, clumping together so that, eventually, each one is completely covered in a blanket of white.

Delwynn's voice breaks the silence. "Arden, go to your chambers. Immediately."

Downtrodden, she looks at Braxton once more. "I'm so sorry. I didn't mean to hurt you. I was only trying to help."

He casts his eyes toward the ground, refusing to respond.

"Go," Delwynn repeats, this time more harshly.

Braxton doesn't lift his head until the sound of snow crunching fades in the distance. He motions to Delwynn to help him to his feet. The queen's advisor obliges, using caution as he lifts him from his crouched position. The blood on his hands is a deep ruby color and is mostly clotted, but he knows to seek attention immediately in order to avoid infection.

Delwynn hobbles along beside him. "Care to explain?"

"Don't act like you didn't see it."

For someone more than three times his elder, the grip on his arm is surprisingly strong. Delwynn gives him a knowing look. "I meant *after* the chakrams sliced the skin from your hands."

Braxton searches for some sort of explanation, for the *truth*—but all logic escapes him. He shakes his head in defeat. "If I knew, I'd tell you."

From the agitated expression on Delwynn's face, his answer isn't what he'd expected, but he carries on anyway. "Let's head inside and get you cleaned up." He glances at the injuries one more time. "You are aware that Arden's ability to heal will be much faster than the traditional route?"

Braxton nods dismally as he continues to follow Delwynn to the healing ward. He scans the deserted training grounds once more, but, much to his dismay, Felix is nowhere in sight.

Later that evening, Braxton stirs from a sleep he doesn't remember falling into. It's only when he notices the bandages wrapped around both of his hands that he recalls the events from the day.

Training with Arden. His inability to deviate. The gushing blood. The immense pain.

What the hell happened out there?

His head in a fog, he slowly rises from the bed. A shiver cascades down his spine as a draft sweeps through the room. For some reason unbeknownst to him, the window is wide open. In the dead of winter. Irritated, he marches over to it, but as he raises his hands to close it, he remembers the bandages. With a sigh, he uses the sleeve of his shirt, near his elbow, to hook the latch into its proper place.

Much better.

His stomach growls. *When's the last time I ate?*

Suddenly feeling famished, he turns away from the window, scanning the room for food. It's then he notices something out of place. One of the doors to his armoire is slightly cracked. He specifically remembers securing it before he'd left for training.

Odd.

He approaches the armoire with caution, carefully opening the other door. Atop a neat stack of linens is an envelope. With unease, he glances over his shoulder, but no one is in the room. He's alone.

He slides the envelope from its place and flips it over. His blood runs cold at the familiar crest in the wax seal. Two swords crossing through an oval shield encased in human bones, a skull adorning the top.

The Tymond family crest.

He debates on whether or not to open it, but his curiosity gets the better of him. He slides his finger underneath the flap, loosening the wax from the paper, to find a handwritten note.

From Queen Aldreda Tymond herself.

His estranged mother.

ARDEN ELIRI

I LAY ON my back, staring at the ceiling in my chambers, hoping that my mind will still long enough for me to fall asleep—but the thoughts keep rushing in like the tide. First Rydan, now Braxton? In less than a week, I've managed to push away two people I actually care about . . . two people that actually *mean* something to me.

I sit up suddenly, for no apparent reason, other than to frighten Juniper. Clearly alarmed by my outlandish behavior, she scampers off the bed and scurries over to the opposite side of the room. As I turn to face her, I catch a glimpse of myself in a gold-plated mirror that's leaning against my three-tiered bookshelf. My hair, which was once secured in a tight bun, is now disheveled and knotted. Strands stick out every which way, reminiscent of my Cruex days. I sigh, blowing a tendril out of my face as I focus on Juniper. "I'm sorry, Juni. I didn't mean to scare you."

She stays put, eyes wide with fear. It makes me feel even guiltier for frightening her. "Looks like no one wants me nearby this week, not even you, huh?" I let out another sigh before falling into the warm, fluffy blankets on my bed. As I'm staring at the ceiling, I attempt to replay the all-too-recent events with Braxton, but the imagery leaves me feeling baffled.

It's almost as if *I* were the one causing his pain—like with every step I took, I caused him more and more agony. *It doesn't make any sense. I'm a Healer. I have restorative abilities. My gift is to make people feel better, not worse.*

I'm not sure why, but my gaze lands on the bookshelf. I flip over onto my stomach and crawl to the edge of the bed before hopping over the frame. Before I know it, I'm kneeling right in front of the wooden structure. I peruse the many titles, then pull a few from the shelves. I carry them over to my desk and open the first one, *The Power of Illusié*. I scan the first couple of chapters—preface, introduction, history—before finally settling on a more interesting topic.

Chapter Seven: Light Magick and Dark Magick.

My skin crawls—or at least it feels like it does—as I'm consumed by the accounts of dark mage after dark mage. It's utterly fascinating. With each word I absorb, a strange sensation surges through me—so strange that it causes me to break away from the text. In a way I cannot explain, I suddenly feel the need for . . .

Destruction.

Chaos.

An uprising.

But why?

The question remains unanswered as all logic and reasoning escapes me—as if it were never there to begin with. The faces of the Soames family float across my mind, but the empathy I once felt transforms into a faint echo, desperate to be heard—to be *noticed*. I'm urged to ignore it. I ricochet back and forth across my mind, over and over, until I'm finally released into an awareness that isn't my own. An attack on my subconscious would be far too kind—and whatever *this* is . . . isn't kind.

I come back to, my fingertips tingling, alive with newfound energy. The sensation continues to intensify, migrating to every muscle, every fiber, of my body—to my arms, my legs, my neck, my face. My fingers curl into my palms as I relish the way this new, yet somehow darker, energy feels.

Where is this coming from? What is happening to me?

A single blink, and I've suddenly landed in the middle of a field. Confused, I peek over the long strands of grass. Even though everything around me is hazy, I can see a small child—a young boy—running around with what appears to be a gold figurine of a dragon. Something catches his attention, and he darts off.

I get my wits about me and follow him.

I observe the area around me, trying to gain some semblance as to where I am, but it remains unclear. The boy vanishes from my sight as he enters a small cottage. I spot an open window on the side and, as discreetly as I can, run over to it, crouching just underneath the overhang. The voices carry from inside, although they're mostly muffled.

I rise just high enough to see over the ledge.

I spot the young boy sitting on the floor, moving his toy dragon along a handwoven rug, and to his left, a woman with dark brown hair—most likely his mother. As she turns to the side, her belly protruding, I realize she's pregnant.

"Go wash up," she instructs the boy.

Without any reservation, he does what she says.

I scan the small cottage, looking for clues as to who this family is, but nothing pops out at me. And yet, it feels eerily familiar in a way I can't explain.

My eyes are glued to the scene, watching, waiting for *something* to reveal itself, but just as quickly as I'd been brought here, I'm whisked back to the present—sitting at my desk, the book still splayed on Chapter Seven.

"What the hell?" I mutter to myself. Mouth dry, heart pounding in my ears, I look down at my hands, expecting them to be trembling, but they're not.

They're completely still.

I look around the room, but I'm completely alone.

And that's when I realize that something is very, very wrong.

RYDAN HELSTROM

RYDAN'S NOT SURE how many days have passed, or how long both he and Vira have been asleep, but he's almost certain they've stayed past their welcome. Using caution so as to not wake her, he pushes himself up from the makeshift bed of pine needles, leaves, and wool patches. Vira remains sound asleep. Who can blame her, especially after being locked away in the Trendalath dungeons? As someone with first-hand experience, he certainly can't.

Dim specks of light twinkle along the walls, leading him to the front of the cave. He tiptoes in that direction, shivering as a cool gust of wind sweeps through the enclosure. He crosses his arms to warm his skin, but the effort is futile.

It doesn't take long to reach the section of the cave where the path diverges. Instead of making a left to where Haskell's sleeping quarters are, he shifts his gaze to the right—to the corridor he hasn't yet ventured down. Not that he should be venturing anywhere since this isn't his home, but technically it isn't Haskell's home either.

It's a cave, formed by nature.

Nature is everyone's home.

Sound logic.

His curiosity gets the better of him as he turns away from the direction he *should* be heading. His mind taunts him to not trip and fall, which causes him to spiral even further into worst-case scenarios. If he does trip and fall, he'll likely make an obnoxiously loud noise and wake both Haskell and Vira. There's no doubt he'd lose Haskell's trust, and he and Vira would end up right where they'd started—in the midst of a snowstorm.

His paranoia begins to fade as something flashes in the distance. One step leads to another, and another, and as he draws closer, a flickering torch comes into view. He briefly wonders how it's been burning for this long, in the dead of night—but, nevertheless, he removes it from the wall sconce and continues down the cave's corridor.

As he approaches what appears to be a dead end, the sound of rocks scattering stops him in his tracks. He whirls around and holds the torch out in front of him, moving it swiftly back and forth to locate the source of the noise.

A shadowed figure looms before him. He shuffles backward, frantically groping the wall for a loose rock to use in his defense. As it gets closer, the shadow grows from large and ominous to petite and gentle. He breathes a sigh of relief at the familiar voice.

"What are you doing back here?" Vira asks with a yawn. "And what is this place?"

"Lords, Vira. You scared the living daylights out of me!" A small laugh tumbles from his lips. "For a minute there, I thought you were Haskell. I would have been in real trouble then." Even in the dim lighting, he can tell that she has no idea what he's talking about. "Come on," he urges as he walks toward her and gently pulls on her arm. "Let's head back."

A sleepy grin crosses her face. "Funny. I don't know where 'back' is."

"Not to worry." He flashes her a smile. "We'll return undetected."

If not for her half-asleep state, he's almost certain she'd be pressing him with questions—questions he'd be smart to dodge.

Not tonight.

With her arm looped through his, they walk back in the direction they came, but every now and again, Rydan finds himself glancing over his shoulder at the mysterious space he'd almost discovered. Even though everything in him tells him there shouldn't be a next time, he's convinced that there will be.

DARIUS TYMOND

ANOTHER DAY, another meeting with his Savant. Darius pauses as he reaches the doors of the Great Room, knowing full well what awaits him on the other side.

A group of men eager for his direction.

More heated arguments than he's prepared for.

An evening of squabbling and disagreement.

And Clive's leering face.

The last one sends a shiver down his spine.

He sets his shoulders back and lets out a long exhale before shoving the doors open. The men rise and all eyes turn to him, making him feel even more powerful and in control—something he hadn't thought possible until this very moment.

Avoiding Clive's lingering stare is intentional as he glides to the head of the table. It would seem his Savant expect him to sit, but the king remains standing.

"Since we last spoke, you're probably under the impression that you won't be in Trendalath for longer than a fortnight." He moves his gaze around the table. "However, given recent events, it appears we have a much larger problem on our hands." From the far end of the table, he can hear snickering—most likely from Clive— but Darius has the good sense to ignore it and continue on. "Just because securing Braxton is now first priority, do not assume that Arden's capture falls to the bottom of the list. I have a feeling wherever we find Braxton, we'll find Arden, too—as well as the rest of them."

The table murmurs in agreement as they nod their heads—all except one.

Of course.

"If I may," an all-too-familiar voice says, "what does the queen think about all of this?"

A knot forms in Darius's stomach. He resists the temptation to fidget with his amethyst ring as he moves his gaze to Clive.

The bastard who had an affair with my wife.

Clive's face is hard, weathered even more from the past two weeks. Sprouts of gray attempting to blend in with his unruly copper hair only make his age more obvious, and his tattered and stained tunic hangs from his thinning frame. It would appear this assignment has taken quite an unexpected toll on him.

Good.

Darius tries to hide his smile as he finally takes his seat, placing his hands on the table in an authoritative manner. "I don't know why you'd feel so inclined to ask such an irrelevant question, seeing as this is Savant business, for my"—he gestures at the table—"and your ears only."

Clive fumbles for his words. "I was . . . well, I was under the impression that the queen would be informed of such activities."

The king remains stone-faced, hoping his current disposition expresses his level of supremacy. By the look on Clive's face, it does. "And *why* would you be under such an impression?"

The shift in the room is palpable as a couple of the Savant members whisper to each other.

"Forgive me, sir," Clive says slowly, "for my lack of judgment."

Darius ignores him, turning his attention back to the rest of the table. "Would anyone else like to question my decisions? Or can we focus on the assignment?" Out of the corner of his eye, he can see Clive slink down in his chair.

"What do you suggest as our plan of action?" Benson pipes up from the seat next to Clive.

Darius scoffs at his ignorance. *Clearly I have to do everything around here.*

Benson seems to take notice of the disdain on the king's face because he hurriedly adds, "All I mean is that we don't want to do anything rash. As always, we'll wait for your direction, Your Majesty."

Darius eyes each one of them until a glint from his ring diverts his attention. He stares at it for a few moments to finalize his thoughts. "Julian and Landon, you will be stationed in the southwest region of Aeridon." He shifts his focus to Clive, who's still pitifully slumped in his seat. "Clive and Benson will take the northeast—"

Benson seems surprised at his assignment. "Your Majesty, is it at all likely that the Caldari are in the north? The temperatures are below freezing. I can't imagine they'd be able to survive—"

Before he can finish his sentence, a member of the King's Guard bursts into the Great Room, unannounced. The entire table turns to face the intruder as he approaches Darius and takes a knee. He removes his helmet and sets it on the ground.

"My King," he says through ragged breaths. "Pardon the interruption, but I have news that I trust you'll want to hear right away."

Darius swiftly rises from his seat, resting his hands on the table. His Savant follow suit.

"We've spotted some unusual activity up north," the guard sputters, "near Lirath Cave."

"What activity do you speak of?"

The guard hesitates. "We found traces of magick— scorched trees with smoke still warm and rising—in the middle of a winter snowstorm."

The king's demeanor doesn't falter as he absorbs the information. The room falls silent. Finally, he says, "You are dismissed."

As if realizing that he may have overstayed his welcome, the guard rises, fumbling to pick up his helmet, then hurries out the doors.

Darius looks at the men around him. "Given this new information, we must change course. Disregard everything we've discussed here today, except for this."

From the way Benson looks around the table, eyes wide with ignorant hopefulness, Darius almost feels sorry for him. His Savant won't like what he's about to say, but what choice does he have?

"Each and every one of you will be stationed in the northeast near Lirath Cave," he orders. "And you will only be permitted to return when you've found my son."

CERYLIA JARETH

OPAL STANDS ACROSS from Cerylia in the bell tower. Cerylia can't help but feel shocked—confused, even—after what they'd just witnessed.

Opal had taken them back in time, to just moments before Rydan's decision to flee. Arden *had* been there. And, not only had she been there, she'd also witnessed Rydan's first encounter with his own illusié abilities.

She lied to me.

Cerylia presses her palms against the sides of her robes. "So Rydan is—"

"—one of us," Opal finishes.

"And Arden—"

"—is a liar and unworthy of your trust." She pauses before adding, "Nor ours, for that matter."

Cerylia wonders if her words fall as harsh on Opal's ears as they do hers. "I don't understand why she would lie. She's been truthful—dare I say *loyal*—up until this point."

Opal blows a stray hair from her face as she leans against the open tower window. Against the backdrop of the glimmering starlight, she looks as though she belongs to another realm. "Do you *really* know that? How can you be so sure she's been truthful? What if everything she's told you has been a lie?"

"How can you say that?" Cerylia demands with a shake of her head. "She's one of your own. Why are you suddenly so quick to doubt her intentions?"

Opal regards the queen with solemn eyes. "I'm doubting her because of what I just saw—what we *both* just saw."

Cerylia tries to push the scene from her mind, but it's too fresh—too vivid—for her to escape. "Perhaps she has a good reason for keeping it secret."

Opal smirks. "It's not exactly a secret any longer."

A stretch of silence passes between them before Cerylia says, "And it will remain a secret, between us, until I say otherwise."

Opal turns to face the queen, lips pursed. "I'm afraid I can't do that. I'm loyal to my Caldari, and once I know something that they need to know, I tell them. I am them, and they are me. We are one."

Cerylia takes a deliberate step forward before grabbing the girl by the arm. She winces at the pressure. "As long as you reside here, in *my* castle, you will do as I say." And then, through clenched teeth, "If you'd rather leave and freeze to death, go right ahead. But while you're here, my wishes take precedence. You are one with *me,* and me alone. Understood?"

Opal nods quickly before gently tugging her arm away from the queen's grip, her eyes misty from embarrassment. "Will that be all?"

Cerylia gestures toward the staircase. "Yes. You are dismissed." She's not sure why, but a pang of guilt strikes her right in her chest as she watches the distraught girl flee down the winding staircase.

A gust of wind diverts her attention, beckoning she come closer. She approaches the opening until her bare toes almost hang off the edge, the ground below a heavy blanket of powder. As she lifts her gaze, a full moon appears from behind a dense cloud. "Tomorrow will be a better day," she assures herself.

She stills, captivated by the sight of Sardoria, before finally turning to make for the staircase. It's long and winding, and just as she's about to reach the landing, she's surprised to see Arden climbing the steps. Their eyes meet instantly. Cerylia searches her expression for a sign of running into Opal, but she looks as oblivious as ever.

She gives Arden a calculated, but warm, smile. "Just the person I was hoping to run into."

Arden climbs a single step, so that she's almost eye-level with Cerylia. For someone who's supposed to be unaware of the current situation, she radiates self-assurance. "You were hoping to speak with me?"

Cerylia nods before briefly glancing over the girl's shoulder. Arden follows her gaze. "Am I interrupting something? Were you meeting someone?"

Cerylia's not sure if her imagination's taking over, but she swears Arden's face is slowly draining of color.

"Delwynn mentioned you were up here."

There's no break in her voice. No strain. *She must be telling the truth,* the queen thinks to herself. But then again, didn't she just witness what a skilled liar she is?

Trying not to read too much into it, Cerylia continues to descend the staircase, her shoulder brushing against Arden's as she swiftly passes her. "Follow me."

Arden seems to keep pace with her as they walk the long corridors to the White Room, but Cerylia purposely manages to stay just a couple steps ahead of her. When they arrive, the queen gestures for her to take a seat in one of the armchairs near the fireplace. As Arden makes herself comfortable, Cerylia pokes her head into the hallway. No movement—just silence.

She closes the doors, waiting until they shut securely in place. When she's absolutely certain that they're alone and no one can hear them, she takes a seat in the chair opposite Arden.

The girl's been watching her with grave intent the entire time. She's the first to speak. "Is something troubling you, Your Greatness?"

Cerylia studies Arden's body language. Hands on her lap, head held high. Even though she's leaning back into the chair, her posture is impeccable. She looks, unsurprisingly, as an assassin would—poised, confident, and fearless. Cerylia catches herself straightening her own posture before answering her question. "Yes, actually. There is something troubling me." Her eyes shift from Arden's posture to her face—not even the slightest change in her expression.

"I want to apologize for earlier when we were discussing the whereabouts of Rydan and Elvira."

Arden's expression remains the same, however she does tilt her head slightly. "Apologize? I'm not sure I understand. There is nothing to apologize for."

Her response is steady and unwavering, which makes Cerylia even more irritated. "Oh, but there is," she continues with an artificial sigh. "I shouldn't have directed my interrogation at you, especially not in front of the Caldari. For that, I hope you'll accept my sincerest apologies."

Arden merely shrugs. "I didn't see it as an interrogation. You were simply asking a question, seeking answers."

Cerylia hesitates, waiting for Arden to give some sort of indication that the conversation is making her uncomfortable—to prove that she did, in fact, lie earlier—but no such indication is given. She just sits there with the same faultless look on her face.

It's infuriating.

"Well, then" Cerylia says, trying to stifle her rising anger, "don't I feel foolish?"

Arden smiles. "There's no need to feel foolish. I truly appreciate the gesture, but like I said before, there's no need for an apology."

"Of course." Cerylia presses her lips together before forcing them into a smile. "Well, I suppose that's all I wanted to speak with you about. Unless," she lifts a brow, "there's something *you'd* like to discuss?"

Now *this* seems to catch Arden slightly off guard. She swallows as her hands fall to the sides of her lap, but she maintains eye contact. "Not that I can think of."

Why does she feel the need to lie?

Why is she hiding this?

The fire in the hearth crackles and pops, but the only thing Cerylia hears is resounding hesitation. She tries to hide her disappointment. "Well, in that case, I bid you adieu. Goodnight, Arden."

Arden nods, then rises from her seat. She gives the queen a half smile before exiting the room. Cerylia sits back in her chair, stumped. She eyes the doors as Opal's concerns echo in her mind. It's the first time Cerylia doubts whether or not she's made the right decision in opening her home to the Caldari.

BRAXTON HORNSBY

WITH HIS EAR pressed against the door and his mother's note burning a hole in his pocket, Braxton's not exactly sure what he's expecting to hear, but it doesn't seem to matter because the voices on the other side are muffled beyond comprehension. If he hadn't seen the queen leading Arden into the White Room, he never would have known anyone was in there.

But, even from afar, he could tell by their quick strides and hurried pace that the topic of discussion was urgent. To his knowledge, the only urgent thing happening in Sardoria was the news of both Rydan and Elvira fleeing the premises—pretty easy to put two and two together.

Just as he's leaning away from the door, his ear almost numb from the cool metal detailing, the secondary door swings open. Startled, he finds himself face to face with Arden. The look on her face is more surprised than irritated, but that quickly changes as she shuts the door behind her. "What are you doing here?"

Braxton lifts his bandaged hands. "I came for a proper apology."

She seems to sense his sarcasm. "Very funny. If I remember correctly, you want nothing to do with me."

"What happened out there . . . it was unexpected. I may have overreacted."

"You think?" She glances between him and the oversized doors. "Wait, were you eavesdropping?"

"I couldn't help it. I saw you follow the queen in there and wanted to make sure everything was okay."

Her mood suddenly turns sour. "Everything's fine. I should probably get back—wouldn't want to hurt you again."

She pushes past him. As much as he wants to grab her arm, the bandages keep him from doing so. "So you injure me and *I'm* the one who's supposed to apologize? I didn't realize we were in Trendalath."

At this, she stops in her tracks, slowly turning to face him. "You wouldn't let me *near* you, Braxton. I was trying to heal you, trying to right my wrong, and you chastised me as if you were . . ." Her voice tapers off.

"My father," he finishes.

She sighs. "It was horrible seeing what happened, knowing that *I* did that to you. That I *could* do something like that to you—"

"It was an accident," Braxton interrupts. "I know it wasn't intentional."

She doesn't seem to hear him. "But when I approached you, wanting to heal you . . . It was almost as if *I* was the one causing you pain—as if my mere presence was more harmful than any blow of a weapon could ever be." There's a faraway look in her eyes, as if she's stuck, floating in the memory.

That's exactly what it'd felt like, but he keeps his mouth shut.

Her eyes draw back to him—searching, studying.

Neither says a word.

After some time, Braxton speaks. "I forgive you, Arden."

"Thank you." She lowers her head. "And I'm sorry for whatever happened out there."

"Don't let it happen again."

A wordless exchange of shy smiles.

They're about to say goodnight when Braxton remembers the reason he'd been looking for Arden in the first place. His hand goes to his pocket as he fishes around for the note. "Can I show you something?"

Arden angles her head, then shrugs. "Sure."

Realizing their proximity to the White Room, Braxton motions for her to follow him. They round a few corners, luckily not running into Estelle or Felix along the way, before arriving at his door. He opens it, gesturing for her to come inside, before securing it behind him.

"What's the urgency?"

Her tone is playful, and as much as he wants to reciprocate, he can't. He pulls the note from his pocket and hands it to her.

"What is this?"

Braxton tilts his head, keeping his eyes on the folded parchment. "Open it."

She does as he says, reading through the lines of text.

My dear son,
The time has come to return to Trendalath. There is much to be said for the past, and even more to be gained for the future. I hope you both can forgive me one day.

Only when she gets to the end does she read aloud, "Your loving mother, Aldreda."

Braxton lets out an uneven breath that he hadn't realized he'd been holding in.

As if she has access to his every thought, Arden rereads the line that also has him stumped. "I hope you both can forgive me one day? What does she mean by both?"

"I wish I knew."

Eyes alight with curiosity, she asks, "Why are you showing me this?"

He shrugs. "Well, you were around her longer than I was . . . more recently, too. I thought maybe you'd have an idea."

She reads the note again before folding it up and returning it to him. "I'm sorry, I don't. Sounds to me like she just wants you to return to Trendalath. I mean you are her only son, the heir to the Tymond throne."

"Maybe so."

An uncomfortable silence stretches between them.

Her eyes flit from his to the floor. "Are you going to?"

"What?" he asks, taken aback. "No. Absolutely not."

"Just checking." Her lips tilt in a faint smile, but it fades almost instantly. "Are you going to show Cerylia?"

His eyes fall to his hands. He hadn't really thought about that until now. "No."

As soon as the word leaves his mouth, he's filled with absolute certainty. He makes for his armoire, shuffling his clothes around one of the drawers until he finds a perfect spot. He tucks the note in the very back before shutting the drawer. "You're the only one who knows about this, Arden. I'd like to keep it that way."

A shadow flickers in her eyes. "Looks like we both have secrets to keep."

ARDEN ELIRI

AS I SHUT Braxton's door behind me and head down the hall to my rooms, a wave of guilt washes over me. Even after the unfortunate incident during our training session, he'd still felt comfortable enough to confide in me—to share something that, if found out, would likely get him exiled from Sardoria. He'd trusted me enough to read a letter, from his *mother*, in full . . . and what had I chosen to confide in him?

Only half the truth about Rydan.

Only half the truth about what I *actually* know.

A part of me yearns to turn around and tell him everything—the other to never mention it again. I don't even recognize the person I'm becoming. Deep down, I know I can trust him and still, my feet pull me farther away.

Disgusted with myself, I continue onward toward my chambers, hoping that I won't run into anyone along the way. I'm in no mood for feathery conversations with the handmaidens, nor a tale of enemy surrender from the ill-tempered guards. I'm almost stopped by one of the servants, but he breezes past me as if he, too, wants to be left alone.

I breathe a sigh of relief as I make it to my rooms unbothered. The door closes gently behind me as I bend down to pet the circling fox at my feet. I scratch Juniper behind the ears, then pick her up and set her on top of my desk. As per usual, she curls up into a little ball with her nose tucked underneath her fur, eyes watching me like a hawk's.

I take a seat, surveying the second stack of books I'd plucked from the shelf the other night—the ones I haven't yet jumped into—and sigh. My gaze lands on the first stack, furthest to the left—*The Power of Illusié.* My hands ball into fists, and before I can understand what's come over me, I lean forward and knock the book off the stack with so much force that it scatters to the floor.

A clink sounds then, causing me to lean back in my chair and peer underneath my desk. I strain my eyes to see what looks like a silver chain peeking out of the book. Confused, I push my chair back, patting my pockets as I rise, but they no longer carry the weight of the item from my encounter with the mysterious man.

My pocket watch.

I walk around the side of the desk and kneel to examine the specimen further. As I pull on the metal chain, releasing it from the pages' grip, I start to feel lightheaded. I turn it over in my hands a few times, hardly believing what I'm seeing. It's *my* pocket watch . . . but it's no longer gold.

It's now silver with rust around the edges.

There seems to be something etched into the front, but I can't make out what it is—it's just a dark, nondescript blur. A familiar sensation creeps down my spine as whispers begin to float in and out of my mind.

As if I'm being summoned to do so, my hand suddenly flings the watch away from me. It skitters across the room as I tread on my heels until I've backed myself into a corner. The whispers grow harsher, more insistent—pleading with me, begging—as I sink to the floor and pull my knees to my chest, all the while staring at the rusted timepiece lying desolately on the other side of the room.

How did this happen? What's causing this?

I retrace my steps. I know for an absolute fact that my encounter with the two men had been real. The pocket watch had indeed exchanged hands, from the mysterious man's to my own. Rydan, too, had seen it as we'd both mounted the dragon's back. He'd thought it strange and even mentioned how I *never* brought it on Cruex missions. And when we'd arrived in Sardoria, I'd hid it in the pocket of my favorite trousers—the ones I'm wearing at this very moment.

That watch had been *gold.*

Not silver.

Not rusted.

I continue to rack my brain for a logical explanation, but it's no use. It doesn't make sense.

I gingerly place my hands on the side of the wall to push myself upright before scanning the room once more. My eyes are frantic as they land on the tousled rug, the slightly shifted armchairs, the half-open drawer in my armoire, and finally, the loose hinge on the door.

Someone was here.

How had I not noticed it before? I'd been so distracted thinking about Braxton and *his* safety that I'd completely foregone my own.

Someone knows I'm here.

Someone went looking for me, and, lo and behold, they'd found me. I'm not sure whether to flee, stay put, or hide. An unwelcome, self-imposed interrogation begins, the questions popping up so rapidly, I can hardly keep my head on straight.

Do I tell Queen Jareth? Do I tell anyone? What in lords' name am I supposed to do?

I glance from the door to my desk, feeling unusually on edge as Juniper continues to stare at me with wide, questioning eyes. Even though I'm focused on her, I can see the spherical shape of the watch glimmering out of the corner of my eye—provoking me. I march over to it and place it back where I'd found it, then firmly secure the book back on the shelf. Until I can figure out what's going on, I don't want that thing anywhere near me.

In two swift strides, I'm back at my desk. I take a deep, steadying breath in the hopes that I can tuck my thoughts and feelings away. To distract myself, I reach for a book from the second stack. Without even glancing at the title, I open it to the middle section. I scan the pages, not fully certain what it is I'm looking for, which makes it even harder to process the information I'm reading. Not like it matters though—because I can't stop thinking about that damn pocket watch.

I finally get so frustrated with my own thoughts that I slam the book shut and scoot backward in my chair. Somehow, I fight the urge not to look back over at the bookshelf. Since I clearly have no control here, my mind unwillingly wanders back to the first unusual encounter I'd had in Orihia, just after I'd met Estelle—more specifically, the dark mist that had slowly transformed into a cloaked figure.

Ribbons of crimson weave through my thoughts. At the time, I'd been warned—told I didn't belong there, with *them*—which I assume means the Caldari. But when the figure had asked me to join them . . . now that, I still can't wrap my head around.

Join who?

Not long after that encounter, Felix had opted to show me his abilities as an Amplifier, but instead of seeing him, I'd seen Rydan and the Soames boy. Rydan's persistence in completing the mission had haunted me, and so I'd wrapped my hands around the neck of the young boy, squeezing until I was certain I'd kill him. And then, as quickly as the scene had arrived, it had vanished, leaving me with an irate Felix, gasping for air.

Next—the incident with Braxton. His failure to deviate my attack had led to a gruesome injury, and even though he'd been completely aware of my healing abilities, he wouldn't let me anywhere near him. With every step I'd taken, it'd seemed I was somehow hurting him more and more—that my presence was, for lack of a better word, *painful*.

I lean forward in the chair so that my elbows are resting on my knees. I relax my neck, allowing it to hang loosely above my forearms, and slowly bring my hands together. These three scenarios—with Estelle, Felix, and Braxton—continue to replay over and over again in my mind. I desperately try to discern a pattern. I tap my thumbs together, growing impatient with the fact that nothing seems to be revealing itself.

Whether I want it to or not, enough time goes by to warrant shifting my focus to something else. Reluctantly, I lift my head. Exhaustion begins to set in as I rub my eyes. *That's enough stewing for tonight.*

I'm three quarters of the way through getting ready for bed when I hear a knock. Not bothering to wrap a blanket around myself, I go to the door and open it. When I see who it is, I immediately wish I had.

Felix leans against the doorframe. His eyes flick to my lace camisole, but his gaze doesn't linger. "Is this a bad time?"

My first instinct is to cross my arms over my chest, but I stop myself because I have nothing to be ashamed of. It's late. I'm getting ready for bed. I wasn't expecting any visitors, and yet here he is, unannounced. Although if I'm being totally honest . . . I'm actually kind of glad to see him.

"I was just getting ready for bed," I say a little too boldly, "but no, it isn't a bad time." I step to the side, trying not to notice the intoxicating scent of sandalwood as he walks by.

"Funny how I always seem to catch you when you're getting ready for bed. At this point, you're probably having nightmares about me."

"I wouldn't call them that." My candid response causes a faint warmth to bloom in my neck. *Great, so now he thinks I dream about him.* I raise my hand and pretend to scratch at something as I pass by him and take a seat in one of the armchairs.

He follows and takes the one across from me, sitting slowly—deliberately. He places his hands on his lap, one at a time, before setting his russet eyes on mine.

Even through my blunder, I manage to maintain eye contact. "I take it you couldn't sleep?"

He crosses one leg over the other. "Who says I was trying?"

"Night owl?"

He tilts his head. "Something like that."

The warmth returns. "So," I say, trying to recover from my wayward thoughts, "you decided to come *here*?"

His mouth rigs to the side. "I was hoping to pick up where we left off."

My thoughts flash to the last time he was here.

His palms on the bed.

Heat radiating through the blanket.

My legs curling up beneath me . . .

Much like they want to do right now.

"Oh?" I lean forward just enough to seem confident, but not overly interested. "And where was that?"

"As I recall, we agreed to start over." The feral look on his face takes me by surprise, but I don't show it. I can tell he feels exactly what I'm feeling.

The rising tension.

Our inexplicable connection.

I briefly wonder if I'm misjudging the situation.

I'm not.

His eyes say everything, reflecting my every thought.

It's enough to make me want to jump from my seat and go to him—but I stay where I am.

"I brought you something." He only breaks eye contact to stand and dig around in his pocket, from which he produces a small wooden carving of a ship.

As he approaches, I regard him with complete calm, but internally, my thoughts are here, there, and everywhere they shouldn't be. My breath hitches as he kneels before me, gently taking my hand and turning my palm upward. He places the ship right in the center.

I raise my hand to eye level, reluctantly shifting my gaze to the carving. It's so intricate, so precise in it's detailing, that I recognize it immediately. "Your ship."

He nods. "The one I brought you to Lonia on."

I briefly recall that Rydan was *also* on that ship, but I keep my mouth shut. "It's stunning," I say, running my finger along the side. "Truly."

"I'm happy you like it."

Only when I lower my hand do I realize he's still kneeling before me. My voice catches. "You carved this yourself?"

A proud nod. "It took me a while to make since I had to teach myself, but once I got the hang of it, it wasn't so bad."

I look at him, dumbfounded. Not only did he make something by hand for me, he also took it upon himself to learn a new skill.

Lords help me.

Even though I'm certain my heart is beating faster than a hummingbird's, my voice comes out surprisingly steady. "Thank you, Felix."

A lazy smile. "You're welcome, Arden."

The way he says my name sends an immediate chill down my spine, but not in a bad way—not in the way I'm used to. "Why this? Why your ship?"

He doesn't hesitate in the slightest. "Because it's where we first met."

I close my fingers around the carving, suddenly wishing it were his hand instead.

"And," he says, his voice lowering to a whisper, "I want it to serve as a reminder that when you need someone most, I'll be there for you."

My blood heats and it takes every fiber of my being not to pull him onto this chair and kiss him.

Our eyes lock.

A slow blink. Once. Twice. His gaze travels downward to my lips. Naturally, I feel mine do the same.

I hardly notice him rising from his knees as he leans in to brush a soft kiss to my cheek.

I close my eyes. When I open them, his face is lowered, just inches from my own. I can feel the warmth of his breath on my neck, my ears.

"Goodnight, Arden."

I watch in stunned silence as he retreats to the door, his back facing me. I want him to come back—to stay—but I can't bring myself to verbalize it.

Just as he opens the door, he turns to face me. "Is it too much to ask for a proper adieu?"

I angle my head, unable to hide the all-consuming smile on my face. "Pleasant dreams, Felix."

Later that night, I dream—but not in the way I'd hoped. Beady black eyes stare at me from the windowsill. I stay still for a moment before whispering, "Xerin?"

Alarm surges through me when the creature doesn't move, but then it hops from the windowsill onto the back of an armchair, and finally down to the ground. The transformation begins and Xerin appears, his head the only thing exposed from behind the chair.

I rise from my seat, but keep my distance. "How'd the search go? Did you find them? Are they here, in the castle?"

Those blood-red eyes focus on mine, but something has replaced their usual neutrality. *Guilt?*

Xerin shakes his head. "I wish I had better news, but the search hasn't been as fruitful as we'd hoped." He grabs hold of the fleece blanket on the back of the armchair and starts to wring it between his hands. "I don't know what to tell the queen. I can't return here as a failure."

His meaning sinks in. "Cerylia doesn't know you're here?"

"That is correct."

I give him a perplexed look. "You came to me first?"

Xerin rolls his eyes. "Again, you would be correct."

"But why?"

He glances over his shoulder at the door. "We're alone?"

I gesture at the room somewhat sarcastically. "Does it look like anyone else is here?" His gaze shifts to Juniper, who's regarding both of us with suspicious eyes. "That's a fox, not a fox pretending to be a human. You're the only Shaper here, Xerin."

He gives the fox another onceover before returning his attention to me. "I came here first because I needed to speak with you."

I muster a reassuring nod, although I feel anything but. "Which is?"

Something ominous flickers in his eyes.

I reach out to lay a comforting hand on his arm, but he retreats. "Is everything okay?"

His eyes fall to the floor. "Funny. I should ask you the same question."

His curt response catches me off guard. "Pardon?"

When he lifts his gaze, I can't help but gasp. A chill lodges in my chest. I no longer know who it is I'm looking at. Xerin's once blood-red eyes seem to have been swallowed whole by his pupils. A sea of black stares back at me.

Emptiness.

Loneliness.

Darkness.

When he speaks again, his voice is low, guttural. "You've experienced it too, haven't you?"

I stumble backward out of shock, my arms flailing behind me as I try to grab onto anything that will help me keep my balance. He takes a step forward as I continue to move back, back, back—fearing I may fall into an invisible oblivion. Finally, my hand finds the edge of a chair. I cling to it for dear life, as if it's the only thing keeping me upright. "Have I experienced . . . what?" I ask, trying to keep my voice from shaking.

He angles his head at me, and it feels as though I'm staring into the soulless existence of some deeply disturbed creature. "You know *exactly* what I'm talking about."

He's not wrong because I *do* know what he's talking about. The darkness. My twisted visions. The terrible thoughts and images that constantly plague my mind.

But how does he know?

"Xerin, this isn't you," I say, trying to be the voice of reason. "Come back."

He reaches out for me with both hands, fingers extended, palms up, and I desperately search behind me for something I can use to defend myself. My hand makes contact with what feels like a bookend and, just as I'm about to fling it at his head, a different thought crosses my mind instead.

Heal him.

I release the bookend, staring my possible demise right in the face, and lurch forward. With locked arms, I clasp both of my hands around his forearms so that he can no longer advance. I use all of my strength to keep him still before closing my eyes to focus on my ability.

Heal.

The intermittent force grows stronger.

Heal.

The tether whips and lashes, pulling me in deeper.

Heal.

I keep my eyes pinned shut until a flow of warm energy courses through my veins. I don't open my eyes until I'm certain that it's reached my hands. I peek through an eyelid, relieved to see that my fingers are glowing their stark white, although it is fainter this time than the last. I continue to call on my ability for as long as I possibly can, but when I look back up at Xerin, I begin to panic. While he appears to be somewhat placated, his eyes are still black as night.

In that brief moment, with my mind elsewhere, he breaks through his quasi-healed state, putting undue pressure on my arms all over again. I try to hold him off, but it's no use. With all the strength I can muster, I push him backward, but the force I'm met with is greater than my own. Regardless, I manage to hold my ground, the light from my hands flickering in and out of healing.

Through gritted teeth, I cry out in angst as the muscles in my arms begin to give out. He senses my weakness and pushes harder until we lose contact. As we both shuffle backward from the impact, I sense my opportunity.

Swift as lightning, I swivel a quarter-turn so that I'm adjacent to the side of my desk, grasping the bookend in the process. I look at those dead, soulless eyes and whisper, "I'm sorry," before heaving the bookend straight at his temple.

RYDAN HELSTROM

RYDAN'S GAZE FOLLOWS the bright flickering of the fire as Haskell prepares the game he'd caught earlier that morning. Vira sits across from him with her elbows on her knees, chin resting in her palm, looking even more bored and tired than usual. She seems to sense his stare because she abruptly turns toward him with her brows raised.

Cheeks burning, he offers her a small smile.

Before she can return the gesture, Haskell clears his throat, interrupting their awkward exchange. "You've barely spoken a word since you arrived."

Rydan opens his mouth to respond, assuming the comment is directed at him, but Haskell's full attention is on Vira.

She breaks eye contact with Rydan to look at their host, shoulders shrugging. "I suppose I don't have much to say, except that your generosity is greatly appreciated." She nods her head toward the game that is now roasting over the fire. "From a stamina standpoint, I clearly wasn't prepared for this journey."

"Indeed. You were severely fatigued when you first arrived," Haskell points out. "I'm glad to see that the color has returned to your face and that you're spending more time awake rather than asleep. It's nice to have company, besides just us brutes." He winks at Rydan while a deep shade of pink blooms along Vira's neck.

In an obvious attempt to save her from further embarrassment, Rydan rises from his seat and moves closer to the fire. "I know how hard it is to come by a proper meal, especially during the winter season," he says, eagerly changing the subject. "If you'd be so inclined, I'd jump at the chance to pick your brain and learn your tactics."

This doesn't seem to faze Haskell. His attention remains completely focused on Vira. "We can discuss that later." The response is jarring, but Haskell carries on anyway. "Now that you've been here for a few days, I'm keen to learn more about the two of you—and why you're heading to Chialka, of all places."

Vira shoots Rydan a worrisome glance before clearing her throat. Even so, her voice is strained. "I have family there, or at least, I *did* at one point. I'm hoping to find them."

Haskell appears to be intrigued, but skeptical. "And if you don't?"

She gives him a pointed look. "Then I'm hoping *someone* there will know *something* that will point me in the right direction. Is that okay by you?"

Rydan sucks in a breath. While that's no way to talk to their host, he understands where her frustration stems from. Her family life is clearly private and she wants to keep it that way. Haskell's intrusive questions aren't warranted—but, by the same token, Vira isn't exactly in a position to be rude. Intrusive or not, Haskell has been gracious enough to offer them the three things they currently don't have access to—shelter, food, and warmth—and Rydan prefers to maintain that access until they have concrete plans regarding what to do next.

Much to Rydan's surprise, Haskell raises his hands in surrender. "Touchy subject, I see. My apologies. I didn't mean to pry."

Vira's expression softens almost immediately. Before she can say anything else, Rydan interjects with a question. "Have you ever been to Chialka?"

A long silence stretches between them. Haskell strokes his beard, deep in thought, before saying, "I have, but it's been quite some time."

With the shadow that falls over his face, Rydan knows better than to ask more questions. He swiftly diverts his attention toward the fire. "Well, would you look at that? Our next meal awaits."

At this, both Haskell and Vira perk up, readying themselves to eat.

"If I may do the honors," Rydan says as he gestures toward the meat.

Haskell nods. "By all means."

Rydan serves each of them a portion of rabbit as Haskell pulls a couple of loaves of bread from a nearby cabinet. "I hope these aren't stale."

Vira eyes her plate hungrily.

"Well, go on. Dig in," Haskell urges as he heads back to his seat, passing out the bread as he goes.

It doesn't take long for all three of them to devour the food with not even a single string of meat on the bones left behind. Haskell lets out a belch so loud that it bounces off the cave walls, echoing down the many corridors. Rydan glances over at Vira, expecting to see a look of repulsion, but instead, she's laughing.

"That was delicious," she gloats as she wipes the corners of her mouth on a spare linen. "Thank you for sharing your hard-earned meal with us."

A spark of mischief dances across Haskell's eyes. "It wasn't as hard-earned as you might think."

Rydan briefly wonders what he means by this, but his curiosity flees as Vira says, "I apologize for the way I behaved earlier, Haskell. I've never been in a situation where I'm malnourished and my body is fatigued. I suppose it has a greater effect on the mind that I'd realized."

Haskell waves her apology away. "There's no need to apologize. I'm just grateful you're feeling better." He slaps his hands on his knees, startling Rydan, then stands up. "I'll be at the northwest end of the cave if you need me."

He smiles. "I've also left some maps and a few texts at your disposal. Feel free to do with them as you please."

Rydan follows the direction of his gesture, his gaze landing on a wooden table across the room. The candles sitting atop it are already lit. He can't tell if this is Haskell's indirect way of trying to get rid of them, or if he's simply being hospitable. Based on what he's seen so far, he wants to assume it's the latter. "Thank you."

Haskell nods before grabbing a torch from one of the wall sconces, then disappears into the darkness.

ᛋ   ᛋ   ᛋ

Hours later, after poring over text after text and map after map, Rydan can't help but feel somewhat disheartened by the progress—or rather, lack thereof—he and Vira have made. The journey to Chialka is by no means a difficult one, but they'd be a lot better off if a) there wasn't a horrendous blizzard afflicting the northern half of Aeridon, and b) if they had some other form of transportation besides their own two feet.

When he looks up, he's surprised to see Haskell approaching them . . . with a full burlap sack over his shoulder.

"Is it already time for dinner?" Vira asks as she shuts one of the books. "I feel like we just ate." She opens her mouth to say something else, but stops herself, as if realizing what she's just said is rude.

"What are we having?" Rydan asks for her.

Haskell heaves the bag off his shoulder and sets it down near the fire pit. "Salmon," he says with a goofy grin. "Lots of it."

Rydan slowly rises from his chair, watching intently as Vira skips over to Haskell and begins sorting through the fish, admiring his catch. Rydan takes a few steps toward them, using caution not to get too close. He's not sure why, but something doesn't feel right. "Did you catch all of that today?"

Haskell hardly pays him any attention as he and Vira begin to organize their next meal. "I sure did. Aren't they a beaut?"

Rydan continues to approach them, meticulous with his next words. "So you're telling me that you caught that entire sack of salmon in the waging blizzard outside?" He points to the entrance of the cave. "Care to explain how?"

This finally seems to get Haskell's attention. He stops what he's doing, then looks up at Rydan, his expression darkening. "I don't appreciate my methods being questioned. I've been doing this for a very long time. I've gone ice fishing in much worse."

"Haskell . . ." Rydan shakes his head, his eyes growing wide. "You never left."

He merely shrugs. "You must not have noticed me slip out. You and Vira were nose-deep in those texts."

Rydan looks from Haskell to the cave entrance, picking apart his words. "That can't be. I would have seen you. I'm sure of it."

An uncomfortable silence.

Haskell straightens so that the edge of the sack falls at his feet. "Is there something you'd like to ask me?"

Vira glances over her shoulder, shooting him a bewildered look. Between Haskell's tone and the stench of fish, Rydan can't help but feel overwhelmed—and yet, he stands firm, even though he feels anything but. "I'm only going to ask this once. Who are you, really?"

"Rydan!" Vira cautions, but Haskell raises an oversized hand. She immediately falls silent.

"Who am I?" he repeats with a small laugh. "If I'm not mistaken, I've already provided that information."

Rydan grits his teeth. "I'm starting to think it's only half of the story." He moves closer to Vira as if to shield her from a lurking danger. "Tell us the truth."

The corner of Haskell's mouth twitches as he looks Rydan up and down. "I'm not the only one who hasn't been forthright. Why don't you go first?"

Usually, Rydan doesn't shy away from confrontation, but this seems . . . wrong. Like a mistake somehow.

"We shouldn't have come here," Vira says under her breath, barely loud enough for him to hear. "We need to leave."

Rydan gives a slight dip of his head to indicate he's heard her, but keeps his gaze locked on Haskell. The man's just standing there, with a few flopping fish at his feet, the others still as stone. He lifts his boot and presses down lightly on each fish until the movements cease. The only thing standing between them and the exit is this jumbled web of ambiguity.

Who's going to go first?

Although Rydan knows better than to speak again, he does it anyway. "I find it almost impossible for a group of people, let alone one person, to successfully catch the amount of fish you seem to have caught in the middle of a torrential blizzard." He takes a steadying breath. "I was facing the cave exit the entire time Vira and I were studying those maps." He points at the table for good measure. "I would have seen you leave. So why didn't I?"

Vira nudges him from behind. Another warning.

He doesn't listen. "So how did you do it?"

Haskell regards him with solemn eyes before tugging on the end of his beard. "I suppose you've given me no choice."

His sudden act of surrender isn't the least bit expected. Rydan braces himself for what he assumes will be an attack of some sort, but instead finds himself eye to eye with . . . no one.

What the . . . ?

Vira's voice is panicked. "Where'd he go?" She sweeps past Rydan and dashes over to the graveyard of fish. Her blonde hair billows behind her as she spins in circles, desperately looking for their host. "Where the hell did he go?"

Before Rydan has a chance to respond, a low chuckle sounds from behind him. He whirls around to find Haskell standing near the cave's entrance holding . . . two carafes of red wine.

"Go on you two, have a seat," Haskell says cheerfully. "We may as well discuss this over a drink. I find it's easier to absorb this sort of information after a few glasses of fine verdot."

A wordless exchange passes between Rydan and Vira as they walk over to the benches surrounding the fire pit. Haskell waits for them to get situated before sitting across from them. He pours the wine into two goblets, then leans over, extending them to his guests.

A peace offering, perhaps?

Wisps of dark smoke from an earlier fire travel up the stems of the glasses as Rydan takes them in his hands. The embers underneath the logs continue to glow, albeit faintly. He hands one of the goblets to Vira, all the while keeping his eyes on their host.

Haskell takes a brief swig of his wine before saying, "Now that we've gotten that out of the way, I suppose I'll just come right out and say it." He swirls the crimson liquid around in his goblet, glancing at both Rydan and Vira, as if urging them to drink faster.

Rydan takes a small sip. The taste is heavy and bitter on his tongue. He sets his glass down, hoping no offense will be taken.

Haskell doesn't seem to notice. "You are correct in that you would have seen me leave the cave to go ice fishing." His eyes land directly on Rydan's. "You are also correct in that ice fishing, especially in weather like this, is nearly impossible." He taps the sides of his glass with his fingertips. Hesitation lines his voice as he says, "I'm what they call a Transporter."

Vira looses a breath. "You're illusié?"

A slow nod. "Indeed. I am."

Vira nudges Rydan, as if telling him to reveal himself. He shoots her an icy glare before looking back over at Haskell. He chooses his words carefully. "And what exactly can a Transporter *do*?"

"Well, for starters, I'm able to fast-travel anywhere in the world—so long as I've been there before—and return with whatever I'd like." He gestures to the heaping pile of fish strewn about the cave, then to the half-empty bottle of wine. "Having this ability comes in handy when you've lived in seclusion for so many years."

At first, Rydan's not sure how to respond. He could tell Haskell about his own abilities, but what good would come of that? Two people—Arden and Vira—already know, and, in his mind, that's two people too many.

"It's nice to be in the presence of one of our own," Vira says with a warm smile. "I'm a Summoner."

Rydan lowers his head. *How could she give it up so quickly?*

"Ah, I see," Haskell says with a quick stroke of his beard. "Dragons are truly majestic creatures. I could have sworn I saw one flying around here recently."

A coy smile tugs at her lips. "That's because you did."

"Well I'll be damned! So they *do* still exist in Aeridon," Haskell exclaims, childish wonder written all over his face. And then, "What about you?"

The question is obviously pointed at Rydan. Seeing no other choice, he pushes himself up from the bench and kneels by the pit. He puts his hands near the logs.

When nothing happens, he reverts to his last infuriating memory.

Betrayal.

Desertion.

Imprisonment.

Arden Eliri.

Sparks instantly shoot from his fingertips, orange flames dancing wildly on the logs. He turns to face the audience he never asked for. "Does that answer your question?"

DARIUS TYMOND

"WHEN WERE YOU going to tell me?"

Darius glances up from the wooden table that's currently covered in flattened parchment scrolls and sketches of maps. He watches intently as Aldreda glides into the room, her lower abdomen protruding even more than the last time he'd seen her—when she'd screamed at him to leave.

What a pleasant memory.

He picks up a nearby magnifying glass to review one of the scrolls before answering, "And to what might you be referring?"

She swiftly strides over to the table before slamming her hands down on the wood. "Do not take that tone with me."

Darius's mouth curls into a sneer. "My Queen, with you I'll take whatever tone I please."

Given the doe-eyed look on her face, she appears to be taken aback by his cold remark, but within mere moments, she's composed herself. "I asked you a question, My King. I would appreciate a forthright answer."

His patience wearing thin, he throws the magnifying glass onto the table, almost expecting it to shatter, but the metal merely clangs against the ligneous surface. It lands just inches from her hands. His gaze travels upward—from her fingers, to her stomach, to her bosom—until it finally reaches a familiar, unyielding expression. "Your question," he says flatly, "was vague. Be more specific and perhaps I'll consider answering."

Small threads of assumption begin to weave through his thoughts. Hopefully she hasn't found out about the altercation with their son in the town square. *No, she seems much too calm for that.*

Aldreda's fingers curl into the table, but she manages to speak with unwavering resolve. "When were you going to tell me that you were sending the entire Savant to the northeast?"

Darius looses a small breath, hoping the relief he currently feels isn't written all over his face. "I'd planned to tell you," he lies, "but I only recently made the decision."

"And why, might I ask, was I not involved?"

Darius pauses to look deeper into her eyes. There's something uncanny reflected in the light blue of her irises—guilt, perhaps? He purses his lips as another, more disturbing, thought occurs to him. "Who have you spoken with?"

Her eyes widen slightly, and she bows her head before shaking it. "I'm not sure what you mean."

"Yes, you do." He gives her a menacing look even though they're not making eye contact. "*Who* have you spoken with?"

She doesn't lift her gaze. With much trepidation, she says, "Sir Hale."

Darius twists the amethyst ring on his finger round and round, his disdain growing with each passing second. "Are you sure that *Sir Hale* is who you spoke with?"

She nods unconvincingly.

He sees right through her poorly executed façade. In an effort to torment her, he murmurs, "Perhaps I should have a word with him."

"That won't be necessary," Aldreda says hurriedly. "I was just surprised that you hadn't informed me of your decision to send the Savant northeast. That's all."

"Well then, if that's *all*, I suppose you can leave."

From the pained look on her face, he can tell his words have struck a nerve, but for the first time in a long while, he doesn't care in the slightest.

Without another word, she turns to leave, but Darius's words catch her just as she's about to open the doors to the Great Room. "I hope Clive left before you had a chance to say a proper good-bye."

She stills, but as any prideful woman would do, doesn't dare look back before slamming the doors shut behind her.

CERYLIA JARETH

"WHAT WOULD YOU do if you discovered one of your own was lying to you?"

Delwynn's mid-pour when Cerylia asks the question and nearly spills the kettle's contents as he sets it on the end of the table. "I suppose that depends, Your Greatness. Do you speak of the Queen's Guard or one of the servants . . . or one of our guests?"

His attempted quip irritates her. "The Caldari," she replies curtly.

Delwynn bows his head, as if surrendering to her tone, then gathers the canisters of honey and sugar. "Did this alleged member of the Caldari approach you with their wrongdoing?" he asks as he stirs the syrup and small granules into the steaming liquid.

"Not exactly. Let's say I caught them in a lie."

"To what extent?"

Cerylia sighs. "Are the exact details relative to this conversation?"

"Forgive me, Your Greatness, but I am much more forthcoming when I have specifics to work with."

"Valid point." A coy smile tugs at her lips. "But I still can't give them to you."

Now it's Delwynn's turn to sigh. "Well, even without the specifics, I'd hope this person comes forward."

"And if they don't?" Cerylia presses.

"Simple. You approach them." He says it so calmly, as if he's stating the obvious.

"You're to say that I should . . . accuse this person outright?"

He lifts a brow. "I hope you'll spare me in twisting my words. I would advise against finding fault and pointing fingers, but instead, have a thought-provoking conversation. Ask the right questions and you'll get the answers you seek."

"And if I've already tried that?"

He smirks. "Try again."

She nods before taking a sip of her tea. "Very well."

Later that evening, Cerylia finds herself aimlessly wandering the castle grounds. Her conversation with Delwynn hasn't left her, and it continues to jab at her subconscious. Those involved in this predicament have made what should be a seemingly simple answer so much more complex. Perhaps she should have given Delwynn—seeing as he *is* her most trusted advisor—the specifics. But with Opal already privy to the information, she thinks it best not to add to the list—at least, not until she determines how to properly handle the situation at hand.

A cool gust of wind sweeps through the courtyard, sending a chill down her spine. There's a break in the seemingly endless snowstorm, but the ground is still covered in a blanket of white. Hundreds of tiny stars dot the translucent sky, each one twinkling in and out of sight—here and then gone.

She spots one that's brighter than the others, and it immediately reminds her of her late husband, Dane. His eyes used to gleam just as vividly, brighter even. An image of his face crosses her thoughts—the strong contour of his jaw; his deep-set eyes resembling that of the Great Ocean; the curve of his lips when he'd flash his trademark side smile. They'd been nearly invincible.

Until . . .

The mere thought of her past causes her to crumple onto a nearby bench. She doesn't even bother brushing the flakes of snow from the surface. So much betrayal as of late. So much unwelcome discovery. And with her recent focus on Arden's deceit, she's subconsciously brushed over the grisly actions that had led to her husband's death.

Aldreda.

The name tastes sour and rotten on her tongue. Aldreda's thirst for power has never been a secret, but to go to lengths such as this? To scheme and murder without even a fair fight? Cruel and unusual punishment—even for a Tymond.

And then there's Arden. Her need to lie—not only to Cerylia, but also to the rest of the Caldari—remains shrouded in mystery. Why would she lie about Rydan? Why would she keep such vital information not only from her, but from the rest of the Caldari? What is she so afraid of?

The thought crosses her mind to give Arden a brief visit in her chambers, but given the late hour, she's probably asleep. Or, perhaps she's awake, plotting her next lie—her plan of escape.

A chill lodges in her chest at the thought of Arden fleeing. No, she mustn't take her anger for Aldreda out on the girl. She must find a way to keep her here, to keep her secure and safe. She owes the girl that much.

The queen's thoughts dissipate as she gazes up at the night sky, looking for that single shimmering star. It flickers in the distance—a ball of fire in a sea of black. It's been quite some time since she's sought guidance, but sadly, the one person she used to go to is no longer here.

What do I do?

Everything around her stills until a mist, darker than the night sky itself, rolls over the current blanket of stars, snuffing out everything except for the moon. For hours she sits on that bench, the faint glimmer of moonlight her only company. Eventually, a long stretch of shadow casts itself over the grounds. It's there, in the absence of light, that she finally finds the clarity she's been searching for.

BRAXTON HORNSBY

BRAXTON'S SURPRISED TO hear a knock on his door, given the late hour. He tosses in his bed, hoping that whoever it is will go away, but the knocking persists. With a sigh, he slips out from under the covers and wraps a blanket around himself before approaching the door. "Who is it?" he asks irritably as he rubs the sleep from his eyes.

"It's Queen Jareth."

Suddenly fully awake, he flings the door open. "Your Greatness, my sincerest apologies. I wasn't expecting you."

She dismisses the apology with a graceful wave of her hand. "May I come in?"

Feeling like an imbecile, Braxton realizes he's standing right in the middle of the doorway—essentially blocking her from entering—and quickly moves to the side. With a sweeping gesture of his hand, he invites her to come in.

"Please forgive the late hour, but I haven't been able to sleep." He can feel her eyes following him as he attempts to light a fire in the hearth. "As much as I wish this were a friendly visit, I'm afraid my coming here tonight is of a more serious nature."

Braxton hesitates before setting the rest of the logs in place. It doesn't take more than a couple of minutes to light it—although he wishes it'd taken longer—after which he glides over to the empty chair across from the queen.

"I have something important I need to ask you."

He does his best to keep calm, but his thoughts are like the flames he'd just brought to life—sparking all over the place.

Is she going to ask me about Rydan?

Does she know what Arden and I both know?

His eyes flick to the armoire.

Does she know about the note from my mother?

"It's about your family."

He stares at her, stifling any trace of emotion on his face. A long silence stretches between them. "About the . . . King and Queen of Trendalath, you mean?" he finally stutters.

At this, Cerylia frowns—not a sad frown—but a disappointed one. "Yes. If you're up to it."

He's afraid if he looks at the armoire again, where he's concealed his mother's note, she'll catch on to the fact that he's hiding something. He still hasn't had time to sort through all of his feelings just yet—he and his mother had always had a closer relationship than he'd had with Darius. Not nearly as absent as his father had been. He can easily recall many nights where Aldreda would tuck him into bed and read him stories until he fell asleep. Deep down, he still yearns for that sense of belonging—of being loved and cared for . . .

He levels a steely look at her. "I can't guarantee I'll be of much help, seeing as I haven't been around either of them in years."

"That's quite all right," Cerylia assures. "I just have one question."

Braxton doesn't move, doesn't break eye contact.

"To your knowledge, has Queen Tymond ever acted of her own accord?"

Braxton studies her for a moment, brows furrowing.

Why is she asking about my mother?

He stalls, hoping to buy more time, his thoughts whirling like the blizzard outside. "Forgive me, Your Greatness, but I'm not sure I understand what you're asking. I'm afraid you'll have to be more specific."

She lowers her voice to a whisper. "Does King Tymond give . . . *direction* to the queen, or does she act on her own?"

The rephrased question doesn't do much to clarify, but it's more than obvious that *something* is gnawing at Cerylia's conscience—something serious.

Suddenly, he feels protective over the queen. "Your Greatness, are you in some sort of danger? Because if you're referencing something in particular, it'd be helpful to know what that is."

She regards him with sullen eyes. "I just need to know if she always takes instruction from the king, or if she has a tendency to stray from his wishes."

The way she says it is so flat, so devoid of emotion, that Braxton honestly can't determine what her end game is. He leans back in his chair, choosing his words carefully. "Your Greatness, if there's one thing I can tell you about my mothe"—he catches himself, not wanting to show his hand—"*Aldreda*, it's that she does whatever she wants, when she wants, whether or not the king approves." He stifles the slow smile tugging at the corner of his lips. His parents weren't ones to put their disagreements on display, but, the few times they had, Aldreda had always won. She'd never known this, but Braxton had always looked up to her, especially in the way she'd handled Darius during their more trying times—unruffled with unyielding calm. The words leave his lips before he can stop them. "Growing up, I sometimes got the feeling that she was the one running the kingdom, not Darius."

She lifts her chin. "What makes you say that?"

He glances at the door, wishing Opal would appear so that he could go back to the moment prior and keep that last spoken thought to himself. He thinks twice before responding, his mind floating once again to the cryptic note—the one that's sitting just steps away from where they sit. "All I meant is that Aldreda is influential in her own way." He pauses, hoping it'll be enough for Cerylia.

It's not. She raises a brow, waiting for him to continue.

Braxton fumbles for words. "As his queen, it's always seemed like she can get away with just about anything with no consequences."

She considers this. "On the contrary, every action has consequences," she murmurs. "Sometimes it takes longer than it should for those punishments to be realized."

Blunt, honest words. Braxton opens his mouth to speak only to find that he's tongue-tied. *What has my estranged mother done to warrant such a conversation?*

The words from her note weave through his mind. *I hope you both can forgive me one day.* He steals a look at Cerylia. The vacant, faraway look in her eyes. The slight frown pulling at the corners of her mouth. The underlying sorrow in every word she speaks.

Is it possible that 'both' refers to me and . . . Cerylia?

Cerylia suddenly breaks from her daze and shifts her sights on the window. "I have one final question for you, Braxton." As her eyes fall on him, so does an unusually harsh expression. It makes her almost unrecognizable. In a flat, unwavering tone, she asks, "Are you loyal to your family? To Trendalath?"

Caught in the midst of crippling indecision, he falters. He knows exactly what she wants to hear, but he's not sure if it's the truth. He needs more time, but time is a luxury he doesn't have. If he lies, how many more lies will he tell? Can he really keep up this charade and continue deceiving her? Moreover, will he ever have the courage to stop lying to himself?

If he waits any longer, she'll start to draw a conclusion he won't be able to come back from. So, he does the only thing he can think of. He goes back to his feelings *before* he'd found his mother's note. The reason he'd fled Trendalath in the first place. The anger. The betrayal. The isolation.

His resentment for his past drives his response. "My loyalty lies with you and Sardoria, Your Greatness. I am at your service." He gives her an affirming nod. "Whatever you may need."

Her eyes rove his face, as if looking for some indication of deceit. She seems pleased with his answer because she sits back in her chair and smiles.

Never in his life did he think one conversation could make him feel so conflicted.

Does he trust Cerylia?

For the most part, yes. She'd taken him in, knowing that he was her sworn enemy—or, at least, that his family was, but the bigger question remains . . .

Can he trust her intentions?

Now *that's* something he'll have to find out for himself, even if it means doing things the hard way.

ARDEN ELIRI

A FEW DAYS have passed since my late evening visit from Felix . . . and subsequently, my strange dream involving Xerin. I'd be lying if I said I didn't wish Felix would show up every night, if nothing more than to talk. Our last conversation is the only thing keeping me from feeling rattled—that, and my growing feelings for him. Even so, I find my subconscious encounter with Xerin slip back into my mind. I'm fully aware that it was just a dream—that it wasn't real . . . and yet something tells me there's more to it than that.

I snap back to attention as Delwynn says my name. I give him a quick nod to show that I'm paying attention (even though I'm not), feeling relieved as he drones on and on about something that has nothing to do with my training. I glance to my left at the empty seat next to me. Braxton's more than twenty minutes late, which is uncharacteristic of him. My frustration gets the better of me when forty minutes pass and he's still a no-show. It's difficult to practice my healing abilities when I don't have anyone to practice them on. With this in mind, I can't help but sigh as Delwynn brings yet another injured animal to me. Within minutes, I've healed the small creature, watching apathetically as it hops along on its merry little way.

I'm tempted to remind Delwynn that *this*—what we're *currently doing*—isn't helping me to improve. If anything, it's *reducing* my abilities. I need a challenge—something more fruitful in which to apply my efforts. Just as I'm about to open my mouth, Delwynn starts up again, and it takes everything in me to not get up and march away from this damn courtyard.

Only ten minutes left of training for the day and we've spent the latter half away from the courtyard and inside the training room. It's still just Delwynn and me. I've channelled all of my efforts into listening to today's lesson, but my mind has been completely preoccupied, what with Felix and Xerin—and now Braxton.

Fortunately, Delwynn concludes today's lesson early and even acknowledges me for attending. Just as I'm about to leave, I hear his staff clink against the floor. I turn over my shoulder, watching as he hobbles toward the door. An idea strikes me—but whether it's a good one or not eludes me.

"Say Delwynn?" My words come out slick as butter.

He seems to sense my intentions because he immediately stops and straightens. He turns to face me, eyeing me curiously. "Yes?"

A hint of a smile touches my lips. "Would you mind terribly if I had a look at that?" I angle my head at his staff.

He looks at me warily. "May I ask what for?"

I don't say anything in response, just gesture for him to take a seat. He sighs, but hobbles back over to where I'm standing. I notice he's reluctant in handing over his staff—even more so when I drag an extra chair over and ask him to extend both of his legs out in front of him—but nevertheless, he listens.

I can feel him watching me as I kneel and lightly place my hands on his knee. "Has anyone ever tried to heal you?"

He regards me with incredulous eyes and, just as I think he's about to scold me for such an outlandish proposal, he does the one thing I never would have expected.

He laughs.

"Oh, Arden, my dear." He shakes his head. "Where do I begin? I have tried everything under the sun and *more*. Concoctions of herbs, brews of minerals, and every traditional medicinal technique you could possibly imagine."

I wait for him to continue, but he doesn't say anything else. "And?" I press, trying not to sound too impatient.

"Obviously none of it worked, otherwise I wouldn't need this." He gestures to the staff I've placed against the far wall.

"And what about with illusié? Have you tried healing that way?"

He immediately draws his legs from the chair. "No, I have not." His gaze flicks to my hands as he says, "Even that would be a stretch."

I look at him questioningly. "How so? You've seen what I can do with animals. And if you ask Estelle, she'll tell you I healed—"

"The answer is no."

His voice matches his expression—stern and steadfast—so I don't dare ask again. Instead, I try another tactic. "Very well. It really is a shame though," I say as I stand up and begin to walk away from him. "I can just imagine how happy Cerylia would be to see her most loyal advisor able-bodied and healthy again. Or has she never seen you that way?"

His face pales at the assumption, leaving me to believe it's true.

"I suppose she hasn't."

Knowing I've almost ensnared him, I continue, "I must ask, as her most loyal advisor, did you swear an oath?"

He doesn't object.

"Did you?" I ask again.

"You know as well as I do what the answer is."

"Then why the reluctance in pursuing another avenue to heal your injuries? Especially when it's almost certain that it will be successful?"

He seems to consider this. For one minute. Two . . .

Before he can think himself into oblivion, I ask, "What's the harm in trying?"

A muscle feathers in his cheek. Finally, he extends his left leg and places it back atop the chair. "You get one chance, Eliri," he murmurs. "Use it wisely."

I nod graciously before placing my hands over his knee. I close my eyes. A deep inhale follows as I hurtle into the essence of my ability, hunting for that familiar feeling, that stark white light. I can feel it rising within me, swift and sudden, like the wind with the tide.

But as I grab hold of it, something unsettling occurs—something I can't explain. It's like there's a block that's keeping me from accessing the bulk of my strength . . . a distant entity I'm entirely unfamiliar with.

A black mist seeps into my thoughts, nesting deep within the confines of my mind. I try to focus on the white light—on expanding it and pulling those healing tethers upward, but they remain just out of reach. I press my eyelids together even more, doing everything I can to concentrate on the light, but the dark shadows encroach, taking over.

Seeing. Feeling. *Wanting.*

Cries of agony force my eyes to open and I quickly realize that they're coming from Delwynn—Delwynn, who is no longer conscious. Delwynn, who is now seizing. His body shakes uncontrollably as his eyes roll into the back of his head.

"Delwynn!" I yell. I look down at my hands and immediately begin to panic. Where there *should* be a soft white light lingers an impenetrable black fog.

What in lords' name have I just done?

I yank my hands away from his knee, but the fog doesn't dissipate. It hovers, growing denser and darker with each passing second.

"Guards!" I scream as loud as I can. "Someone, help!" I reach out to Delwynn, who is now foaming at the mouth, but immediately pull back when I realize that I'm the cause of his seizure.

I did this. I brought this pain onto him.

I look from him, to my hands, then back to him again, not knowing what to do. I rush for the door and call out again, torn between staying and leaving to get help. I begin to pace back and forth in front of the door, afraid that if I go anywhere near him, I'll somehow deliver the final blow that will end his life.

After what feels like an eternity, two guards arrive . . . with the queen on their heels. She rushes to Delwynn's side, then turns to me, her face a mask of cold indifference. "What the hell happened here?"

I open my mouth to respond, but no words come out.

"Call for the Herbalist!" she barks at the guards.

I watch in a haze as one of the guards scurries off to the healing ward.

"Arden," Cerylia says, "tell me what happened. Now."

I look down at my trembling hands and close them into fists. Tears prick the corners of my eyes. "It's my fault . . . I did this."

"Look at me." Her voice is frank and cold. I don't dare disobey. "Tell me what happened—and do not make me repeat the question."

I clench my jaw, fists curling and uncurling at my sides. "I . . . I tried to heal him."

"Heal him?" The queen scans Delwynn's body for a sign of injury. "Of what?"

I shake my head. "Not a new injury," I whisper. My eyes drop to his knee.

The queen follows my gaze. "I see." And then, "Did he ask you to do this?"

I shake my head again. "It was my idea. I convinced him to let me try."

Just as she's about to ask another question, the guard arrives with the Herbalist. I quickly scoot to the side as he approaches and takes my place. He checks Delwynn's vitals before preparing what must be a healing brew.

Cerylia clears her throat. "We'll take it from here."

I look up, at war with the bristling rage inside of me—not at her, but at myself.

"You are dismissed, Arden."

I look at the sight before me, feeling helpless. "Your Greatness, I'd like to make sure he's okay."

"We will send word," the queen says through clenched teeth. "You are dismissed."

I rein in the sudden need to scream. Without so much as another breath, I turn to head back to my chambers. Tears continue to cloud my vision as I hastily wipe them away with the back of my hand. I pick up my pace, not wanting anyone to witness my current state.

Weak. Fragile. *Guilty.*

I'm just steps away, but as I round another corridor, I bump headfirst into Felix. *Great.* I stagger backward, my hand flying to my forehead. I blink rapidly to clear the tiny dots floating in my already foggy vision.

Felix regards me with wide eyes as he opens and closes his jaw. It seems I'm not the only one caught off guard. I must look distraught because he immediately asks, "Is everything all right?"

I should be happy to see him. At *any* other point in my day, I *would* be happy to see him. But not right now—not as everything crumbles around me.

Without thinking, I force a smile. I wonder if he can see the quiver in my lips. I feel the urge to lie to him—to tell him everything is fine—but one look into those deep chestnut eyes holds me back. My mind flashes to when we'd first met—how inexplicably close I'd felt to a total and complete stranger—and then to our most recent conversation and how much stronger our connection has grown since then.

"Actually," I say, somewhat hesitantly, "can I talk to you?"

He arches a brow before giving me a small smile. He takes a step closer. "Isn't that what we're doing right now? Talking?"

Even though it's meant to be playful, I can't find the humor—not in my current state. I can't seem to focus on anything else right now except for the fact that I've hurt Delwynn—that I *keep* hurting people. "Can we talk privately? In your chambers?"

His face falls at my solemn tone. "Sure. But we're closer to yours."

I realize he's right, then nod before leading the way, even though he clearly knows where we're headed. I'd been in such a rush to get to training earlier that I'd left the door unlocked. I gently press it open, then walk to the center of the room. He joins me, but I don't speak a word until I hear the door creak shut.

His eyes leave mine as they scan the room. The desk. The bookcase. The table. The bed. "This is the first time I've been in here while the sun's still up."

Even though I want to, I can't seem to smile. I feel like if I show emotion, or express anything other than what I'm truly feeling, my face will crack. I stay quiet.

"Looks different," he continues as he walks past me and glides his hand along the desk. "I'm not sure which I prefer, day or evening."

I turn, exhaling when I realize his back to me. What I'm sure is a flurry of different emotions dances across my face, but I manage to rein them in right as he turns to face me. His gaze locks on mine as he situates himself on the edge of the desk, arms folding over his chest. Eyes alight with concern, he says, "Something's wrong."

I fidget with my hair, my words just as jumbled as my thoughts. "Do you remember when we met?"

An ethereal flicker dances across his eyes. "I would hope so, since I gave you something to signify that very moment."

"That came out wrong," I recover, carefully crafting my response. "What I'm trying to ask is . . . did you know then what I was capable of?" I hate how much my voice shakes.

He looks at me long and hard before saying, "I knew enough."

Not the response I expected. "What does that mean?"

And just as I'd deflected, so does he. "Why are you bringing this up, Arden?"

"That day, in the Thering Forest," I whisper, "I hurt you." Although he remains silent, I can sense the painful memory flash across his mind. "It was a mistake," I continue. "But ever since that day, things have only escalated. And it's happened again. And again."

He breaks his silence. "How many times?"

I don't want to answer—to reveal the truth—but one look at him pulls it out of me. "Three."

His back stiffens as his eyes fall to my hands. He gets up from the desk and begins to pace, scratching the back of his head as he goes. "Who were the afflicted?"

"You. Braxton. And now Delwynn."

He stops. "What do you mean 'And *now* Delwynn'?"

I angle my head toward the door. "What did you think I was running from in such a hurry? What did you think had me so distraught that I didn't even see you walking down the hall?"

"Are you going to tell me what happened?"

The way he's looking at me—with such intensity and concern—I wouldn't dare lie. "Not long ago, Braxton and I were attending our usual training session with Delwynn, but there was nothing usual about it. There was an incident"—my eyes blur as I remember my chakrams flying straight for his head—"but Braxton managed to get out of the way, just barely." I pause. "His hands were sliced up pretty bad, so I attempted to heal him—"

"Attempted?" Felix interrupts.

I nod, blinking back any sign of weakness. "When I tried to heal him, it seemed to do the opposite. He was in so much pain . . ." My words falter as Braxton's screams echo in the depths of my mind. "He yelled for me to get away from him, to not come near him." I try to shake the memory, but it won't budge. "I caused it. I was the reason for his pain." My voice cracks with the last word.

It's then I feel a gentle tug on my arm. Suddenly, Felix's fingers are interlaced with my own. I gaze into those large almond-shaped eyes, my eyes moving to his mouth as he asks, "And Delwynn?"

My emotions are far too strong for me to focus. I try to gather my thoughts, but they're fleeting. Every time I attempt to grab onto a new memory, it disappears, like fireflies scattering to and fro in a dark field.

"Just now," I manage to say, squeezing his hand tighter, "I tried to heal him so that he'd no longer need his staff to walk." My tears burst through the barrier I've tried so hard to maintain. "I just wanted to help. But he started seizing, uncontrollably . . ." Saying the words out loud makes them real—*too* real. I crumple to the floor, but not alone. Felix is right there with me.

"How can someone with healing abilities," I sputter, "do the exact opposite and cause pain instead? My whole life I've killed and killed and killed . . . and now I have the chance to heal, and I can't even do that right." I lower my head in shame. "Am I destined to become as cruel and unforgiving as the Tymonds? Is that the fate that awaits me?"

I'm not sure when it happened, but his arm is now over my shoulders, cradling me like a small child. Never have I felt so weak and so safe at the very same time.

We sit in silence, my head against his chest, as he slowly rocks me back and forth. My tears cease with each subtle movement, but even as I begin to feel better—more controlled—I don't want to leave the comfort of his arms.

Felix's voice is quiet. "Is it redemption you seek?"

His question is somewhat jarring. I lift my gaze, searching his face for answers I know aren't there. "I don't know. I don't know anything anymore."

Words seem to escape the both of us. As I curl into his chest, he leans his head against mine, his arms tightening around me. And it's there we remain, on the floor, unencumbered by a need to be anywhere else but together.

RYDAN HELSTROM

"AN IGNITOR," Haskell murmurs to himself, still in disbelief. It's been a little over a week since Rydan had revealed his abilities to Haskell, but instead of welcoming his talents—like he had Vira's—he'd been keeping Rydan at arms-length. At first, his reaction hadn't been all that surprising—now it's just downright aggravating. No time like the present to address it; if Haskell will let him, that is.

As if she's set up post in his mind, Vira asks, "So, are you going to talk to him?" She's sitting on the bench across from him, eyes flitting back and forth.

Rydan shoots a quick glance over his shoulder. Haskell is still muttering to himself, diligently organizing the contents of one of the wooden cabinets. He can make out some of the phrases, but the rest are indecipherable. "Trust me, I want to . . . but look at him." Vira's eyes travel to Haskell. "He's distraught and talking nonsense."

Her gaze lingers for a moment. "He'll drive himself mad if you don't say *something*."

"If it's so easy, then why don't you try? He seems much more fascinated by your summoning abilities— mine, not so much."

"You and I both know he's not going to be able to talk about anything else until you clear the air. He keeps repeating '*an Ignitor*', so no matter what I say, his focus will remain solely on that until you find a way to snap him out of whatever trance he seems to be in."

Once more, Rydan turns over his shoulder to get a better look at Haskell. Their host is red in the face, grunting as he shuffles multiple stacks of papers before attempting to maneuver them into an overstuffed drawer.

Rydan faces front again before sighing loudly. "Fine."

Vira smiles, then makes a shooing motion with her hands. He intentionally gives her an exaggerated eye roll before rising from the bench. There isn't much time to consider what he should say or how to best approach the situation because he quickly finds himself standing in front of a muddled Haskell, wordless and thoughtless.

After a lengthy stare, Haskell takes the liberty of speaking first. "Yes?"

The words he couldn't seem to find just a few moments prior suddenly flow effortlessly from his mouth. "It's been a little over a week since I showed you my abilities as an Ignitor, and it seems that you're not too keen on this discovery, and I—well, I want to know why."

The dark circles under Haskell's eyes become more prominent as he steps into the natural light that's pouring in from the cave's entrance. "The storm seems to have ceased. Now would be a good time for you to leave."

He says it loud enough that Rydan is certain Vira's heard his request. He takes a quick peek over his shoulder and, from the look on her face, knows that he's guessed correctly. "Please don't shut us out. We've opened up to you. We're one in the same—"

Without warning, Rydan finds himself stumbling backward as Haskell begins to shout, flipping the wooden table over on its side and slamming chairs against the walls. The wood splinters from the impact, raining down as it covers the cave floor in miniature death spikes.

"Don't you dare," he yells with terrifying authority, "compare my abilities to yours *ever again.*"

Rydan's certain he's going to fall into the fire pit at any moment, but Vira intervenes—and fortunately before his body can be consumed by the hungry flames. He kneels beside her, hands shaking.

"What the hell did you say to him?" she hisses into his ear. "Why is he so angry all of a sudden?"

"I honestly have no idea."

"Well do something!" she urges, giving him a shove back onto his feet.

Rydan finds his balance before daring to take a step forward. The rapid rising and falling of Haskell's chest is enough to make him cower and gently lay both hands over his own chest. He gazes up at their burly host-turned-tyrant before shaking his head in surrender. "I apologize," he says quickly, hoping Haskell has calmed enough to let him finish. "I wasn't trying to compare anyone or anything. It's just . . . what you said when we first met . . ."

Haskell's fists loosen at his sides, his shoulders no longer tense. "I apologize for my outburst. It's just been quite some time since I've seen . . . well, one of *you*."

"A fellow purveyor of illusié?" Vira interjects.

Rydan can't help his jaw from clenching at the word.

Haskell shakes his head. He draws an uneven breath, his response merely a murmur. "An Ignitor."

His curiosity piqued, Rydan rises and takes a step forward. "You've met another Ignitor before?"

Haskell remains quiet, his eyes cast toward the ground.

Vira steps beside Rydan. "Please tell us. We're new to all of this. We need to learn whatever it is you know."

Haskell lifts his head, then very begrudgingly mumbles, "Follow me."

Rydan and Vira exchange a shrug, but gladly follow him down one of the cave's corridors. As they make a sharp right turn, Rydan realizes exactly where they're headed—it's where he'd originally tried to venture off to when they'd first arrived. Vira seems to remember the incident as well because she nudges him in the side before shooting him a pointed look.

The pathway grows darker until a soft glow comes into view. It's a torch—the same torch he'd stumbled upon that night. Haskell grabs it from the wall sconce before plunging further into the darkness. After a few minutes, they finally reach what appears to be another room. Rydan squints, trying to make out the various shapes in the dim lighting, but it's no use. It's too dark.

"I can't see," Vira whispers a little too loudly.

"Hold on," Haskell grunts.

Vira clutches onto Rydan's forearm. They stand there, apprehensive and blind, waiting for whatever's about to happen. A number of scenarios fly through Rydan's mind, most of which are unsettling. But as more torches are lit, the room comes into view. It takes a moment for his eyes to fully adjust, but once they do, he can hardly believe what he's seeing. The scene before him is astounding.

Various pieces of parchment are tacked to the cave walls—page after page of drawings and text that have been ripped from the spines of books. Battle ornaments are scattered atop a number of tables, from helmets and swords to shields and armor. Rydan runs his hand along one of the tables, accidentally ruffling some loose papers with the motion. "What is all of this?"

Before Haskell can respond, Vira draws closer to one of the pages tacked on the wall. "The King's Savant," she whispers.

"I'm afraid so," Haskell confirms.

Rydan looks back and forth between the two of them, confused. "So it's not just a rumor. It's true?"

Haskell gives a solemn nod. "I've transported back to Trendalath a few times, mostly for fresh game. I've overheard some of the guards talking. If what I've heard is true, King Tymond has successfully gathered his Savant for the first time in a decade."

Rydan takes a sharp breath, feeling an unexpected sense of betrayal at the news. For years he'd only considered the Cruex as the King's primary source of protection and intel. Seems Tymond's had something else up his sleeve all along.

"What for?" he asks.

Haskell furrows his brows. "Are you asking why Tymond has gathered his Savant?"

"Yes."

"It's obvious, isn't it?"

Rydan glances over at Vira, whose blank expression matches his own.

While Haskell's response is quiet, it's unmistakeably clear. "They're after illusié."

DARIUS TYMOND

THE PAST FEW nights have been longer and lonelier than usual. With Aldreda refusing to sleep in their chambers, Darius has been forced to sit with his thoughts. Normally this wouldn't bother him, but seeing how they'd last left things, there's only one conversation replaying in his mind.

His nights seem to have taken on a monotonous routine of their own, starting with pacing at the foot of the bed, staring aimlessly out the castle windows at the kingdom below, and then, once in bed, tossing and turning, unable to still his thrashing mind.

Tonight will be no different.

Darius throws the covers off of him before grabbing the robe he'd carelessly strewn over the back of the armoire. He shivers, bundling the layers of plush fabric even tighter over his chest as a cool draft sweeps through the open window. He eyes his shoes, which lay at the foot of the bed, but doesn't bother.

A quick tug and the door creaks open. Quietly, he steps into the hallway, grabbing one of the lit torches along the way. At first, he has no sense as to where he wants to go, but hastily decides on the library, for no other reason than to get away from the hollowness lurking in every corner of his chambers. Perhaps filling his mind with other useless information will bore him right into a deep slumber.

As he's about to round another corner, nearby voices stop him. The words are hushed—faint—but he's almost certain it's two women talking. He glances behind him, searching for an empty sconce, so as to not cast a shadow and give away his presence. He spots one and glides over to it as quietly as he can manage, securing the torch in place.

He returns to the edge of the wall and presses his back against it before peering around the corner. The hall is dimly lit, and the two figures are shadowed, but the fullness in shape of the left figure points to none other than his wife, Aldreda. The figure on the right is harder to discern—probably just one of the handmaidens.

Darius strains his ears, but to his dismay, only hears bits and pieces of the conversation.

"I know there's something he's not telling me," Aldreda says. "But I can't get a word out of him edgewise."

"My Lady, have you spoken with the others?"

"A futile attempt, I'm afraid. I'm completely in the dark." She sighs. "And now they've all left on yet another mission in the northeast."

"Do you know of their expected return?"

"Unfortunately, I do not"—she pauses—"but I know this isn't just about apprehending the Caldari. It goes far beyond that."

"How can you be so sure?"

Darius cranes his neck as the voices lower even more.

"Call it an inkling, but there's something important he's not telling me." She reaches out and takes the woman's hands in hers. "If you knew something, you'd tell me. Wouldn't you?"

"I would tell you as much as I'm permitted to."

A long silence stretches between them.

Darius waits impatiently for the conversation to continue, but the only response is that of shuffling feet along the corridor. Unable to discern which direction they're headed, he swiftly turns back, grabbing the torch once again, and hurries around the next corner. When he peers around the edge, he's relieved to find that they aren't behind him. He takes his time walking back to his chambers to allow the conversation to sink in.

Who had Aldreda been talking to so openly? Sure, she's always been friendly with the servants, but this conversation . . . it'd had an underlying tone of . . . *trust*.

It crosses his mind to gather all the servants and interrogate each and every last one of them, but quickly realizes he hasn't followed Aldreda closely enough to even begin to guess which of the staff she's formed close relationships with—not that he truly has anything to worry about. The servants are just as naïve as his wife.

And yet, even after settling back into his chambers, one sentence echoes in his mind. *I would tell you as much as I'm permitted to.* It's then his eyes shoot open and his blood runs cold. Because if there's one person on his staff he *should* be worried about . . .

It's Gladys.

CERYLIA JARETH

CERYLIA SPOTS ESTELLE from afar, dashing from the courtyard into the castle. It's another dreary winter day, and with the thickening snowfall, she can't be sure *what* she's seeing. From her current post in the courtyard, it looks as though someone's waiting for Estelle inside the castle walls. If the assumption is correct, it's likely to be one of two people—Arden or Felix.

As the Caldari's stay in Sardoria continues, she's come to notice that the group frequently splits off into pairs—Arden and Braxton, Estelle and Felix, Rydan and Elvira—although the latter are no longer under her supervision. Opal and Xerin tend to break off separately, which isn't surprising, given their abilities—the more individualistic aspects of their talents call for more singular activities, whereas the others tend to stay in closer quarters.

Removing herself from her station, Cerylia trudges across the snow toward a shortcut that leads to the hallway Estelle had run off to. The moment her feet hit solid ground, she gives a vigorous shake of her robes, freeing the fabric of its fresh coat of white. She's disappointed to discover she's already gone, but a trail of footprints surrounded by melting snow gives her a renewed sense of hope. Like a leopard in pursuit of its next meal, she follows the footsteps until she reaches . . . the dining hall. Not nearly as climactic as she'd hoped.

She waltzes in, not at all surprised to see Estelle and Felix sitting at a nearby table, shoveling heaping spoonfuls of porridge into their mouths. It's only been an hour or so since she'd last eaten, and by no means is she hungry, but for the sake of gathering information, she calls over a servant and requests that he bring her a tray of fresh fruit.

"May I join you?"

Both Felix and Estelle look up from their half-empty plates, giving the queen their undivided attention. Felix flashes a toothy grin before sliding further down the bench. Cerylia gathers her robes, and as she takes a seat, her tray of fruit is set in front of her. "Thank you," she says dismissively.

"So," Estelle starts, leaning forward on her elbows, "to what do we owe the pleasure, Your Greatness?"

Cerylia looks between the two of them, suddenly at a loss for words. Sure, she'd prepared the topic of conversation on her way to the dining hall, but she hadn't quite worked out exactly *how* to breach the subject. "I've come to speak with you about a . . . pressing matter."

They shrug simultaneously before wiping their hands on their trousers and pushing their plates aside. Even without a verbal response, the looks on their faces tell her to continue.

"I need to know what communication you've had with your fellow Caldari."

Estelle exchanges a look with Felix. "Do you have someone particular in mind?"

"Not necessarily," she lies. "I just want to remain informed. Xerin hasn't returned with any news, and the longer Rydan and Elvira are out there . . ."

Estelle glances toward the window at the imminent snowstorm and nods in understanding. "Well, I haven't heard from Xerin. Haven't spoken much to Braxton. And, seeing as you and Opal are close, I'm sure you've already spoken with her."

Were close. Past tense. It pains her to think of her last interaction with Opal and how foolish they'd both behaved. She shakes the thought away. "And what about Arden?"

"Nothing out of the ordinary."

Cerylia looks beside her. "And what about you, Sir Barlow?"

Felix has his hands clasped underneath the table, eyes lowered. He doesn't speak right away, but when he finally does, it comes out as little more than a croak. "Your Greatness, may I speak with you in private?"

Estelle bristles at his request. "Excuse me, but anything you'd like to discuss with the queen regarding our fellow Caldari can be said in front of me—seeing as I *am* one."

Felix bows his head at her. "I'm sorry, Estelle, but I think this information should be for the queen's ears only."

They both turn their gaze toward Cerylia, clearly waiting for her to make an executive decision. Much to her dismay, it's not so cut and dry. On the one hand, if she asks Estelle to excuse herself from the conversation, she's almost certain Estelle will go straight to Arden— which is the exact opposite of what she wants. On the other, if Estelle stays and Felix reveals some . . . *sensitive* information, well, that could result in unnecessary tension. It's a risk, but one she'll have to endure. "That's quite all right. Estelle can stay. I'm sure we can both benefit from any information you may have."

"If you're sure." Felix looks from Cerylia to Estelle, then shrugs. "The other day, I ran into Arden while she was rushing away from the courtyard. I could tell by the expression on her face that something wasn't right. So I confronted her about it."

"Is this about Delwynn?" Cerylia interrupts.

He hesitates, as if he doesn't want to say. "It goes beyond Delwynn. Arden explicitly expressed that she's having difficulties with her abilities and that, as a Healer, she's actually been doing more harm than good."

Estelle looks at him as if she can't believe what she's hearing. "Did she tell you this in confidence?"

Felix gives her a pointed glare. "I'm sure you remember the incident in the Thering Forest when we first met Arden."

Her face falls.

"Well," Felix presses, "do you?"

Estelle gives a silent nod.

He turns his attention back to the queen. "This isn't a standalone incident. It's happened multiple times, most notably since we've arrived in Sardoria."

"Forgive me," Cerylia says as she lifts a hand, "but I am not privy to the incident that occurred in the Thering Forest."

Felix opens his mouth to respond, but Estelle beats him to it. "It's not important. It was a misunderstanding."

"Estelle," Felix pleads, "she needs to know."

She shakes her head but doesn't try to stop him.

"Arden attacked me in the forest—tried to kill me, actually. The rage in her eyes was . . ." He swallows, mouth rigging to the side. "It's hard to explain, but I get the sense that something's gone awry with Arden's abilities."

Cerylia takes his account into consideration as she recalls the more recent incidents involving Braxton and Delwynn. Her heart sinks as a stark realization dawns on her. She knew it'd come to this at some point, but it's much too soon. She can only do so much to protect Arden from herself . . .

"If you need the Caldari to leave," Felix continues, "we'll understand. The safety of Sardoria—of your people—comes first."

Cerylia nods at Felix before shifting her gaze to Estelle. "Lady Chatham, do you have anything to add?"

Estelle furrows her brows as she weighs the question. "Arden can come back from this, Your Greatness. With the right training, the right tools, and the right guidance . . ."

Cerylia nods. "I hope you're right. In the meantime, we'll keep a watchful eye." She senses discomfort from Felix as he shifts in his seat. "I appreciate your forthrightness, Sir Barlow. It certainly makes up for Arden's other transgressions—" She bites the inside of her cheek.

Before she can recover, Felix asks, "What other transgressions?"

Cerylia hesitates. An urge to hide behind a lie surfaces—but she cannot act on it, not when Felix has so willingly shared the truth. Her tone is bleak. "It's an unspoken rule that the Caldari need to inherently trust each other, correct?"

"Right," they both say in unison.

"Arden knows why Rydan fled." Cerylia's voice catches. "Which means she not only lied to me . . . she lied to you, too."

BRAXTON HORNSBY

THE SHEER WEIGHT of the queen's request plagues Braxton's mind. At some point, he figured he'd have to face his estranged mother and father again, but not this soon. What would it be like going back to Trendalath after a decade? Would he be welcomed with open arms? It's entirely possible Aldreda would be happy to see him, but his father? Highly unlikely, especially after their last encounter. If he's going to get through this in one piece, he must learn to view it as an opportunity. A way to get clarification on his mother's note—and hopefully to find out how it got to Sardoria, in his chambers.

A twig snaps in the distance, jolting him from his absentminded stare. Tracing the source of the noise to a nearby oak tree in the courtyard, his gaze is led to the highest branch, atop of which a snowy owl has perched. It opens its wings, almost blinding him with its white canvas of feathers. The sight immediately reminds him of his mother, but, for some reason, he can only recall her long white-blonde hair and how it was always styled in loose braids. The features of her face escape him. Thin or full lips? Freckles or porcelain skin? Pointed or round nose? His recollection of her, and their time together, has only grown worse the older he gets—the more time he's spent away.

Raised voices yank him from his thoughts. He glances at the tree, but the owl is gone. Estelle and Felix come into view, bickering about something (yet again), followed by Delwynn, who is now in a wheelchair, and yet is still inserting himself into their scuffle, trying to break it up. They're probably headed to training.

Speaking of which, skipping out on his last training session *had* been intentional. Even though his injuries had since healed—and Arden had apologized—Braxton hadn't exactly been excited to face her again, especially in a training setting. It dawns on him that he hasn't spoken to Arden since that day.

He watches the interaction below with a soft gaze, thoughts flitting between his old home in Athia and new home here, until his surroundings grow dark. The once translucent sky is now coated in a dense gray fog, the shimmering light of only a few stars poking through. Delwynn bids Felix and Estelle farewell as they head toward opposite ends of the courtyard.

With nothing left to entertain him, Braxton turns away from the window, facing the dim corridor he's holed himself up in for the night. He sighs, knowing this time would come—when he'd no longer have something to distract him, leaving him to confront his thoughts. It's then that a flickering torch catches his eye, beckoning him to come closer. Arden's room isn't far from where he stands.

The real reason he's remained here most of the night.

Although the queen hadn't explicitly asked him to keep their conversation to himself, it's easy to gather from the nature of her lofty request that he should.

Gray area, perhaps?

Before his mind can catch up with his feet, he finds himself barrelling down the corridor. It only takes a minute for him to reach Arden's chambers. His eyes scan the wooden panels of the door as he raises his hand to knock, but something stops him. His fist floats in the air until he gently lowers it and brings it back to his sides.

An internal argument commences.

If I'm about to leave to fulfill Cerylia's request, I should at least say good-bye . . . but how would I explain my reason for leaving? What would I say?

He can feel the decision eating away at him until, finally, he musters up the courage. With a steadying breath, he once again raises his fist, followed by three bold knocks. When the door doesn't open, he knocks twice more.

But, much to his chagrin, the door remains shut.

ARDEN ELIRI

THREE KNOCKS AT my door, followed by two more. For a brief moment, I consider answering. It could be Felix, and I could really use a pick-me-up at the moment. As much as I crave comfort, especially *his* comfort, there's always a chance it could be someone else. Braxton. Delwynn. Cerylia.

I decide against it. Keeping to myself as of late has been intentional. I've been feigning ill in order to avoid my training and my fellow Caldari. Until I can get whatever is going on with me under control, it's not worth putting everyone I care about at risk.

Over the past week, I've managed to play back every peculiar incident in my head. A desperate attempt to connect the dots—to make some sense of it all—but I've convinced myself that there is no logical explanation. As a Healer, I should be making things *better*, not causing even *more* pain and suffering.

The thought has me hastily turning over in my bed so that I'm facing the window. The sheer white curtains rustle in the breeze, puffing outward before resuming their original shape. I bring the covers up tighter around my chin, keeping my eyes locked on the glass. For some reason, my thoughts shift to Xerin. I wonder if anyone's seen him—if he's been back to the castle since leaving to look for Rydan and Elvira . . . which then brings me to wonder where they are. If they're safe. If Tymond's apprehended them.

Another breeze, harsher than the last, dances around the room. Even though I love the cold, a shiver dances down my spine. Something about that open window is disturbing. I count to three before forcing myself to climb out of bed and swing it shut. The room immediately feels warmer as I clamber back into bed, but instead of lying down, I remain upright. I turn behind me and grab one of the pillows, watching as Juniper hops up onto the bed. She curls up beside me as I lean forward, hugging the pillow between my knees and chest.

My gaze shifts back to the window. It's so quiet. The only thing I hear is the breeze rapping against the glass, the curtains eerily still. In that stillness arrives a stark realization.

I can't stay here.

As if in agreement, Juniper paws at me. I look down and scratch her behind the ears. She lifts her little head and looks at me knowingly with those big eyes.

"But where do we go?" I whisper. She looks at me a little while longer before lowering her head again and drifting back into her nap. "Yeah. I don't know either."

I lift my gaze from the furry little creature to the desk across the room. My eyes land on the stack of books, on *The Power of Illusié*. Slowly, I slide out of bed and tiptoe over to the desk. I pull the book from the pile and open it to where it's bulging, gingerly lifting the pocket watch from where I'd last placed it, in the middle of the page. My fingers close around it, and I can feel its rhythmic *tick, tick, tick* against my skin.

My eyes close. In mere seconds, what I must do becomes painstakingly clear. Things started taking a turn for the worse after my first encounter in the Thering Forest, just outside of Orihia. It was the first time I'd ever seen the cloaked figure, and ever since then, darkness seems to follow me whether I like it or not.

I have to go back there. To Orihia.

Without a second thought, I swipe an empty knapsack from the floor and ease open the doors to my armoire. I throw some wrinkled tunics and trousers into the bag, followed by some wool socks and gloves. I don't even bother to change out of my current ensemble, which is purposed for sleep, and instead throw on a heavy overcoat and my boots. I fashion a belt around my waist before securing each chakram into its holster.

I've almost finished packing most of my things when my hands run across something small and familiar. I pull the object out and hold it up to the light. The wooden carving Felix had made me.

My heart flutters at the sight of it, but the feeling quickly dissipates as what I'm about to do sets in. I secure the wooden ship in an inner pocket before glancing over my shoulder at my desk. Two books catch my attention. *The History of Trendalath* and *The Power of Illusié*. Although I want to travel light, I also don't want to leave anything behind that might prove useful once I arrive in Orihia. And, seeing as Cerylia had all of the texts brought to Sardoria *after* we'd arrived, it'll be slim-pickings once I get there. I toss both books into my bag, throw it over my shoulder, then reluctantly remove Juniper from the bed. At chest-level, she nuzzles her head into the side of my coat.

Dawn hasn't broken yet, so it should be early enough for me to leave undetected. I take one last look around my room to ensure I haven't forgotten anything before slipping out the door. The halls are silent as I pass room after room. First Opal's, then Estelle's, then Braxton's, then . . . Felix's. I stop at his door, frustrated that I'm letting this get to me so much. I realize that I've never been inside his chambers—that I probably never *will* be inside. I turn to face his door, fighting the urge to knock, to ask him to come with me. Doubt creeps in.

What if I don't say good-bye?

What if this is the last time I'll ever see him?

What if this is a mistake?

Crippled by my own indecision, I stand there. Half of me prays that he'll sense my presence and fling open the door; the other half tells me to get moving. This internal battle wages on for what feels like hours until I finally lower my head and press it against the door.

"I'm sorry," I whisper, wishing that he could hear me, wishing that I could say this to his face. "I want to stay, but I can't risk hurting you again." I squeeze my eyes shut as tears threaten to fall, then brush my fingertips to my lips and press them to the door.

Silently, I retreat. With each step, I have to force myself not to turn back. I pick up the pace as the dawn encroaches. I know not to exit through the front, but through the courtyard instead. It's mostly enclosed, except for a small area in the northeast corner. I sneak along the outermost part, hoping that the lack of light and my dark coat will keep me hidden.

Visibility is better than I thought it would be as I step out of the confines of the castle and into the bitter wind. The sun has just started its ascent, providing clear direction as to which way is south. I hike my knapsack up on my back and press Juniper deeper into my coat. The little fox doesn't resist, but instead nuzzles into the warmth, her head now buried in layer after layer of thick fabric.

I trudge along in the dense snow in a race against the rising sun. A groan escapes me as a harsh wind whips at my face. My eyes begin to water from the sheer cold. As long as I'm out of sight, away from the castle's view, my plan should carry on without a hitch.

A few minutes later, the bell tower chimes. I glance back over my shoulder, hoping that I haven't been spotted, but surprisingly, I'm farther from the castle than I'd originally thought.

It takes longer than I'd hoped to reach the snow-covered thicket of the Roviel Woods. I pull out my pocket watch to check the time. The falling snow seems to be lessening with each hour that passes, and thankfully, it seems the sun is going to burn right through this blustery haze. I run my thumb along the inscription on the back of my timepiece, ready for some answers.

I turn around once more to look at the castle—at the place that houses the very people I now consider family . . . plus the one who's stolen my heart. In my mind, I promise him that I'll return soon—but something tells me otherwise. That this could be the last time.

Before I can talk myself out of my decision, I duck underneath one of the oversized branches, pushing onward as the castle, and all of Sardoria, fade from view.

RYDAN HELSTROM

"WE HAVE TO go back," Vira says for what must be the eighth time that day. "We have to warn the others!"

"Shhh, keep your voice down." Rydan glances over his shoulder at the darkening cave surrounding them, but Haskell is nowhere in sight. "How many times do I have to tell you we're *not* going back?"

Vira slumps in her seat, her lower lip protruding in a well-versed pout. "Whether you like it or not, Rydan, you're illusié. You have unique abilities. And that group of people back there—the Caldari—they *saved* you. They saved me, too."

Rydan shakes his head as he squeezes the bridge of his nose. He knows she's right, but he doesn't dare admit it. His behavior may seem selfish and uncalled for, but there are two sides to every story; and on his side of the story is one simple fact: that he didn't ask for *any* of this. If he ever hopes to get Vira on his side, she'll have to understand what he's been through. "Do you even care to know how I ended up here?"

Vira straightens in her seat, clearly taken aback by his harsh tone. "Why would you say it like that? Of course I do."

His chest tightens at what he's about to reveal. "I was sent to Lonia on a mission by King Tymond. The directive was simple: assassinate the targets and return with their heads." At this, Vira cringes, but she doesn't interrupt. "Upon completion of the mission, training would resume until the next directive. But someone I *thought* I could trust abandoned me and essentially left me for dead. The person who *saved* me is also the same person who betrayed me."

"Arden," Vira murmurs.

He rakes his hand through his matted hair before giving her a pointed look. "She left me to fend for myself *and* took the evidence of the assassination with her, full well knowing that not completing a mission in its entirety is punishable by death in King Tymond's eyes."

From the look on her face, he can tell that this isn't news to her. "So your plan is to pretend like we don't know the King's Savant is after them—after *us*? To just go along on our merry way like we don't have this huge black cloud hanging over our heads?"

Rydan feigns consideration. "Precisely."

The disdain in her voice is palpable. "Seems perfectly logical to me," she scoffs.

"If you'd rather not continue with our original plans," Rydan counters, "then, by all means, feel free to head back on your own."

If she wasn't riled up before, she certainly is now. "Don't be unreasonable, Rydan. I'm not heading back to Sardoria on my own. After fleeing, who knows if we'd even be welcome again?"

His point exactly.

"So we're heading to Chialka," she continues, "with the Savant out there . . . who are after illusié—after *us.*"

"Yes."

Vira leans forward and bops him on the head. "Have you really thought this through? Even a little?"

Rydan raises a brow as he rubs his forehead. "Of course I have."

"We can't just leave for Chialka—not with the current state of things, anyway. We need to have some sort of precautionary plan in place. Just in case we run into the Savant."

He angles his head. "What would you suggest?"

She gives an exasperated sigh before throwing her hands in the air. "For lords' sake, Rydan, I don't know! That's exactly why I'm bringing it up *before* we leave."

Although her tone is unyielding, he softens. "You're right, Vira. I'm sorry. It's a good idea—one I probably should have thought of before."

Vira rolls her eyes. "*Finally.* I have your attention."

He winks. "Undivided."

꿍   꿍   꿍

"You two have been awfully quiet."

Rydan glances up at Haskell from their cluttered workstation. "What time is it?"

"Late enough for your meal to have gone cold." He points to the table.

Vira stifles a snort. "Looks like we missed dinner."

"Not to worry," Haskell quips. "I transported earlier and picked up some fresh fruit, cheese, and bread. It's on the table whenever you get hungry."

Before Rydan can thank him, Haskell slides around the desk, peeking over his shoulder at the scattered pieces of parchment. "What's all this?"

He's not sure why his initial reaction is to gather the papers and leave the room, but Haskell's tone indicates he's genuinely willing to help. "It's a strategy for how we're going to get to Chialka and what to do if we happen to run into the Savant."

"More like *when*," Vira scoffs with a shake of her head.

Haskell smiles. "Why not save yourselves any potential trouble and allow me to help you?"

Rydan gawks at him as if he's just been hit between the eyes, then laughs. "I can't believe we didn't think of that." He looks over at Vira. "He's a *Transporter.*"

"You'd be willing to do that for us?" she asks.

"Of course. It's dangerous to be traveling during times like these. Do you know exactly to which part of Chialka you're headed?"

"Bayside," Vira responds without hesitation.

"When?"

A wordless exchange passes between Rydan and Vira—the one part of their now-useless plan they hadn't confirmed. "Tomorrow?"

Haskell nods. "Tomorrow it is then." Just as he turns to leave, he stops. "I'd recommend eating as much as you can and getting a good night's sleep. Get your strength up. If you've never transported before, it can be quite"— he pauses, searching for the right word—"nauseating."

Rydan gives him a two-finger salute. "Understood."

"Oh, and even though it's not as cold down south, bring some warm clothes. I'll see what I can gather around here for you." As if realizing he may have overstepped his duty as their host, he quickly turns and walks out of the room.

"Aww," Vira says once he's out of earshot. "I think Haskell might actually *care* about us."

Rydan smiles to himself. At least they have one person on their side.

DARIUS TYMOND

WITH HIS SAVANT away in the northeast, there's no better time to clean up house in Trendalath. An opportune moment to speak with Gladys after overhearing the conversation between her and his wife hasn't yet presented itself—yet another thing on his list—but first, a less confrontational matter awaits him.

A meeting with the Cruex.

With startling conviction, Darius strolls into the Great Room and, as expected, the members of the Cruex are lined up before his throne, waiting for him. The balance is tipped more to the left, seeing as two of his Cruex members are no longer welcome here.

Traitors.

The murmurs come to a halt as Darius takes his place in front of them. "By now, I'm sure you are all well-aware of the situation at hand." He looks to his right at Percival, Ezra, and Cyrus, then to his left at the cousins, Elias and Hugh. Their faces remain stoic, except for Percival's. Darius notices a small smirk quivering at the corner of his mouth. "Sir Garrick, have I said something to amuse you?"

Percival's face falls, his amber eyes widening. "No, Your Majesty."

"That's what I thought. Anyone else have anything to say?" As it should, the room remains silent. Just as he's about to continue, the most senior member of the Cruex, Cyrus, steps forward. "Your Majesty, if I may."

In an effort to hide his dismay, Darius makes a wide sweeping gesture with his hands. "By all means, Lord Alston."

"As your hand-selected group of assassins, I believe I speak for us all when I say our responsibilities seem to have diminished." He then adds, "By no fault of your own, Your Majesty."

Darius takes a step forward and clasps his hands in front of him. "And how is that?"

Not even a glimpse of hesitation. "We know you've called in your Savant, and for good reason. Let us help you in retrieving Sir Helstrom and Lady Eliri."

Hearing their names used with such formality sends a surge of bile up the king's throat.

"If there's *anyone* who knows the two of them—how they think, how they behave—it's the people they've trained alongside with for years," Cyrus explains. "By keeping us partially in the dark, you're refusing to utilize the greatest asset available to you."

Darius passes his gaze over each of the Cruex as he considers the proposal. Even though there is no verbal sign of agreement, one isn't needed. He can tell—just by the stern looks on their faces—that it's unanimous. They *all* feel this way.

"In what way would you suggest the Cruex be involved?" When Cyrus regards him with a blank stare, he feels no choice but to rephrase his question. "What are you proposing, Sir Alston?"

Cyrus looks to the others before saying, "As long as there isn't a dire mission at stake, a few of us would be more than willing to search the grounds outside of Trendalath."

Out of habit, Darius twirls the amethyst ring around his finger. "Who among you would be willing to stay behind?"

Another look at his fellow Cruex. The majority have their heads down. He sighs before answering, "I'll offer to stay behind. The others are welcome to go."

"Sir Garrick, Denholm, Kent, and Darby," Darius addresses each one of them with a nod. "Are you willing to search the grounds outside of Trendalath with the utmost scrutiny in search of Arden Eliri and Rydan Helstrom, as well as my estranged son?" He waits for each one of them to provide a verbal acknowledgement. "And, if you happen upon any three of these individuals, by the lords themselves, do you promise to uphold your duty of returning said individuals to Trendalath unharmed?"

Again, another round of verbal affirmatives.

"Seeing as the Savant is stationed in the northeast, I'll agree to divide the four of you amongst the other regions. Sir Garrick, you'll cover Athia."

Percival grunts, clearly not pleased with his assignment, but accepts it all the same.

"Sir Denholm, you will be stationed in the south, covering Declorath, Miraenia, and Chialka."

Ezra nods his head before bending into a low bow.

"Sir Kent and Sir Darby," Darius continues on, "will take the eastern regions, Eroesa and the Isle of Lonia, although I'm fairly certain you'll find only waste and ruins in the former." The cousins nudge each other, smiles plastered on their faces.

As Darius reviews the map of Aeridon in his head to ensure he's covered each region, Cyrus interrupts. "What about Drakken Isle and the Crostan Islands, Your Majesty?"

A hush falls over the room.

Darius narrows his eyes. "What about them?"

Cyrus doesn't so much as flinch at the king's condescending tone. "You didn't assign anyone to either region," he says flatly. "I'd be happy to go—"

Darius gives him a knowing look. He lowers his voice before saying, "You and I both know that we must protect what is already here."

Cyrus clamps his mouth shut as another uncomfortable silence falls over the room.

Just as the king is about to dismiss them, Percival speaks up. "When shall we depart for our stations?"

If there's one thing Darius is certain of after this meeting, it's that he wants the Cruex away from the castle as soon as humanly possible.

"Tomorrow. At daybreak."

CERYLIA JARETH

"ARE YOU SURE you want to do this?"

Estelle, Felix, Opal, and Braxton stand in a semi-circle in front of the queen. Estelle leans forward and makes eye contact with each of her fellow Caldari before giving a firm nod of her head. "Yes. She lied to us. She knew that Rydan and Elvira fled and didn't admit to it."

"She also discovered Rydan's illusié abilities and failed to tell us," Opal chimes in.

"You understand what this would mean?" Cerylia grasps at the small thread of hope, but it quickly unravels as she's met with an overwhelming response of bobbing heads. "Very well. After you."

Estelle takes the lead, followed by Opal, Felix, and lastly, Braxton. Cerylia intentionally stays a few paces behind the group. They pass by one of the many openings that leads into the courtyard. Dawn is just breaking and Cerylia almost swears she sees a shadow lurking in the far northern corner. She shakes her head, reasoning with herself that her eyes must be playing tricks on her, given the recent myriad of sleepless nights.

She averts her gaze and focuses on the back of Braxton's head instead. The white-blond color produces an unwelcome image of Aldreda holding the dagger that killed her husband. It stills in her mind, and she stops walking for a moment, profusely shaking her head to fend off her rising emotions.

Finally, they arrive at the end of the corridor, at Arden's door. "Shall I do the honors?" Estelle asks. Before she has a chance to protest, Felix jumps in front of her and knocks loudly on the door. "Real nice," she scoffs with a roll of her eyes.

When there's no answer, he knocks again.

"Where could she be?" Opal wonders aloud. "And at such an early hour?"

"I'm sure she's just deep in sleep," Cerylia says.

"Do you have a master key?" Estelle asks.

Normally, Cerylia would have Delwynn fetch such things, but given his current condition—thanks to Arden—it appears she's on her own. "I do. I'll be back momentarily—"

"There's no time for that," Felix interrupts. He gives the door a swift kick—once, twice, three times—before it swings open. The hinges creak in angst.

The first thing Cerylia notices is the bed—it's unmade. The doors to the armoire are wide open, and the flickering candle sitting atop the desk appears to have been lit for some time, what's left of the wax barely visible. She pushes past the Caldari, heading straight for the armoire. The clothes have been rifled through, as if in a hurry . . . to leave.

The shadow in the courtyard wasn't a figment of my imagination—it was Arden.

"She's fled," Cerylia says with absolute certainty. A faint warmth blooms in her neck, traveling upward to her cheeks. Only once it passes does she turn back around to face the group.

Braxton seems the most distraught. Without so much as a word, he bolts out the door, no doubt going to search for her. Felix follows him.

Fine, let them.

Opal walks over to the desk, eyeing the flickering candle. She blows it out with a single huff. "Another one gone," she whispers. "Makes you wonder why everyone is fleeing."

Cerylia gives her a sharp look. "It makes me wonder *why* I offered you all asylum in the first place." Her gaze falls on Estelle. "We were supposed to be allies—not keep secrets from one another."

"I'll see what I can find out," Estelle murmurs, clearly bothered by the queen's sudden unwarranted change in tone. She turns to head out the door.

Opal is the only one who remains.

"Aren't you going with them?" Cerylia waves after them flippantly before falling into one of the oversized armchairs. "I'm sure they can use all the help they can get."

"They'll be fine on their own for a little while." She slinks over to the open chair across from the queen. "I was hoping to speak with you . . . alone."

Her tone immediately gives Cerylia a flashback of their prior conversation in the bell tower. Intrigued, she leans forward. "What about?"

"I wanted to show my appreciation to—well, for choosing to tell the rest of the Caldari about Rydan." She pauses, fiddling with a stray thread on the arm of the chair. "And Arden."

"It was the right thing to do," Cerylia admits. "If only I had listened to you earlier, perhaps we wouldn't be in this predicament now."

"Wishing won't make it so." A small smile tugs at her lips. "We know now, and that's what's important." Her eyes flick to the window. "Any word from Xerin?"

"I'm afraid not," Cerylia says with a sigh. "Xerin hasn't made contact since he left on his crusade to find Rydan and Elvira."

"But that was weeks ago," Opal points out.

Cerylia gives a solemn nod. "He'll return when he has news. I trust him."

A pained look crosses Opal's face, but only momentarily.

"I take it you haven't heard from him either?"

"No," Opal says with a shake of her head, "but there is something I think you should know. About Arden."

The way she says it sends a chill down Cerylia's spine. "I'm listening."

"During my walk the other night, I happened to pass by Arden's window." Opal rises and crosses the room to stand by it, as if to emphasize her point. "It was open and the curtains were drawn, but even through the sheer fabric, I could see that there was another figure in her room."

"Who?"

Something malevolent flashes in her eyes. "It was hovering over her bed . . ."

Cerylia straightens in her chair. She knows before Opal even speaks the words.

"The Mallum."

Terror ripples through her, but she cannot speak.

Opal regards the queen with grave intent. "It's coming for her, Your Greatness, and if you're not careful, it'll come for Sardoria, too."

Somehow, Cerylia manages to find her voice. "I will not allow it." She makes for the door. "I must protect what I have worked so hard to build."

Opal is just steps behind her. "How?"

"We lock the doors," Cerylia orders. "From this point forward, no one comes in or out."

BRAXTON HORNSBY

BRAXTON'S FIRST INSTINCT after learning of Arden's fleeing was to go after her; but once Cerylia declared lock-down of the castle, he knew it was too late. The queen's decision in doing so would undoubtedly delay the last conversation they'd shared—about his discreet mission to Trendalath. Although he doesn't have all the details—just a vague directive to retrieve an amethyst ring—somehow, it's everything he needs.

He peers around the edge of the hallway that leads to Arden's chambers, watching as Opal and Cerylia trail out of the room and down the corridor. Even though he's only known Arden a short time, it seems so unlike her to just leave without telling anyone. Sure, they'd had their fair share of differences as of late, but even so, he'd sensed that she trusted him enough to share her decisions with him—especially a decision as monumental as this one. Then again, he *had* been about to flee without telling Arden—but that was different, seeing as he'd promised Cerylia he'd keep quiet and slip away without anyone knowing.

What if Cerylia is behind this?

What if she's the one who sent her away?

Could Arden potentially be on the same mission I've been asked to complete?

His thoughts having wholly consumed him, he suddenly finds himself standing in front of Arden's door. It's slightly ajar, damaged from the forceful entry Felix had inflicted earlier. He runs his fingers along a few splinters of wood before gently pressing it open.

Speaking of Felix . . . he's here.

In Arden's room.

What his fellow Caldari is doing here, and what he seems to be searching for, Braxton can't be sure. Perhaps he's just looking for some indication pointing to where Arden's run off to. But, by the way he's rummaging through the disorderly armoire drawers, Braxton senses there's more to the story.

Felix stops suddenly, noticing his presence. He turns away from the drawer to look at Braxton, a ravenous gleam in his eye. "What are you doing here?"

His tone is unwelcoming. Braxton has no problem matching it. "I should ask you the same thing."

Felix doesn't respond. He marches away from the armoire to the desk, then to the main living area. He drops to his knees, looking underneath the armchairs, and even going so far as to crawl over to the fireplace and comb through the neat pile of logs. Finally, his head droops as a long sigh escapes him.

Even when Braxton clears his voice, Felix refuses to look up. "Perhaps I can help you find whatever it is you're searching for."

"Doubtful," Felix scoffs, eyes focused on the ground.

"If you'd just tell me what it is . . ."

He lifts his chin, levelling a steely gaze. "Your assistance is not required, nor did I ask for it. You should leave."

Braxton stiffens at his tone. "If you don't want my help, that's fine, but I didn't come here to be chastised—I came here to find out where Arden went. She could be in danger."

Felix murmurs something indecipherable.

"I don't need anyone's permission, including *yours*, to be here." He angles his head at Felix. "Perhaps you're the one who should be leaving."

Felix rolls his eyes, then makes a sweeping gesture with his hand. "Have at it."

Realizing he's been lingering near the doorway this entire time, Braxton walks to the center of the room. He scans Arden's belongings, eyes roving over the clothes on the floor, the armoire, the table, the fireplace . . . the bed.

As he stalks over to it, he can feel Felix watching him. Nevertheless, he gives the sheets and pillows a quick fluff, eyeing the space just below the ceiling. A layer of dust and animal hair surrounds him, tufts of stray fur floating to the floor. In that moment, things suddenly become crystal clear.

Juniper.

He knows exactly where she's gone.

Orihia.

But why? What could she be searching for?

From across the room, Arden's bookshelf catches his eye. He hurries over to it and begins inspecting the neatly stacked titles. He pulls a few of the texts out, manically flipping through them. He's still not entirely sure what he's looking for until skimming a book entitled *The Archmage.* One passage in particular jumps out at him . . . about an *amethyst* ring.

Forgetting that Felix is also in the room, he slides his back down the side of the bookshelf, devouring every last word on the page. According to the text, only a handful of copper rings welded around an amethyst stone have been uncovered, providing a protective shield to those who wear them—although the text doesn't say *from what.* He can briefly recall, as a young boy, his father wearing a similar ring. It always seemed to catch the light in astounding ways—splashing glimmers of indigo against the castle walls as he moved from room to room.

Come to think of it, he can't remember a time where his father *wasn't* wearing that ring. He'd always thought it was just for show, but perhaps it was more valuable than his father had let on.

Rereading the text once more, Braxton flips forward a page, then backward two pages, disappointed to find that there's one measly paragraph covering these rare—yet allegedly protective—rings. Frustrated, he slams the book shut and throws it at his feet. He rakes a hand through his hair before closing his eyes.

Yes, Arden possesses this book, and yes, it was on her desk, meaning she must have read it—but the probability of her reading *that* particular passage *and* remembering that Darius wears something similar is unlikely.

Unless Cerylia told her.

Felix's voice breaks his train of thought. "Find something interesting?"

Braxton grunts as he pushes himself to his feet. He steps around the haphazardly strewn book and, without hesitation, makes for the door.

"Braxton?"

With his fingers grazing the handle, he stops.

"I know you're worried about her. I am, too." Felix's voice is unusually strained. "But if you've found something useful, something pointing to where she's gone, you need to share it. There's strength in numbers. We can all benefit from knowing."

A lump forms in Braxton's throat as he considers this. The likelihood that Felix knows what Cerylia's asked of him—what she's after—is slim to none. And if Arden's been tasked with something similar, there must be a reason. If Cerylia had explicitly wanted everyone to know, she would have called a meeting. It seems she's only chosen specific Caldari, although the reason behind *why* remains unclear.

The decision comes easy. "You should be happy, Felix. I'm doing exactly as you asked," Braxton says as he yanks open the door. "I'm leaving."

ARDEN ELIRI

TWO DAYS INTO traveling, and already Juniper and I have been in the presence of a windstorm and a subsequent thunderstorm. We've mostly stayed on the outskirts of the Roviel Woods until happening upon the wastelands of Eroesa. I will admit, I hadn't quite thought ahead to the fact that I'd need to board an actual *ship* in order to get to the Isle of Lonia, and seeing as there's little to no civilization in Eroesa, finding a functioning ship (and a captain) is out of the question.

With this in mind, I make a swift change of direction to head west, knowing that either Chialka or Miraenia are my best bet. Then again, I should probably take Trendalath and Miraenia's complicated past into consideration. The last thing I need is to be taken hostage—or worse, murdered—before reaching Orihia. It's settled, then. Chialka is my preferred port of departure.

Approaching Chialka happens more suddenly than I'd anticipated. Ever since leaving Sardoria, sleep has escaped me, so upon first glance at the bayside town, I've almost convinced myself that it's merely a mirage. For one, it's not snowing here. The trees are still plush with leaves—a mix of golden browns and bright canary yellows—and the temperature is significantly warmer than in the woods. The cobblestone streets are mostly empty, but lining the walkway are narrow cauldron-like stands with glowing orange orbs to light the way, even in the blinding sunlight. I pass by a few of the cottages, noticing that the shutters are closed and large barrels are stationed in front of the doors.

I try to ignore the hollow feeling in my stomach as I remove my coat and sling it over my shoulder, coaxing Juniper not to stray too far. I continue to head south toward where the docks should be. The void only grows when I realize there's not a soul in sight. I abruptly change direction until I spot a bank of water to my left. The alleyway between the two cottages is narrow, so I turn sideways, inching slowly along the brick wall, until I finally emerge on the other side.

Juniper follows. I brush the debris from my pants before scooping her up into my arms. As I lift my gaze, my jaw drops—not at the number of ships docked at the harbor, but at the giant Yoshino cherry tree sitting in the middle of the water. Its branches extend so far outward that, if I could jump high enough, I'm almost certain I'd be able to pick one of the leaves. Even in the midst of what should be winter, the tree is in full bloom, its magenta leaves hovering over the entire wharf. I'm so mesmerized by its beauty that I hardly notice the young man standing right in front of me.

"Excuse me, miss? Is there something I can help you with?"

Startled, I take a step backward. Juniper jumps from my arms and scurries behind my heels. "I'm sorry, I didn't notice you standing there." I fumble for words, repeating his perfectly normal question in my head. "Can you—er, would you be able to tell me when the next ship is scheduled to leave?"

The young man tilts his head to the side, eyes traveling to my boots. "Is that . . . a fox?"

I nod feverishly.

"Thought so. How interesting." He chuckles to himself before meeting my gaze. "As for when the next ship is scheduled to leave, well, that depends. Where ya headed?"

I can feel my cheeks burn, no doubt the same color as the leaves on the tree above me. "The Isle of Lonia."

He flashes a toothy grin. "Looks to me like you're in luck. The next ship to Lonia leaves in about five minutes."

Confused, I glance over his shoulder at the multitude of vessels. "Um, from which port?"

His olive eyes twinkle as he says, "Nine."

"Great. Thank you. I appreciate your help." I stumble over myself as I make to leave, but something in his tone stops me.

"Unfortunately, that ship is only carrying cargo. No passengers—and certainly no animals."

My shoulders slump as he says this. "I suppose that doesn't help me much, now does it?"

Another toothy grin. "Fortunately for you, I'm the captain of said ship."

My demeanor changes entirely. "I know we've only just met, and I hate to ask this of you, but . . . is there any way you could, you know"—I pause in an attempt to judge his reaction—"stow us away?"

He looks me up and down with narrowed eyes, considering my proposal. "Not from around here, are ya?"

I shake my head, hoping it'll be the last of this unnecessarily long interrogation.

He drums his fingers against his chin. "I don't know why, but I like you. And I like your pet fox." He says it so casually, it makes me wonder if all the people in Chialka are this trusting. "I'll let you stow away on my ship under one condition."

I look at him hopefully.

"Tell me your name."

My stomach twists into knots. I know better than to reveal my true identity. King Tymond has surely sent word to the surrounding regions of my alleged betrayal. What I say next could either save me or ruin me. I'm so, so close to getting on this ship—getting to Orihia.

I use the first name that comes to mind.

"Opal," I say with the utmost conviction. "My name is Opal Marston."

≪ ≪ ≪

About an hour into the voyage, I've learned that the young lad's name is Avery Bancroft. With an abundance of freckles on his cheeks and auburn hair, he comes from a merchant family who used to reside in Declorath, but moved shortly after due to its proximity to Trendalath. His obvious distaste for King Tymond is just one of the many things working in his favor. He can't be older than eighteen and yet his father has appointed him captain on numerous expeditions. The compassion with which he speaks for his family makes me wish I had the chance to know my own.

"Hungry?" Avery shouts from the helm of the ship.

I turn my gaze away from the cobalt sea and climb the steps toward him, Juniper on my heels. "Famished, actually. What do you have?"

"Not much," he admits begrudgingly. "To be honest, I like to wait for my trips to Lonia before stocking up. Since they experience a better winter than Chialka—and most other regions, for that matter—the fruits and vegetables are impeccably ripe nearly year-round. Grains are always fresh, too."

I nod hungrily, my mouth watering.

He smiles. "In the pantry on the lower deck, there are a couple loaves of bread. Should be some grapes, a couple of apples, and possibly some dragon fruit."

"Dragon fruit?" My eyes grow wide. "I don't think I've ever had one, let alone even seen one."

He looks at me as though I've just spoken to him in foreign tongue. "Well, we must change that immediately. Come on." He leaves the helm, pulling me along behind him.

"But who's going to steer the ship?" I ask.

"It'll be fine for a few minutes," he assures me. "The tricky thing about dragon fruit is that you have to cut them properly, otherwise it's impossible to get to the good stuff." He releases my arm before taking off down the stairs.

I coax Juniper to follow me before heading to the lower deck where I watch in amusement as he raids the pantry, swiping his hands back and forth across the shelves. "There's got to be one in here," he mumbles to what he probably thinks is himself, but it's loud enough for me to hear.

"It's okay," I say trying not to sound too disappointed. "Perhaps we can get a fresh one once we get to Lonia."

"Found it," he interrupts, holding out a tall, spiky-looking pink fruit. But when I take it in my hands and examine it further, I realize that the spikes are dulled— and actually aren't spikes at all. They're leaves.

"By the way, we can't get a fresh one in Lonia because they don't grow there," he remarks. "They're actually native to—"

"It's unlike anything I've ever seen," I interrupt as I lightly press my thumbs into the skin, leaving small indentations. "Is the inside as pretty as the outside?"

Avery extends his hand. "Here, allow me."

I hand the dragon fruit back to him, watching as he grabs a sharp knife from one of the drawers and levels it overhead. Mesmerized, I watch as he slices it right down the middle to reveal bright white flesh dotted with tiny black seeds.

As he hands me the fruit, along with a wooden spoon, the ship suddenly jerks us both forward. His eyes flick to the top of the stairs. "If you'll excuse me for a moment . . ."

I give him a concerned look. "Is everything all right?"

He nods, but his eyes don't leave the stairs. "I'll be right back."

I have an unexplainable urge to follow him as he makes for the stairs, but I stay put. I busy myself with the fruit, digging my spoon into it. I give Juniper the first bite before trying some myself. The taste is hard to pin down. It's not tart enough to make my lips pucker, but not sweet enough to crave it.

My thoughts scatter when I hear footsteps bounding down the steps, distracting me from my momentary disappointment. "Avery?" I call out. I peek around the pantry door, but there's no one at the foot of the stairs. My body tenses at the sheer silence. The ship feels as though it's stopped rocking, and I can no longer hear the waves crashing against the hull.

"Stay here," I whisper to Juniper. As if she understands me, she curls up into a ball directly underneath the wooden stools.

I swiftly check the holsters at my sides, my chakrams ready if I need them. Stepping around the pantry door, I press myself up against the wall and inch closer to the stairwell. I want to call out his name again, but I know better. I take a quick gander up the stairwell.

Nothing but navy blue sky ahead.

I climb the steps as quietly as possible, really putting my Cruex skills to use for the first time in a while. Just as I'm about to reach the top, I turn and poke my head up so that only my eyes are slightly above the planks of wood. The ship is completely empty.

As I fully emerge from the stairwell, I can't help but feel a sense of familiarity. It's uncanny. I look up at the mast, the white sails billowing in the fierce wind. The sky grows darker and darker until only the stars are visible. And then those fade, too.

I don't see Avery anywhere.

I rush to the edge of the ship and look overboard. We're obviously on the water, but the ocean is motionless—not a single ripple. If the stars were still out, I'm sure they would have reflected with immaculate precision in the water, seeing as the ship is also stationary. Everything surrounding me is immobile.

And that's when I feel it.

An icy wind chips at the back of my neck, causing my skin to prickle. A gloomy mist forms in the sky, somehow making it even darker, which, at this point, seems impossible. I take a steadying breath as I raise my face skyward. I pull my chakrams from their holsters, standing at the ready. I know what's coming for me.

And this time, I'm prepared.

A crimson cloak materializes from the darkness. I don't flinch as it floats down toward me. It stops just inches from my face, its heated breath lingering in the air.

It's time, it says to me.

I remain calm, my fingers gripping the chakrams even tighter than before.

We have everything you could ever need. Everything you could ever want.

I grimace at the pull I feel toward this strange being. Once again, part of me says to listen, to go with them—the other part of me says to stay.

Won't you join us?

I open my mouth to form the word *no,* but it doesn't come out. Suddenly, my throat feels thick, my body paralyzed. My mind tells my arms to raise the chakrams, to attack this *thing,* but I'm frozen.

I can't move.

Panic takes over. I try to call out for help, but the effort is futile.

Join us, it growls, baring its yellowed, jagged, triangular-shaped teeth.

I stand there—unable to move, think, or feel—in front of this terrifying creature that is surely going to kill me. As Cruex-turned-Caldari, assassin-turned-illusié, I have never felt more helpless in my life. I imagine closing my eyes and not staring into the hooded abyss of this *thing,* focusing on anything else, grasping for another vision—one that doesn't feel like it's sucking the very life out of me. I dive deeper and deeper into my own layers of darkness, floating along the edges of my mind—waiting.

But nothing comes.

It's as empty in here as it is out there.

Just as I'm about to give up hope, I stumble upon a soft white glow, hidden in the deepest part of my subconscious. I catapult toward it, moving as fast as my inner drive will take me. I reach for it, extending beyond a length I would have thought possible.

I'm so incredibly close when, suddenly, every part of me is consumed by a chilling cold. I thrash in the water, kicking frantically until I break through the surface, arms flailing as I gasp for air. Wisps of my still-warm breath float in front of my face, growing fainter by the minute. Before my body goes into what I'm sure will be hypothermic shock, my gaze falls on the ship I've just been thrown from. A name comes into view.

The Corsair.

I begin to fall in and out of consciousness as I watch the hooded figure dissipate into the opaque sky. I blink once, twice . . . my breaths growing shallower with each passing second. The return of the twinkling stars is the last thing I see before I fade away.

RYDAN HELSTROM

IT'S THE DAY of their departure, and Vira seems to have made herself scarce, which is surprising and nearly impossible, given the size of the cave. It's not like they're back in Sardoria, where there are seemingly hundreds of rooms to hide in, and yet, there's absolutely no sign of her.

"Vira?" he calls out, checking one of the few closed-off areas.

Silence.

Trying not to let his irritation get the best of him, he swings by another couple of enclosed spaces within the cave, continuing to call out her name to no avail. He decides to walk back to the common area, cursing as he strolls down one of the dimly lit corridors, when he unexpectedly bumps into Haskell.

"There you are!" Haskell exclaims, seemingly unbothered by the collision. He looks past Rydan, clearly perplexed by his lack of company. "Where's Vira?"

"My question exactly," Rydan responds as he rubs the sore spot on his shoulder.

"I bet you I know where she is," Haskell says as he turns and starts walking back the way he came. "Come on."

"That makes one of us," Rydan quips. He follows closely behind him and it's not but three-quarters into their journey that he realizes exactly where they're headed. Haskell grabs a familiar torch from the wall sconce and guides him into the once undisclosed quarters. Sure enough, Vira is there, rifling through multiple stacks of parchment.

"See," Haskell says with a quick glance over his shoulder. "Told ya she'd be here."

Rydan notices Vira stuff a rolled-up piece of parchment into the waistband of her trousers before abruptly straightening to attention. In one swift movement, she glides over to them, swiping her overcoat (that Haskell had so generously provided) from the table before saying, "Ready to go?"

Rydan is tempted to ask her what was so important for her to take without asking their host first, but doesn't want to delay their trip to Chialka any further.

"Well, let's get a move on," Haskell urges. "You sure you have everything you need?"

Rydan holds up his knapsack (yet another gift from Haskell) and Vira holds up a small satchel. "Ready," they say in unison.

Haskell leads them out of the cave into broad daylight. They walk a little ways until they reach a small circular clearing surrounded by trees. Haskell extends his left arm to Vira, his right to Rydan. "Whatever you do, don't let go," he instructs.

Rydan looks across the man's burly chest at Vira, bracing himself for whatever's about to come next. All too suddenly, he feels as though he's been flipped upside down and his insides have been turned inside out. Swirls of gray, navy, and violet surround him, his entire body going numb, except for the contact between his hand and Haskell's arm. A shrill sound penetrates his ears, and he briefly wonders if Vira is the one making the noise, or if it's just part of the transporting process. The distorted noise shrieks on and on for what feels like an eternity until they finally somersault and tumble out of the vortex.

Haskell lands upright, perfectly stable on his feet, while both Rydan and Vira flail, struggling to regain their balance. Just as Rydan opens his mouth to speak, a wave of nausea hits him. Bile creeps up his throat, and he swiftly turns away to release it. The sound of retching seems to be amplified, and that's when he realizes that Vira must be experiencing the exact same thing.

Rydan blinks the wetness from his eyes before wiping his mouth with the back of his hand. Slowly, he pushes himself upright, attempting to stand. It takes him a few tries before finally feeling steady enough to take a few steps forward, and it's then he realizes they've landed in some shrubbery between two cottages.

"That was, by far, the most *dreadful* thing I have ever experienced." He pats Haskell on the shoulder before stepping out of the shrubs, brushing the leaves and twigs from his trousers. "I don't know how you do that on a daily basis."

"Daily. Weekly." Haskell shrugs. "You get used to it."

"I highly doubt I could." Rydan wets his cracked lips before observing their surroundings. "So, where to?"

He'd almost forgotten about Vira, who lets out a small groan as she haphazardly steps through the bushes, following in his footsteps. Her face is completely drained of color, made even more blatant in the afternoon sun. At the sight of her, Rydan makes a mental note to find a fresh fruit stand . . . and to search for a nearby spring to refill their canteens.

"Actually," Haskell starts, returning to his half-hidden state amongst the shrubbery, "this is as far as I go."

"What do you mean?" Rydan asks. "You came all this way just to . . . leave us here?"

Vira looks equally as alarmed. "Very funny. You're just messing with us. Right, Haskell?"

He doesn't respond, just starts digging in his pockets until he pulls something out. Rydan can't discern what it is, so he draws closer. "I need you to take this," Haskell says, handing him a small, circular object wrapped in a handkerchief.

Rydan gives him a sidelong glance before slowly unwrapping the item. It's a silver pocket watch. One that looks exactly like . . .

He turns the watch over in his hands.

The inscription reads *Eliri.*

Rydan looks up, but when he does, Haskell is gone.

Arden's *brother* is gone.

DARIUS TYMOND

WITH BOTH THE Savant and the Cruex away from Trendalath castle, Darius can finally attend to other matters without distraction—namely the indicting conversation that's recently taken place between Gladys and his wife. Aldreda hasn't spoken to him in weeks, nor has she slept in their bed . . . evidence enough that he's still on her bad side.

He'll have to go through Gladys then—getting information, that is. While he'd never admit it aloud to anyone, the woman intimidates him to no end. Perhaps it's because of her sheer size, or her unfazed reaction to the horrific things she's witnessed in the past. Either way, she's not someone he looks forward to interacting with.

But, if he wants the exact details pertaining to the conversation with his wife—and he does—there doesn't seem to be much of a choice. Making nice with Aldreda, especially in her overly sensitive state, is out of the question, and so off to find Gladys he goes.

The west side of the castle is more deserted than he remembers, save for a few guards, but it's also been ages since he's trekked this far away from the Great Room. He'd felt almost foolish asking one of the stationed guards for directions to the handmaidens' quarters, even though they'd been graciously provided without judgment. Given the size of Trendalath kingdom and its many alcoves and dens, it's not surprising he'd almost lost his way.

After walking along what is certainly the longest corridor in the castle, Darius finally reaches a door enveloped in maroon and gold panels. He straightens his robes and clears his throat before knocking. Moments later, Gladys stands before him, clad from head-to-toe in steel armor. When she realizes who it is, she quickly bends into a low bow. "Your Majesty. I wasn't expecting you."

"Gladys." He lifts his chin. "I assume you can forgive my unannounced intrusion."

She bristles at his tone. "Certainly," she says, stepping to the side. "Do come in."

Shoulders back, Darius strolls into the room. With Gladys towering over him by at least half a foot, it's hard to keep his wits about him. The door bangs shut. Gladys takes a seat and gestures to the chair across from her. As much as Darius wants to remain standing, giving the illusion that he's completely in control, he finds himself lowering onto the chair.

"How may I be of service, Your Majesty?" Gladys asks.

Darius had prepared exactly what he'd wanted to say on the way to her chambers—he'd had plenty of time to do so—but his thoughts now escape him. He blurts out the first thing that comes to mind. "How is Aldreda?"

Gladys regards him with an arched brow. "I beg your pardon?"

It's then he realizes how strange the question must sound—why would a former handmaiden-turned-guard know more about his wife's well-being than her own husband? Knowing full well that there's no coming back from that question and its many implications, he decides to be direct. "A week or so ago, I overheard you and Aldreda conversing in the hall." Gladys stiffens at the accusation. "I want to know what, if anything, you've told her."

Her pupils turn to mere slits as she narrows her eyes. "Forgive me, Your Majesty, but that is a conversation that should be had between you and the queen."

"Normally, I would agree." He strokes his chin. "But, as I'm sure you're aware, Aldreda and I aren't on the best of terms right now."

Gladys is quick to respond. "I don't see how that's my problem."

Not only is her response unwarranted, it's entirely disrespectful. He rises from the chair, taking slow, deliberate steps toward her. He leans over so that his hands grip the armrests, his face just several inches from hers. "It's your problem if I say it's your problem."

She doesn't flinch.

"What did you tell her?" he shouts, violently jolting the chair.

She stares at him, not a flicker of emotion on her face. "Screaming at me like I'm an intolerable child is not going to make me feel any more inclined to cooperate."

Yet another infuriating response.

Darius shakes the chair once more, then whirls away from her, smoothing the sides of his hair with trembling fingers. He takes a steadying breath before lowering his hands, balling them into fists. It does little to calm him.

When he turns back around, he almost loses his footing. Aldreda is standing behind the chair Gladys is occupying, arms crossed, lips drawn in a firm scowl. He realizes she must have been hiding somewhere in the room.

How much of the conversation did she hear?

"If there's something you need to ask me, I'd prefer if you came to me directly."

And just like that, his question is answered.

"My Queen, would you mind joining me in the hall for a moment?"

She angles her head slightly before giving it an adamant shake. "If it's privacy you seek, you have it— right here, in this very room. After all, that *is* why you came to speak with Gladys, is it not?"

She has him there. "Very well." A warmth blooms in his neck, crawling all the way up to his cheeks. Even so, he doesn't waver as he says, "As I'm sure you overheard, I spotted the two of you in the hallway the other evening, speaking in rather hushed voices."

"And?" Aldreda challenges.

"*And*," Darius retorts, feeling uncharacteristically flustered, "I demand to know what you were discussing."

"You *demand* it?" Aldreda takes a deliberate step forward. "Is it safe to assume you were *eavesdropping*?"

His gaze lands on her engorged abdomen, which seems to have grown considerably larger since the last time he'd seen her. "Since it wasn't on purpose, no, I was not eavesdropping. I merely overheard a conversation that piqued my interest. That's all."

Aldreda remains silent for a moment. "Well then. I suppose you heard everything you need to know."

"And how is that?"

Gladys answers for her. "Because we haven't spoken since that night."

Confused, Darius flicks his gaze between Gladys and his wife.

"I think the more appropriate question," Aldreda says, taking another step forward, then another, "is what *you've* been keeping from *me*."

Oh lords. He's walked right into this one. "I'm not keeping anything from you." He regrets the lie as soon as it leaves his mouth.

"Funny," Aldreda says as she walks past him and circles an empty chair, "because I certainly wasn't aware

177

that, on the last execution day, our *son* made an appearance for the first time in over ten years."

Well, shit.

CERYLIA JARETH

ALTHOUGH SHE HADN'T publicly announced her decision to lock the castle doors, the upending riots from the townspeople are enough to indicate that the knowledge has indeed spread past the castle walls. Sure, the decision had been made in haste, but it was better than no decision at all—especially with what, according to Opal, was lurking just outside her doors.

Cerylia sits in the White Room, trying to ignore the shouting outside, when a soft rap on the door stirs her from her thoughts. "Come in," she mumbles somewhat absentmindedly.

A silver head of hair pokes through the doors. "Your Greatness, is this a bad time?"

She's happy to see Opal. "It's a fine time," she responds gracefully. "Please, have a seat."

Opal shuts the doors quietly behind her before sitting in front of an empty teacup and saucer. It's the last of the tea, and Cerylia has barely had one full cup, but she's just gotten back on the right foot with Opal. No need to be difficult.

A long silence stretches between them as she takes her time preparing a cup for her guest. Opal nods appreciatively as the queen slides the saucer back across the table. She studies the girl as she takes a couple sips of her tea, noticing that she doesn't exactly appear to be rattled but . . . something is definitely off.

As the silence carries on, it's clear that neither of them wants to be the first to speak. Cerylia has to commend Opal's resolve—it's both terrifying and oddly refreshing. She waits for Opal to set her cup down before finally saying, "To what do I owe the pleasure, Lady Marston?"

"I came here today because I wanted you to know that I went back to that night . . ." Her voice trails off as if she's debating whether or not coming here was the right thing to do.

Cerylia raises a brow, but doesn't press.

Opal swirls her finger around the outer edge of the saucer. "The night Arden fled."

"You saw something?"

"Nothing out of the ordinary, per se, except for her clutching a pocket watch like it was her lifeline. She studied it for quite some time. Does that mean anything to you?"

Actually, it does, but the lie rolls right off of Cerylia's tongue. "No. I'm afraid it doesn't."

"That's unfortunate. I saw her grab that pocket watch, a couple of books, and her clothes before scooping up Juniper and leaving."

Cerylia tries to maintain the blank look on her face, but it isn't easy. Her eyes flick to the empty cup in front of her. Before Opal can pry further, she needs to change the subject. "Shall I have one of the servants fetch more tea?"

Opal doesn't seem to notice anything peculiar in the queen's behavior. She leans back in her chair, stifling a yawn. "That's quite all right, Your Greatness. I should probably head to the courtyard for training."

"Is Delwynn keeping you busy?" As soon as she says his name, an image of her loyal advisor in a wheelchair flashes through her mind, followed by a memory she wishes she could erase—when he'd been writhing and seizing in pain, with Arden kneeling next to him.

Things haven't been the same since.

Opal's voice pulls her from the memory. "Have you decided what you're going to do about Aldreda?"

Cerylia sits back in her chair. The bluntness of the remark leaves her speechless.

Opal must sense her discomfort because she quickly adds, "I know there have been a number of distractions as of late, but I also know how important it is to seek retribution for Dane's untimely death."

My sweet Dane. Memories from long, long ago make a brief appearance before passing her by. Now these— *these* she wish she could stay in, could *live* in. As any wife would, she'd planned to experience it all with her late husband—build a life together, rule a kingdom, produce an heir—but her vision of happily ever after had been swiftly plucked from her grasp by the one family she despised more than the Mallum itself.

The Tymonds.

Fortunately, hope remains. Once she possesses the amethyst ring, she can finally do what should have been done many years ago—and she'll have all the help she needs to do so.

BRAXTON HORNSBY

ALREADY LATE FOR training, Braxton wakes in a haze. He clambers out of bed, rushing to his armoire to get dressed. He throws on an unwashed tunic and a pair of trousers before pulling on his boots. As he's about to close the drawer, his gaze lands on the folded note from his mother. He's tempted to read it once more, but knows better than to keep Delwynn and the others waiting—especially after Arden's failed healing incident.

He rushes out of his chambers, locking the door behind him, and carries on down the hall, when, much to his chagrin, he bumps into the last person he'd expected to see this early in the morning.

Queen Jareth.

"Ah, just the person I was coming to see." She seems to sense that he's in a hurry. "Not to worry, your training has been cancelled. I'd planned to ask you to breakfast this morning in the Great Hall"—she looks him up and down—"but not dressed like that."

Braxton blushes as he glances down at his wrinkled linen pants and ragged tunic. "I'd be honored to join you for breakfast. I'll go change and meet you there in a few minutes."

This seems to satisfy her. She nods and turns away, her footsteps echoing down the massive corridor. He waits patiently until she turns the corner, then dashes down the hallway. He swiftly exchanges his wrinkled clothes for freshly pressed ones, throws on a less tattered pair of boots, runs a comb through his matted hair, and heads back out the door.

Awaiting his arrival in the dining hall is a wide spread of breakfast items—scones, porridge, toast, and an assortment of meats. He gives Cerylia a polite nod before taking his seat. He waits until she takes a bite of her meal before digging into his own. "Will it be just the two of us?"

She arches a brow as if to say, *What do you think?*

He lowers his eyes, tearing into a loaf of bread and stuffing it in his mouth to keep from speaking. *She asked you here. Let her speak first.*

After a drawn out silence, Cerylia says, "I was hoping we could continue our last conversation."

The bread in his mouth keeps him from smiling. With so many questions after their last exchange, he'd hoped he'd get a chance to clarify.

"Just so you're aware, I've advised Delwynn that you are the only person allowed to leave the castle."

He stops chewing, eyes growing wide. "Pardon, Your Greatness?"

"You are the only person permitted to leave during the lock-down," she repeats, more brashly this time.

Now Braxton finds himself with even more questions, like *why* the castle is on lock-down. Something has provoked Cerylia enough to make her feel the need to protect her queendom. His thoughts flick to their last conversation about the amethyst ring. Is this why she's tasked him with retrieving it? Had he assumed incorrectly about Arden?

He debates whether or not to ask, but the words leave his mouth before he can reel them back in. "Forgive me if this is out of line, Your Greatness, but I read something in one of the texts that was transferred here from Orihia. It mentioned the protective capabilities of amethyst rings . . ."

Cerylia's hands freeze at her mouth, mid-bite.

"I'm just curious to know what it is these rings protect from."

"The text is incorrect," she says quietly. "It's only one ring."

Her response doesn't do much to clarify. "What does it protect from?"

Her jaw clenches as if suddenly recalling a horrible nightmare. "Even if I were to explain it to you, you wouldn't understand. Not until you . . ."

He waits for her to continue, but her voice trails off, a faraway look in her eyes.

"Not until you what?"

A long pause. "Feel it."

He knows he's about to press too far, but he can't help himself. "Is it the same reason the castle is on lock-down?"

It's then Cerylia snaps out of her daze, narrowing her eyes at him. "You will leave today."

Braxton looks at her in bewilderment. "I beg your pardon?"

"Today," Cerylia says, nodding her head fervently. She pushes her chair from the table and rises. "You will leave today."

Not knowing how to respond, Braxton swiftly removes the napkin from his lap and tosses it onto the table. He slides his chair backward before standing, gives her a brief and awkward nod, then exits the Great Hall, wondering what in lords' name just happened.

Looks like he's going to Trendalath sooner than he'd anticipated.

◆   ◆   ◆

In the middle of packing his belongings for the journey ahead, Braxton curses himself for not being more forthright with Cerylia. He should have asked about

Arden. He needs to know if the queen's been putting up a façade. Is there a chance he'll run into Arden in Trendalath? First the first time in a while, a sense of hopefulness flutters in his chest.

Without warning, his door creaks open. Braxton briefly looks up from his bag, somewhat surprised to see Delwynn enter. He's so preoccupied with his own thoughts that he hardly notices Delwynn is *walking*—out of his wheelchair. "If you're here to hurry me along, no need. I'll be out of the queen's hair shortly," he says huffily, throwing another pair of trousers into his bag.

When there's no response, Braxton ceases his shuffling and looks up, yet again. His eyes grow wide as he focuses on the man that is standing *fully upright* before him. Without a wheelchair. Without a cane.

"I thought . . ." he starts, unable to find the words to finish his thought.

"I thought so, too." Delwynn takes two fluid steps forward. "But, as it turns out, Arden actually *did* heal me after all."

Braxton looks him up and down, hardly believing his eyes. "But how? How is that possible?"

Delwynn shrugs. "Perhaps we must experience pain in order to know healing—just as light cannot exist without darkness, healing cannot exist without pain."

Funny—he doesn't remember asking the old man for a lecture. "Right. Well, I'm glad to see you are doing better. Truly." He scans the room one last time before securing his knapsack. "I need to get moving or Cerylia will surely have my head." He throws a strap over one shoulder and makes for the door, but Delwynn steps in front of him, completely blocking his path. Until now, he hadn't realized just how tall the queen's advisor is. Suddenly, Braxton feels very small.

Delwynn stands firmly in place. "That's partly the reason I'm here. Cerylia was hasty in making her decision to force the castle into lock-down, just as she was hasty in telling you to leave."

Braxton recalls that Delwynn wasn't present for that conversation, but perhaps Cerylia filled him in right after he'd left.

"While her former decision is smart, I'm afraid the latter is not. I implore you to stay here until it is safe."

Braxton eyes him warily. "Has this new plan been cleared with Queen Jareth?"

Delwynn chuckles softly, leading Braxton to presume he's here of his own accord. "Not to worry. You can stay in my quarters. Cerylia can think you've gone. I can't allow another one of you to leave . . . not with the current state of Aeridon."

Braxton drops his bag to the floor. "So you're suggesting that I *don't* leave and then when I pretend to return—*without* the amethyst ring—what then? Do I act like I've failed her when I haven't even tried?" He shakes his head. "I may be many things, Delwynn, but I am not a coward."

Delwynn shushes him. "No one said you were." He glances over his shoulder, realizing the door is still slightly cracked. "Staying here doesn't make you a coward—it makes you smart. Going out there now is like inviting death straight to your door."

A lump forms in Braxton's throat. *But Arden's out there.* "I'll have to leave eventually."

Delwynn nods. "Yes, when the time is right—but that time is not now." He grabs Braxton's left hand and closes his grip. "You will not leave until I say so. Shake on it."

Braxton gives him an idle stare as a plan begins to take shape in his mind. "Fine. I won't leave—on one condition."

"What's that?"

"You're going to tell me everything you know about Cerylia's decision to lock down the castle *and* why she wants me to retrieve the amethyst ring from Trendalath."

Delwynn gives a long sigh, but the corner of his mouth twitches upward. "Very well. I suppose it's only fair."

"Do we have a deal?"

"Against my better judgment, yes," Delwynn says with a firm grip, "we have a deal."

ARDEN ELIRI

WHEN I REGAIN consciousness, I find myself back aboard the ship, wrapped in a wool blanket with Avery hovering over me. Despite the warmth of the blanket, I'm still shivering, my teeth chattering against one another.

"Opal, are you all right?"

Avery's voice comes in waves. I look around me, trying to locate Opal, almost forgetting that I'd told him that that was *my* name. I try to respond, but my lungs and throat burn, like someone's lit a furnace right beneath them, so I shake my head instead. I am the furthest thing from okay.

Did Avery see what happened?

I *would* ask him the many questions plaguing my mind if it weren't for the fire I feel like I'm about to breathe every time I even consider opening my mouth. Fortunately, he answers my questions without needing any verbal prompts.

"You didn't tell me you were involved with the Mallum," he whispers harshly. "I would have thought you'd disclose such life-threatening information *before* boarding my ship."

My eyes sting as they widen. I try once again to speak, but the words come out as barely a croak. "The *what*?"

It's then he must realize that I have absolutely no idea what he's talking about because his face turns pallid. "Never mind. It must have been a hallucination." He grabs another blanket and throws it on top of the one that's already wrapped tightly around me. "Why don't you get some rest and we'll talk about it later?"

He doesn't have to ask twice.

◈ ◈ ◈

When I wake again, Juniper is impatiently pawing at my face and I'm even more disgruntled than before. As I make an attempt to bat her away, I realize I'm still wrapped in a double layer of blankets.

One look around indicates that my surroundings have changed. The brightly colored landscape tells me that I'm in Lonia, but I'm nowhere near the harbor, which is on the southwest side of the island. I seem to have been dropped off on the northwest side—where there's no civilization.

Avery is nowhere in sight.

My bag sits next to me, and I immediately notice a folded piece of parchment sticking out of one of the pockets. I hastily unwrap the bundles of blankets from around my body and whip the note open. The handwriting is barely legible, but even through the scribbles, I can make out what it says.

Opal,

This is for your protection—and my own. I'm sorry.

Safe travels,
Avery Bancroft

For some reason the note brings up a swell of unwarranted emotions. Tears prick the corners of my eyes. I take a deep breath, gulping down the familiar feeling of abandonment. This is *not* how I expected to start my journey to Lonia.

I then recall my terrifying experience with . . . well, I'm not sure exactly what it was. A particular word sits on the tip of my tongue, and I can remember Avery saying it when I first awoke back on the ship, but for the life of me, I can't seem to formulate the *exact* word. Whatever it'd been, it'd sounded dreadful, which is exactly how I'd felt when I'd been forced into the icy ocean water. Come to think of it, it's the first time the *thing* was actually able to make physical contact with me—to potentially cause me harm.

I shuffle through the items in my knapsack to make sure nothing's missing: the pocket watch, the books, the clothes—as well as a couple of apples, ripe berries, and a canteen of water that I definitely hadn't packed prior to getting on the ship. Once again, my eyes well with tears knowing that Avery was kind enough to make sure both Juniper and I wouldn't go hungry—but then I think about how he'd just *left* us here, and the feeling is immediately replaced with contempt. I briefly wonder if this is how Rydan felt when I'd left after the Soames mission.

I push the thought away, picking up my pocket watch to check the time—still a few hours of daylight left, so I should be able to make some headway on my journey to Orihia. I do my best to put Avery out of my mind as I feed Juniper some of the berries. I take an apple for myself as I fold the two wrinkled blankets and stuff them into my bag. If I thought it was overstuffed when I'd first packed it, that's nothing compared to what it looks like now—practically bursting at the seams. I hook the canteen onto my belt, secure my knapsack onto my shoulders, and look down at my loyal travel companion.

Juniper takes off in a sprint, and I have to jog to catch up with her. I try to recall exactly how to get to Orihia by retracing my steps the first time around with Estelle. I don't seem to be making much progress until I reach a familiar cliff. The same cliff I'd thrown the Soames's heads over.

My disagreement with Rydan, and everything that's transpired since then, crashes into my mind once again—replaying over and over. I close my eyes, taking a moment to collect myself. I don't know how long I stand at the edge of the cliff, but eventually I shake it off before continuing onward.

An hour passes. The sun has quickly started its descent. The last time I was here, autumn had just begun—but with winter fast approaching, I suppose the sun won't be much help in leading the way. I feel foolish for assuming it would be. Trying not to panic, I grab Juniper with one arm and begin running in the direction I think is east.

I've only been running for five minutes or so when I suddenly lose my footing, accidentally flinging Juniper from my grip. I land face first, spitting out mouthfuls of dirt as I slide with increasing speed along the ground. A gigantic tree comes into my line of vision—I'm heading right for it. Instinct tells me to lift my arms as high as I can to cover my head and brace my body for the impact.

My body jolts as I slam into the trunk, the collision even worse than I'd anticipated. A soft groan escapes me as I press my hands to my temples. Flickering black dots fill my vision. I take a few deep breaths, waiting for my vision to clear, before clambering to my feet. I frantically look around the darkening forest for Juniper. I take a few steps forward, whispering her name, but I don't see her.

My concern growing by the minute, I retrace the indentation of my body as it'd slid along the dirt, feeling thankful we're in the south where the imminent snowfall hasn't already covered my tracks. Finally, a short distance away, I see her, contently munching on some nearby shrubbery. Now that I know she's safe, I begin to look at my surroundings for a different reason.

What in lords' name did I trip over?

I strain my ears as a muffled wail echoes close by. The sound of a twig snapping causes me to freeze, alerting all of my senses. At first, I think it must be a small animal—a rabbit or a squirrel—until I hear another sound, one that is clearly human. I double-check my chakrams—both in place and ready to use, if needed. "Hello?" I call out, my hands grazing the edge of my weapons. "Who's out there?" I slowly begin to walk toward the noise, and as I round a tree, I see . . . a light.

Without so much as a second thought, I dart over to it. I squint as I draw closer, and I'm almost certain I can make out someone sprawled on the forest floor, reeling in pain. It's only when I'm standing a few steps away from a makeshift fire—the source of the light—that I realize whom it was I'd tripped over.

Fellow Cruex member, Elias Kent.

"Elias?" I whisper as I kneel next to him. I glance around, looking for his cousin, Hugh, but he seems to be alone.

He looks at me, his russet eyes widening as he realizes who I am. "Arden?"

I don't even have to ask what he's doing here because I already know. *He's searching for me.*

I bring my blade to his neck. "Where are the others?"

He doesn't so much as flinch as he says, "We've both had the same training. You really think I'd tell you that?"

I press my chakram harder against his skin, right against his Adam's apple. "You really think I won't kill you?" I say through gritted teeth. He growls at me as a streak of crimson trickles down his neck. "Like you said, we've had the same training."

Something resembling fear darts across his eyes, but he doesn't respond.

"Go on. Try me."

I lay off the pressure just enough to allow him to speak. Even so, his voice is strained. "It's just me. I'm alone. The others are nowhere near here."

I don't believe him, so I tighten my grip. "Hugh!" I call out. "Percival!"

I'm met with silence.

"I'm not lying to you, Arden."

I look him in the eye as unwelcome memories of my time with the Cruex infiltrate my mind. *Does he know the king he willingly serves is a monster? Does he know how many innocent lives he's taken? Does he even care?*

Everything I'd ever been taught as an assassin boils down to one thing and one thing only—the essence of apathy. Caring *just enough* to complete the mission, but that's it. No challenging the directive. No questioning why or who. No sense of sorrow or sympathy afterward.

In. Out. Done.

At war with myself, I don't dare look into Elias's eyes because I know what I'll find. My own reflection mirrored back at me. Angry. Heartless. Lost.

I keep my focus on the blade, still determined, and yet deeply confused. I could take his life—hell, I *want* to take his life—especially if it means ridding Aeridon of senseless evil. Long after King Tymond dies, there is no doubt in my mind that the Cruex will continue to pledge their loyalty to Trendalath and everything it's become. They'd rather die than carry the mark of a traitor. I'd felt the same way until I'd found out who I was.

Who *he* was.

Seems I've made quite a compelling argument to justify what I'm about to do.

"It starts with you," I say, "but it won't end with you. I won't rest until all that remains of that entire kingdom—and everyone in it—is ash and dust."

Just as I'm about to lift my blade and lower it in one deft movement, Elias's hand shoots to my wrist. He pushes against me, hard. "It's not the Cruex you need to worry about."

I struggle against him. "Then who?" I press.

"The Mallum."

His words snag on something in my mind.

My weapon tumbles to the ground.

RYDAN HELSTROM

"KNOWING WHAT YOU know now, do you still think not returning to Sardoria was a good idea?"

Rydan gives Vira a pointed look as he adjusts his knapsack. "Don't even for one second act like you knew."

"Oh, you mean that Haskell is Arden's *brother*?" The blunt emphasis on the last word is enough to make them both stop walking. "I'm not acting like I knew, I'm acting like someone who thinks—now more than ever—that we should go back to Sardoria and let her know. If it were you, isn't that something you'd want to know?"

A pang of guilt hits Rydan square in the chest. Vira is absolutely right. Finding a long lost family member after mistaking them for dead? It *is* something he'd want to know, and there's no doubt in his mind that it's something Arden would want to know, too. But the thought of going back—of facing her, especially after the way he's behaved—is out of the question.

"A friend wouldn't even think twice about it," Vira goes on, "and from what you've told me, you and Arden are more like family—"

"Enough!" Rydan stops in his tracks, heaving a jagged breath. "Arden and I are no longer *friends,* and we certainly aren't family. We never were."

Vira presses her mouth shut before stalking ahead of him. They continue walking through Chialka in complete silence. Rydan isn't even sure what they're looking for or where they're headed. Vira doesn't seem to have much of an idea either—that is, until they reach a fork in the road.

"It should be this way," Vira mumbles as she turns left. "I think we should be coming up on my old street soon."

Rydan follows her along the winding cobblestone road, which seems to be growing narrower with each step they take. Rows of similar-looking cottages come into view—they're so close together that they almost appear to be stacked on top of one another. "How can you possibly remember all of this?"

Vira doesn't turn around. "Remember all of what?"

"Your street, your house. Weren't you just a child?"

"When Chialka was invaded, I knew things would never be the same. Even though I was young, I've replayed the image of my street and my house every day since then. I've made sure not to forget any of it." She pauses. "Not a single detail."

Her gaze travels upward when they stop in front of a dark brown cottage with beige shutters. Rydan notices a strange symbol stamped on the door—a black ring with three white circles that also encompass a three-tiered blade. He watches as Vira traces the symbol with her index finger, over and over again.

"What does it mean?" he whispers.

She drags her finger away from it, tucking it back into her fist. "Any dwellings that housed illusié were marked with this symbol. Tymond's intention was never to exile illusié—he wanted them dead."

"How do you know this?"

"If you go to Eroesa, you'll see this symbol on the majority of the rubble. No one's been able to prove it, but the fires of Eroesa were no accident."

"If what you're saying is true, that would mean Tymond burned an *entire* village to the ground. How is that even possible without . . . ?"

Vira simply points to the sky in response.

Rydan understands instantly. "Dragons." And then a terrifying thought strikes him. "But how did he summon them?"

A curtain of despair falls across her face. "Just before my execution date, I learned that my mother was also a Summoner."

"*Was?*"

Vira sighs as she traces the symbol again. Her voice shakes as she speaks. "I'm not sure what happened to her—if Tymond exiled her, killed her, or if she somehow escaped. He then informed me that I would be taking her place."

Rydan's eyes grow wide as he catches on to her meaning. "As a Summoner for King Tymond," he confirms. "Which means you'd become a member of his Savant."

"Obviously I refused. And so he sent me to be executed." A pause as her eyes lift to the sky. "But he failed. My brother—and the rest of the Caldari—came and saved me." She smiles. "You as well."

Rydan feels a long withstanding weight lift from his shoulders. This whole time, he'd thought his conversing with Vira was what had gotten her into trouble. That's what Tymond had told him—that he'd distracted her from her duties as handmaiden.

"That's why I wanted to come back here, to Chialka. I thought perhaps . . ."

"I can understand why you'd hope your mother might come back here, but I doubt she'd risk that. If she *did* escape, Tymond would have found her. You and I both know the first place he would have looked would be here."

She bows her head. "Wishful thinking, I suppose."

"Do you know why he wants a Summoner?"

"Not exactly." Her eyes flick to the door again. "From what I can gather, harnessing the fire from the dragons is the quickest way to eradicate all remnants of illusié, especially those that don't add value to Tymond's Savant.

It's a way for him to start anew—new towns, new people, a new way of life."

"Tymond's way."

Vira nods sadly, then steps back from the door. "The good news is that my abilities are invaluable to him."

Rydan studies her for a moment. Even though he already knows the answer to his next question, he asks it anyway. "And the bad?"

Her voice falls to a whisper. "I wish they weren't."

DARIUS TYMOND

THERE'S NO DENYING what Aldreda already knows. Too many people had witnessed the sudden appearance of Braxton at the failed execution, and whether or not Gladys was the one who'd told her is completely irrelevant at this point. She knows—and she's beyond livid.

Darius stands at the entrance to his chambers, watching as Gladys removes Aldreda's final belongings. He'd falsely assumed that perhaps she'd see his side of things for once, and that they'd carry on with their normal duties as king and queen.

Quite the contrary.

He hastily moves out of the way to allow Gladys to pass through the door, her arms chock-full of random items, but doesn't pass up the opportunity to whisper, "This is your fault," as she exits the room. The words don't seem to affect nor startle her as she continues on her way, which makes him wonder if she'd even heard him at all.

He doesn't bother to watch her round the corner as he slams the door to his chambers shut. There's an irrefutable void in the room—a sort of hollowness that cannot be avoided. Any sort of décor or warm touch had been Aldreda's doing, and with it all gone, the room feels cold—exposed somehow.

With a few quick strides, he arrives at the open window that overlooks Trendalath. The usual bustling of the town is hardly audible. Perhaps it's just the time of day . . . or maybe everyone's finally had enough of his tyranny that they've fled to one of the nearby towns. Even so, it wouldn't matter because they'd still be affected by everything that happens in Trendalath, whether they like it or not. Almost every region in Aeridon depends on Trendalath for . . . well, everything. If he falls, they all fall, too.

It's so silent. Too silent.

The last thing he wants is to be left alone with his thoughts and yet, here he is. He braces himself against the open window, allowing the cool evening breeze to ruffle his hair. With his eyes closed, he takes a deep breath of salty air. Even though the kingdom is quiet, from a distance, he can hear the ocean waves crashing against the shore. The sound instantly reminds him of his son, particularly when Braxton was younger and used to sneak off to go fishing along the side of the castle. Darius never went with him—just watched him from afar through one of the windows.

How had their family dissolved so quickly? As heir to the throne, he'd assumed Braxton would have been smart enough to stick around. While they'd never agreed on much—hardly anything, actually—at least he would have been given the opportunity to eventually run things his own way. The boy had given everything up before even having the wherewithal to get started.

A shame, really.

Perhaps Darius will have another chance with their newborn child—to teach him all the things he'd never been able to teach Braxton . . . to be there as a father figure and not just a sovereign of a kingdom. That is, if Aldreda will give him the chance. Given the way things have gone lately, he honestly wouldn't be surprised if she left him for good. Then again, this life is everything she's ever wanted, a life she's killed for . . .

A deep inhale should help keep his anger at bay.

For now.

His thoughts scatter as the sound of frantic knocks fill the room. When he opens the door, he's surprised to see it's one of the handmaidens.

"Your Majesty, please forgive the interruption, but you must come quick."

Her eyes are wide and her hands are trembling, and Darius knows something must be horribly wrong. Without a word, he follows her down the corridor, keeping his pace steady and his breathing steadier. The silence is replaced with something even more dreadful.

Aldreda's screams.

CERYLIA JARETH

ACCORDING TO HER calculations, it's been at least thirty minutes—more than enough time for Felix to show up—and yet, here she sits, still waiting on his arrival at the White Room. Opal stands on her right, Estelle on her left. She briefly considers calling Delwynn in to join them, but her advisor needs his rest. Come to think of it, she hasn't seen him in weeks.

As she'd ordered, Braxton is no longer in Sardoria. There wasn't so much as a peep after she'd demanded he go—but, in being honest with herself, she would have preferred if he'd dropped by right before leaving, just to clarify her expectations once more—and possibly provide a more concrete timeline. Instead, she'll be anxiously awaiting his return.

Her eyes lock on the doors as she taps her foot against the marble floor. Her impatience with Felix has almost reached its peak. *Where is he?*

Just as she's about to go search for him herself, the doors open and in walks . . . Delwynn. No wheelchair. No staff. Cerylia's eyes widen at the sight of him. She doesn't move—just watches, speechless, as Opal and Estelle run toward him.

"Incredible," Estelle says.

"Unbelievable," Opal echoes.

Cerylia can hardly believe what she's seeing.

Delwynn doesn't hobble even a bit as he walks straight up to her. It's as if he's gliding across the floor without any effort at all—much like the way she's walked her entire life. "Delwynn," she says breathily. "You're . . . healed?"

He glances down at his legs before flashing a wide grin. "It would appear so, Your Greatness. I could hardly believe it myself."

"And this is Arden's doing?" Estelle confirms.

He nods, refusing to shift his gaze from the queen.

"Has she come back?" Opal asks. "Is Arden here?"

"Not to my knowledge." A shadow falls over his face.

It takes a moment for Cerylia to gather her many thoughts. "The pain you endured . . . the suffering . . . I had believed it was all for naught."

"I can't explain it," Delwynn says, gesturing to his legs, "but Arden healed me. Whatever she did *worked*, and it worked better than anything I've tried before." He lowers his voice to a whisper so that only the queen can hear. "And now she's out there, completely alone, with the Mallum lurking."

And so is Braxton.

The sound of a door creaking distracts her from the oncoming spiral of doubt. Heads turn and all eyes land on Felix. His mouth presses into a firm line as he marches toward the queen. Opal and Estelle move out of his way, a wordless exchange passing between them. He climbs the steps until he's just inches from Cerylia's face. "I learned this morning that, per your orders, Braxton is no longer in Sardoria."

Cerylia doesn't break his gaze, but out of the corner of her eye, notices both Opal and Estelle take a step forward.

"What is it, exactly, you're trying to accomplish?" He waves a hand around the room. "I think we have the right to know, Queen Jareth."

The way he says her name is filled with so much animosity that it nearly makes her shrink into her throne. She opens her mouth to speak, but Estelle beats her to it.

"Arden flees, you lock down the castle, and your next move is to send Braxton away?" Estelle steps in line with Felix. "Are you trying to pull us apart?"

Shoulders tensed, she shakes her head. "That is not my intention. You know that."

"Your actions speak otherwise." Opal's voice is flat.

Cerylia's eyes flick to Delwynn, a silent plea to help her—but she's met with nothing more than a steely gaze.

"Whether you choose to believe it or not, my actions will protect Sardoria. If we're to defeat the true evil out there"—her eyes settle on Opal—"there's something I need. Something that only Braxton can retrieve."

She knows she's gone too far—said too much—when an uncomfortable silence falls over the room. It's then she realizes she has no other choice. She must rope the Caldari into this if she ever hopes to find the information she seeks. "Excuse me for a moment."

Before anyone has the chance to respond, she bursts through the doors of the White Room and heads to the castle library, straight for the aisles of books she'd had transferred from Orihia. She scans the titles, running her hand along the spines and plucking more than a few from the shelves. When she returns to the White Room, carrying a stack of books that are at least two feet high, not a single one of the Caldari offer to help her. With a loud thud, she drops the books onto a nearby table. The Caldari, and Delwynn, are still standing near her throne, right where she'd left them. She gives a hasty gesture for them to join her, and albeit reluctant, they oblige.

The queen waits until they're seated before sliding her hand along the table's smooth marble edges, eyeing each of the tattered books in front of her. "What we're about to discuss will not leave this room seeing as it's a force greater than all of us," she begins, pacing back and forth along the side of the table. "A force you may or may not be familiar with, but one that you'll likely get to know very well after today." She shoots Opal a sidelong glance. "We're here to discuss the Mallum."

The mood in the room shifts, but it doesn't stop her. "I need you to forget everything you've been told about the Mallum. Fact or fable—erase it all from your memory." She gestures to the piles of books with a wide sweep of her hand. "The majority of what we need to know should be contained in these texts—"

"I think what most of these texts contain are just stories," Estelle interrupts. "They're just accounts from those who have *allegedly* witnessed the Mallum first-hand."

"You are partially correct," Cerylia says. "The stories that have been passed down in your families and towns through the generations may or may not hold any merit. But these accounts," she emphasizes, placing her hands on top of one of the stacks, "are *true* eyewitness accounts. They have been documented with the utmost precision, down to the very last detail." She pats the top book on the stack, sending a fresh layer of dust into the air. "Quite frankly, *those* are the only accounts I'm interested in hearing."

She pauses, her eyes landing on Felix. There's something in his expression . . . something she's seen before, but can't quite place. When he notices she's looking at him, he lowers his head.

"Any time the Mallum is referenced," Cerylia continues, drawing her attention back to the rest of the group, "I want you to mark the title of the book and the page number. Are there any questions?"

Opal leans forward. "Anything in particular we're looking for?"

Cerylia purses her lips. "Let's just say if you find something of importance, you'll know."

"How?" Estelle asks. "How will we know?"

"When you show me, I'll know. And I'll tell you everything you need to know at that time."

Estelle slinks back in her seat.

"Are there any other questions?"

Complete and utter silence.

"Good." With a flippant wave of her hand, she dismisses Delwynn from the room. "Begin."

BRAXTON HORNSBY

A FEW MORE days of this, and Braxton is fairly certain he'll lose his mind. Not only has Delwynn refused to disclose any new information—he's also, unknowingly or not, created a suffocating environment in not allowing any fresh air into the room. Per Cerylia's lock-down orders, Delwynn's taken the liberty of sealing the windows in his chambers with some type of waxy paste—which would be fine . . . if his furnace wasn't lit at all times. With each new task Delwynn is assigned, it becomes more and more apparent that the queen is desperately trying to keep something out—something no one wants to talk about.

As if sharing a telepathic line, Delwynn suddenly appears through the door, arms shaking from the mountain of books he's attempting to balance on one hand. Braxton jumps from his seat and rushes over to help him, momentarily forgetting that Delwynn's leg is healed.

"I've got it, I've got it," Delwynn murmurs from behind the pile. "It's times like these when I wholeheartedly loathe being the queen's advisor. We should have never sent the Queen's Guard to recover these books from Orihia." He shakes his head. "They don't belong to us."

Although Braxton *hears* him, he's not exactly listening. Curious, he removes four of the books from one of the stacks. His grip slips across what feels like a piece of parchment, and he briefly wonders if one of the books is missing its cover. With surprising eloquence, Delwynn glides across the room, over to the wooden desk, before setting the rest of the books down. Braxton follows suit, then retrieves the loose piece of parchment. He holds it up for the old man to see. "What's this for?"

"Ah, yes," Delwynn says with a nod. He reaches into his back pocket and produces a quill. "Allow me to explain."

"That would be greatly appreciated, seeing as I've been trapped in here—alone—for what feels like a week."

Delwynn shoots him a pointed look. "You're not trapped. And it's been two days."

Braxton rolls his eyes before turning his attention to the heap of books before them. "What is all of . . . this?"

"*This* is a task that the queen has assigned to the Caldari—Felix, Estelle, Opal . . ."

Braxton angles his head. "Well, since I'm *technically* not supposed to be here, why are you bringing this to me?" He eyes the books again, sighing as their purpose dawns on him. He runs a hand down his face. "She needs an extra set of eyes and you're trying to get out of doing it, aren't you?"

A glimmer lines the old man's eyes. "Now that my leg is healed, my attention span for tasks of the mind has diminished. There's so much to life I haven't experienced, particularly in the physical realm." A faux pout lines his lips. "You wouldn't deprive me of such a thing, now would you?"

Braxton taps his fingers on the desk before knocking one of the books off the stack. "We made a deal, Delwynn. If I stayed here, you promised to disclose why Cerylia locked down the castle in the first place and what that amethyst ring allegedly protects from. You haven't done either." He narrows his eyes. "All you've done is left me alone in this room, and now you're trying to put me to work by showing up with a bunch of tattered, old books."

Delwynn straightens slightly, and Braxton is almost certain he's about to be reprimanded, but instead the old man sighs. The defeated look on his face reminds him a lot of Hanslow, and the many requests—mostly ones that fell on deaf ears—to tidy up the inn. The thought sends a pang of guilt humming throughout his entire body.

Hanslow. The man who'd somehow known his secret without Braxton himself even knowing. The man who'd risked his own life to ensure he'd make it out safely—that he'd *survive*.

Braxton immediately softens and replaces the stray book. "Apologies for my outburst, Delwynn. Please forgive me."

"You are forgiven." A wrinkled smile pulls at the man's lips. "And as much as I hate to admit it, you're right. I made a promise and I haven't kept my word."

Braxton holds his gaze, waiting for him to continue.

"I can't tell you much—but what I *can* tell you is that the reason Cerylia put the castle on lock-down is the same reason she so desperately wants that amethyst ring."

"Which is . . . ?"

"The Mallum." A shadow falls over his face.

"The Mallum," Braxton repeats, trying the word on for size. It doesn't feel like something he'd want to say often, that's for sure. "What is it?"

"It's a malevolent force, one that's been lurking amongst the lands of Aeridon for some time," Delwynn answers. "From what we *do* know, the amethyst ring is a means of protection." He seems to want to say more, but doesn't.

Braxton angles his head curiously. "How do we defeat it?"

Delwynn sighs before gesturing to the table and its many books. "That is precisely what this assignment is for."

ARDEN ELIRI

"LET'S BE CLEAR. The only reason you're not dead right now is because you know something that I need to know. So start talking." I sit a few steps away, deliberately sharpening my chakrams where Elias can see them. He sits against the trunk of a massive tree, wearing our earlier altercation as a darkening stain on his neck. I don't think he realizes how lucky he is. It could have been worse—*much* worse.

I don't even flinch as he presses his palms against the ground and tries to stand. He's attempted this a few times over the last couple of hours, but the minute he applies pressure to his left leg, he immediately falls back down—just like the last time. And the time before that.

When I'd tripped over him, I must have injured him pretty good. I try to hide my smirk. He isn't going anywhere.

As I figured he would, Elias slides back down the tree in defeat. "If I tell you about the Mallum," he says between coughs, "can we call a truce?"

I raise a brow. "Meaning I won't kill you?"

He nods.

"We'll see," I say nonchalantly. "Depends on what information you have."

He sighs. "You know, you're not making this enticing for me in the slightest. Is that intentional?"

I ignore his question. "I spared your life, Elias. Tell me what you know."

"I'm not going to hurt you, Arden."

That doesn't change anything. I keep my focus on the blade as I sharpen it. Back and forth. Back and forth.

"Even though you fled after the Soames mission," he continues between coughs, "I still consider you to be one of us. You're still a Cruex."

My eyes shoot up, anger roiling inside me. "I am not now—nor will I ever be—a *Cruex* ever again." I spit the word out like spoiled milk.

His tone immediately softens. "What happened that day? With you and Rydan?"

Well this is unexpected. I try not to freeze at the mention of Rydan's name, but fail.

"There has to be a reason you fled the scene," Elias pries. "There has to be a reason you abandoned your *partner.*"

I blink back my irritation, my hands moving even faster as I work on the blades. "I'm done playing games, Elias. Tell me what you know or I swear to the lords above, I *will* kill you."

He casts his eyes downward. "Fine. Honestly, I don't know much, but I do know there's a greater evil among us . . . greater than King Tymond himself."

To hear his blunt disdain for the king is not only unexpected—it's downright shocking. "I take it you mean the Mallum," I say, turning my head to hide the surprise on my face.

"The only thing I know for sure is that it targets"—he lowers his voice to a whisper—"illusié."

Which is exactly what I am. "Why?"

He raises his arms in surrender. "That I don't know."

"Do you know what it looks like?" I immediately bite my tongue, realizing I sound desperate for information. "I mean, have you ever seen it before or come into contact with it?"

"How could I?" he says glumly. "I'm not illusié."

Again, his tone surprises me. "You want to be illusié?"

He retracts slightly, as if he's just revealed something he shouldn't have. "I thought you just wanted to know about the Mallum."

I shrug. "If you don't know *why* it attacks illusié nor what it looks like . . ."

"It seems we've reached an impasse." He raises a brow. "Might I ask why you're so curious about illusié?"

I bite my tongue, wanting to tell him that I *am* illusié, and that I *could* heal him, if I so choose—but it's a slippery slope. *How much does Tymond know about my abilities? Why wouldn't he reveal this information to the Cruex?* "What did Tymond tell you when he ordered you go looking for me?"

"We're not only looking for you. We're looking for some others, too."

His forthrightness during this entire conversation has me thrown for a complete loop. I have to assume his referring to "some others" must mean Rydan and Elvira. And, if I had to guess, he probably doesn't know that my new *friends* are the ones who ruined execution day and saved both Rydan and Elvira from their undeserved fates.

Then again, maybe he does.

It dawns on me that I don't know Elias as well as I thought I did. I *do* know that I've always liked Elias more than his cousin, Hugh—but I'm at a loss for how to play this, so I stay quiet.

"Lords, with the severity of this injury, I may as well give up now. I'm not going to be able to go far," he admits with a despondent shake of his head. "You may as well run off. We can pretend we never even saw each other."

The thought is tempting, but for some reason, I find myself struggling between wanting to kill him and wanting to . . . *help* him. Not only has he told me about the Mallum, he's *also* revealed his disdain for King Tymond and that he's always held a soft spot for illusié— namely that he wishes he had abilities of his own.

It wouldn't hurt to have an ally on the inside . . .

I haven't the slightest idea whether or not Elias would even agree to something like that. If he's anything like Rydan, then probably not—but it can't hurt to broach the topic. He needs help and I can help him. I need help and he can help me.

I take in an uneven breath, knowing that what I'm about to reveal may very well be the nail in my casket, but before I can give in to my doubts, I say, "Elias, what would you say if I told you I could . . . heal you?"

"Well, that'd be great. You know of a place around here? An Herbalist, perhaps?" He glances around the forest with hopeful eyes. "If you do that for me, I promise we'll part ways. We'll act like this never happened."

I grimace before slowly shaking my head. *Do I really want to do this? Reveal myself? So many things could go wrong . . .*

"I—I don't necessarily know of a place we can go . . ."

He regards me with a docile expression, still hopeful.

Am I really about to tell a Cruex that I'm illusié?

I raise my hands in the air so that my palms are facing me. *Guess so.*

He sits back suddenly as the pieces of my not-so-discreet puzzle fall into place.

"I'm the one who can heal you."

Those deep russet eyes grow so wide, I can see the whites around his eyes. "You mean to say that you're . . ."

I nod in affirmation, a nonverbal finish to his sentence. It somehow makes me feel both lighter and heavier at the same time. "I hope you can appreciate how much peril I just put myself in by revealing that to you."

"But I thought they were all . . . Our Cruex missions were to . . ." He trails off and looks down at his leg, then up at me again. "Does the king know?"

I shoot him a knowing look. "Seeing as you're out here, I'm guessing so."

Elias studies me for a moment. By the slight movements in his facial expressions, I can tell he's weighing his options. I have half a mind to throw my chakrams at him right now and pin him against the tree, but something tells me to wait—that everything's going to be okay.

"So?" I ask, a little too hopefully. "What'll it be?"

"I've never seen illusié with my own two eyes," he starts, shaking his head in disbelief. "And to think, we had one right underneath our noses this whole time." My panic begins to rise again until a boyish grin crosses his face. "Arden, I'd be eternally grateful if you'd heal me. You have my word, I'll walk away from this entire situation without you. It'll be as if it never even happened."

Based on history alone, I know I shouldn't trust him, but, for some reason, I do. It's then I realize that perhaps Elias *can* do a little something more for me. "I'll heal you, but I need something else from you."

There isn't even the slightest bit of hesitation in his voice. "Anything you need."

I look him up and down, hardly believing that I'm about to reveal not just one, but *two* things to him. I whip my knapsack from my shoulders, rifling through the contents before pulling out *The History of Trendalath*. I slide the old photograph from the back of the book.

"Him," I say, pointing to the man with the same emerald eyes as me. "Do you know who he is?"

Elias angles his head, then gingerly takes the photo from my hand. He pushes himself up further on his elbow. He studies the photograph for what feels like an eternity before finally saying, "Sorry, no. I've never seen him before."

I let out an exasperated sigh. Just as I'm about to take the photo back from him, he stops me.

"Wait a second," he whispers. "Is that who I think it is?"

I circle him so I can see to whom he's referring. He points to a man in the front row, on the far right. I bring my face closer to the photo, but I'm at a loss. I have no idea who it is.

"It's a Cruex," Elias confirms. "Look closer."

I look at the photo again. After a few seconds, it dawns on me. The name leaves our lips simultaneously.

"Cyrus Alston."

◈   ◈   ◈

After I've healed his leg injury, it's the only thing Elias can talk about. Apparently, it's no matter we've just discovered the most senior Cruex member in an old photograph—a photo of the *King's Savant*, no less. Elias seems to be taking it well. I, on the other hand, am surprised, but I don't really know why. I feel like I shouldn't be.

It dawns on me that this means Cyrus is also illusié. The evidence is irrefutable, seeing as the King's Savant holds such tremendous power that, apparently, no one's ever heard of or witnessed before. So Tymond has not two, but *three* illusié on the Cruex—well, *had*, seeing as Rydan and I are no longer acting members. *Is it possible we were being groomed to become a part of the King's Savant? Is Cyrus still a member?*

I have more questions than I've ever had before—and no one to answer them. Sure, Elias has revealed the first piece in a very complex puzzle, but he seems just as confused by the whole thing as I am.

"So when did you find out you had these healing abilities?"

Only now do I realize that Elias has been ranting and raving this whole time about my abilities while I've been off in my own world, trying to decipher what all of this means. His question throws me. "I, uh—I started to really notice them right before . . . before I left for the Lonia mission." An image of me bashing Rydan over the head with a lantern at the Soames's residence flashes across my mind. As if that isn't enough, another image replaces it—one where my hands are tightening around Felix's neck as he gasps for air. It's enough to stop me in my tracks.

Elias continues to talk, walking ahead of me, then turns around once he realizes I'm no longer following him. "Hey, is everything all right?"

Juniper runs a few circles around my feet, and if it weren't for her sweet little face looking up at me, I'd probably be in a crumpled heap on the ground. "Just fine," I say as I scoop her up in my arms and nuzzle my nose with hers. I instantly feel better. "What were you saying?"

Elias talks almost the entire way to Orihia. I'm not sure whether I'm allowed to bring non-illusié here, but it's a little too late for that. As I'm about to walk into the endless cave-like entrance, Elias says, "Well, it looks like we've reached a dead-end." He shrugs and turns to walk back the way we'd come.

I look at the back of his head, then at the cave entrance, then back at him. I recall what Estelle had said the first time she'd taken me here. *He can't see it because he's not illusié.*

"Elias," I call after him. "I think I'm just going to stay here." Trying not to be too obvious with my intentions, I quickly add, "I don't think it's safe for me to be trekking back through the Thering Forest with both the Savant and the Cruex out there."

"Oh." He frowns. "I can understand that. But you want to stay here? In the middle of nowhere?"

"I'll be fine," I assure him. "Can I ask a favor of you?"

"You healed me in under a minute." He winks. "What do you need?"

I hesitate, wondering what's come over me the past few hours. I can hardly trust myself with my own thoughts and here I am, spilling everything to someone who's supposed to be the enemy. Even so, I hear myself saying, "When you get back to Trendalath, will you tell Cyrus to . . . meet me here?"

"Here?" Elias looks over his shoulder, clearly confused. "Here as in . . . where?"

"Just tell him to come to Orihia. He'll know where."

Elias gives a reassuring nod. "Sure. I can do that."

"And you won't tell Tymond about this?"

"I've wiped this encounter from my memory entirely."

I nod. "I have as well."

He gives me a genuine smile. "Best of luck to you, Eliri. And thanks again for healing my leg."

"Remember," I say, still feeling a little unsure about everything that's just transpired, "not a word about this to anyone—except for Cyrus."

He stands at attention and salutes me before heading off. I keep my eyes on the back of his head as he hikes farther into the Thering Forest until he's lost from view.

I'd almost forgotten I'm still holding Juniper until she nuzzles against my side. "Well, Juni, would you take a look at that?" I scratch her behind the ears. "It appears I may have been wrong. Perhaps Cruex and Caldari *can* coexist after all."

RYDAN HELSTROM

RYDAN WAKES FROM the most peaceful slumber he's had in weeks—no, months. There's just something so undeniably soothing about sleeping in a village where no one knows him, no one's looking for him, and no one *cares* about him. The crashing of the waves against the docks isn't so bad either.

Upon arriving in Chialka, Vira had been hesitant to enter her childhood home, seeing as it was entirely possible that a new family could have taken residence— but since staying there for a couple of days, no one's come to claim it or kick them out. As far as Vira can recall, the placement of the furniture is exactly the same as when she was growing up. So far, so good.

Rydan stretches his arms overhead before throwing his legs over the bed. The joints in his knees and ankles pop and crack as he traipses to the kitchen. Vira must have just returned from the market, given her flushed cheeks and uneven breathing, as she places the bags on the countertop. His sudden presence seems to startle her, and she almost drops the fresh eggs she's holding.

"Oh, you frightened me," she says with a small laugh. "Hungry? How do pancakes for breakfast sound?"

Rydan rubs the sleep from his eyes. "Sounds perfect." He plops down on a nearby stool, watching as she readies a bowl of flour and eggs. "You know, I was thinking . . . perhaps we could just stay here for a bit."

Vira continues to whisk the eggs, then stops, turning around to face him. "You're wondering exactly what we're doing here, in my old family home, aren't you?"

Rydan just shrugs, because she's not completely wrong.

She sets the bowl down and wipes her hands on the sides of her dress. "Honestly, I was hoping that my father would be here. That my mother had somehow escaped from Trendalath. That Xerin would eventually come back here, and we'd go back to living our life before . . ."

Before me.

He knows that's not what she'd meant, but it's the truth. He'd only met Vira a short while ago. Before him, she'd had a family. Before him, she'd been *happy*.

Not wanting to crush her optimism, Rydan says, as delicately as he can, "Vira, as much as we may want them to, I'm not sure things can ever go back to the way they were before . . . not just for you, but for any of us."

She throws him a harsh glance. "Are you implying that you'd want to go back to being an assassin? Being under King Tymond's reign?"

Well, when she puts it that way—no, absolutely not.

As if she's read his thoughts, she says, "Or maybe you just mean when things were good between you and Arden."

He's not sure if he's upset at her presumptuous tone, or if because what she's said is true. He swivels his body on the stool so that his back now faces her. She's managed to sharpen the one skill he'd hoped no one would ever have the chance to succeed at—reading him. Much like Arden used to do. The thought makes him grit his teeth.

A long, drawn-out silence ensues before the sound of clanging in the kitchen jolts him from his thoughts. With his back still to her, it's hard to know what's going on, but he can hear the batter sizzling over the stovetop. His stomach growls in protest as the scent thickens in the air, immersing him in a delightful aroma of maple and cinnamon. When he finally turns back around to face her, Vira is in the process of setting a full plate in front of him.

"Next time, it's your turn to cook," she says light-heartedly. It's obvious she's trying to salvage whatever's left of the peaceful morning they could have had.

Rydan doesn't have much fight left in him—at least, not until he eats. He picks up his fork and forces a smile before digging in.

◈　◈　◈

Rydan stirs from his nap—realizing it's been about three hours since he'd fallen asleep. It takes him a moment to remember exactly where he is. As of late, waking has been quite a disorienting experience, seeing as he always seems to be in a new setting. He groans as he scoots to the edge of the oversized chair, rolling his neck after sleeping on it wrong. He stops when he hears a pair of voices laughing from the next room over. Vira's and . . . a male's.

He pushes himself from the chair and sets off down the narrow hallway. He follows the sound of the voices until he reaches one of the bedrooms, then peeks his head around the corner. There, sitting on her bed—with his back to the door—is a young boy with messy auburn hair. He turns around when she stops mid-sentence, and Rydan can see he has a face full of freckles and looks to be about Vira's age.

"Rydan, come on in," she says a little too cheerfully. "You won't believe who I found."

Rydan can't help but feel a stab of jealousy as he enters the room—mostly because it feels like he's intruding on a private conversation. It crosses his mind to just turn around and leave, but that would probably make things even more awkward than they already are.

"I was sitting outside on the back porch, looking out at the docks, when my old neighbor, Avery, walked by."

The freckle-faced kid sticks his hand out. "Avery Bancroft. Pleasure to make your acquaintance."

Rydan meets his grip. "The pleasure is all mine," he lies.

"Avery was just telling me about his most recent voyage, weren't you?" Vira goads.

"I was indeed. It certainly was the strangest trip I've had in a long while."

"Is that so?" Rydan does his best to feign interest, when really, he'd rather retreat to his room and fall back asleep.

Avery doesn't seem to notice his indifference. "Well, for starters, I normally only carry cargo on my voyages, but this time, I had someone along for the ride. We ran into some pretty nasty"—he pauses—"*weather* on the way there. It was the first time I had to banish someone from my ship."

"What, you just threw him overboard?" Rydan can't help that his tone is full of blatant sarcasm.

"Not him. *Her*," Avery says thoughtfully. "And that cute little fox of hers."

Rydan stiffens, his gaze locking with Vira's. "That is interesting."

"Told you," Avery quips.

Rydan leans against the bedframe, hoping his question comes off as nonchalant. "Did she happen to give you her name?"

Avery chuckles, waving his hand in the air. "What, you think you know her?" He laughs again, louder this time. When Vira and Rydan don't reciprocate, he puts his finger to the side of his mouth, lost in thought. "She said her name was Opal something. Opal Landen? Opal Cranston?" He shakes his head. "I can't remember."

Rydan exchanges another look with Vira. They both know that Opal doesn't have a fox—Arden does. *And* it would be smart of Arden to give a false name . . . very smart. But to give one of the Caldari's? Why would she put them at risk like that?

"If you don't mind my asking, what did Opal look like?"

Avery narrows his eyes. "Again, it begs the question—do you think you *know* her? Because your piqued interest in the matter suggests that you do."

"I doubt it." Rydan shrugs, trying his best to play it off. "I've just never met anyone with the name Opal. It's a rather unique name, wouldn't you say?"

Avery considers this for a moment. "I suppose so."

"I'm just having a hard time imagining what someone with the name *Opal* would look like."

He takes the bait. "There's not much to tell. She was pretty tall for a girl. Brown hair, green eyes. Nice features overall."

Rydan tries not to look directly at Vira because they both know exactly who fits that description, and it certainly isn't Opal Marston.

"And where did you say you were headed when you . . . banished her?"

Vira's question seems to set him over the edge because Avery swiftly rises to his feet. "The two of you are acting strange. I'd best be leaving now."

Within seconds, Rydan's in front of the door, blocking any chance of an exit. "Sit down," he growls, "and answer the question."

The boy gulps, throat bobbing, as he stumbles backward onto the bed. His eyes flit around the room as if looking for an alternate escape route. They land on the window, but it's far too small to climb out of.

"Where were you headed?" Vira repeats.

A shadow flickers in Avery's eyes. "Lonia."

"And that's where you dropped Opal off?"

He nods.

Vira glances at Rydan to see if this means anything—and it does. Lonia is where his last joint mission took place with Arden—before she'd knocked him unconscious and left him for dead. The thought burns him from the inside—and apparently, from the outside as well. He looks down at his hands as small sparks dance at the tips of his fingers. With his fists clenched, he leaves the room.

DARIUS TYMOND

DARIUS HASN'T LEFT Aldreda's side since receiving the alarming news from the handmaiden. Extreme pain and discomfort, but no signs of internal hemorrhaging. The cause of the symptoms is difficult to diagnose—but seeing as she's able to sleep through the pain, things seem to be getting better.

Conflicting news for a conflicted man.

There were a few nights where, under a heavy dose of herbs, Aldreda had allowed Darius to take her hand. After having more than a few glasses of verdot, he hadn't objected. He'd fallen asleep in the chair by her bedside, holding her hand throughout the entire evening. But upon waking, in his semi-sober state, he'd released it. No need to cause more distress.

One of the handmaidens appears in the doorway, motioning for him to come out into the hall—right when he was getting comfortable for the evening. With a sigh, he gently uncurls his wife's fingers from around his own and swiftly removes his hand. His robes hang lifelessly from the door of the armoire until he tosses them around his shoulders and fastens the brooch in one deft movement. When he arrives at the door, he looks back once more to ensure he hasn't disturbed Aldreda. Her eyes are closed, lips barely parted—sound asleep. He bows his head before shutting the door behind him, then turns his attention to the handmaiden. "Yes?"

His curt tone doesn't rattle her in the slightest. "Your Majesty, I've spoken with the Alchemists and I'm afraid I must deliver some bad news."

Darius runs a hand down his face, pinching the bridge of his nose. He closes his eyes and nods, even though he's not mentally prepared for whatever it is she's about to say. "Continue."

"Because the queen is with child, there are only so many herb concoctions deemed safe. Everything the queen has ingested has been effective for only a short period of time." Her face falls, the color turning pallid. "We're running out of options—and time."

"What do you suggest we do?" he presses.

"We . . ." She struggles to find her words. "Well, we don't know yet."

Darius doesn't hesitate to grab her by the arm and walk her down the hall. He waits until they've rounded the corner before whispering, "What do you mean you don't *know*?"

Unshaken, the woman yanks her arm from his grip and takes a step back. "I suppose there *is* one option, but you're not going to like it. It involves . . . illusié."

Normally, Darius would have anyone discussing magick-related business thrown in the dungeons. After all, he'd been the one to banish illusié a decade ago—save his Savant, of course. But just because he's exiled it didn't necessarily mean it's gone for good . . . or that he'd wanted it that way to begin with, despite the many rumors circulating around Aeridon.

"We need to find a Healer," the handmaiden continues. "Does anyone in your Savant—?"

He interrupts her question with a scoff. "A member in my Savant, a *Healer*? Tell me, what herb concoctions have *you* been taking?"

The handmaiden crosses her arms at his presumptuous tone. Her lips form a firm line as she says, "Looks like having one now would do you a lot of good, wouldn't it?" And with that, she turns on her heel and storms away.

He's about to call one of the guards to go after her and throw her in the stocks, but thinks better of it. *A Healer! What use would he have for a Healer in his great and almighty Savant?*

He shakes his head at the preposterous thought, hoping it'll clear from his mind—but it does just the opposite. Instead, a faint memory surfaces—of a young Arden kneeling before him, emerald eyes wide as she pledges her loyalty to the Cruex, to Trendalath . . . to him. She hadn't been given much choice, and for good reason. If she'd known about her past, her family, who she really is . . .

The thought alone is enough to have him reeling back to Aldreda's ward. He pushes the door open, standing under the archway for a few moments. She looks so peaceful lying there with her eyes closed, hands crossed over her stomach. A part of him wants to go to her, to fall to his knees at her bedside and take her hand, like a loving and caring husband would do. To kiss her forehead, to feel the baby kick, to hold her until she wakes—but he can't. Not after what she's done. Not after what she's put him through.

From where he stands, he can hardly see her chest rising and falling. To an outsider, it would seem as though she's already dead, already passed on to the next realm.

How he wishes that were the case.

CERYLIA JARETH

"PLEASE TELL ME you've had more luck than Delwynn has," Cerylia says to no one in particular as she enters the castle library. Felix rises immediately at her presence and bows, whereas Opal and Estelle remain seated, nose-deep in separate books. At least they're engrossed in the topic. The more they find out, the better off Cerylia—and Sardoria—will be.

Seeing as the other two Caldari are completely ignoring her, she looks at Felix and smiles. "Let's start with you. What do you have for me?"

His face falls, and any hope she once had vanishes entirely. "Right, well, the majority of the texts I was assigned to spoke very briefly on the subject—"

"Brilliant," Cerylia interrupts. "What did they say?"

Felix grimaces as he makes a back-and-forth motion with his hands. "They don't exactly specify *the Mallum* in the legends. I've marked plenty of pages on dark magick and similar forces, but nothing on the Mallum itself."

"I see," she says with a sigh. "Well, keep looking. I'll come back for an updated report tomorrow."

The abruptness of this new assignment seems to fluster him because he immediately sits back down and opens up one of the books.

Cerylia moves down the table until she's standing in front of Estelle and Opal. "Lady Chatham? Lady Marston? Anything of interest?"

Estelle doesn't even look up from her text before saying, "I need more time."

Opal seconds her motion.

Cerylia tries to hide her disappointment and frustration, but it's plain as day in her voice. "When I come back tomorrow morning, I want *something*. A legend, a tale, a mere paragraph that specifically focuses on the Mallum. Understood?"

"And what if there isn't one?" Opal retorts. "What if none of these texts reference the Mallum? What then?"

"It has to be here," Cerylia murmurs, but not quietly enough.

"What does?" Estelle asks. "What has to be here?"

"Are you looking for something specific?" Opal asks.

Cerylia bristles at the sudden interrogation. "All I meant is that these are illusié texts. The information we need *will* be in of these books. Now find it."

And with that, she turns and walks straight out of the library, unavailable for further questioning.

BRAXTON HORNSBY

"THE QUEEN IS getting restless."

Braxton looks up from the current text he's been devouring on dragons. He has to blink a few times before he can fully focus on Delwynn.

"Have you found anything?"

Braxton slams the book shut, coughing as dust particles fill the air. "Nope."

"What were you reading there?" Delwynn prods, drawing closer to the desk.

"Nothing," Braxton says, trying to slip the book underneath one of the many piles, but Delwynn beats him to it.

With his handing resting firmly atop the book, he reads aloud, "*The Siege and Storm of Aeridon's Dragons.*"

He arches a brow. "I'm pretty sure this isn't what Cerylia had in mind when she asked us to conduct research on the Mallum."

Braxton crosses his arms. "Asked *you*, not me," he corrects. "She doesn't know I'm still here, remember?"

Delwynn removes his hand from the book and pulls a nearby chair over to the desk, shaking his head as he sits. "So you've found nothing."

It's not so much a question as it is a statement of fact. But Delwynn just so happens to be right—he *hasn't* found anything. "Unfortunately, that is correct."

Even though he's only just now seated himself, Delwynn gets up and puts the chair back in its proper place. "The queen will return again tomorrow asking for an updated report. I advise you to look harder—if not, then perhaps it *would* be best for you to just leave."

Mouth agape, Braxton stares at the back of the old man's head as he exits the chambers. "Well, that was rude," he says aloud once the door shuts. But maybe Delwynn has a point. If he's not of service here, why stay? Then again, to leave, knowing something as dangerous as the Mallum is out there, without having any background, understanding, or knowledge as to what it's capable of?

Not a risk worth taking.

With a long-winded sigh, he pulls another book from the stack. Thirty minutes of flipping through page after page, and nothing's jumped out at him. He repeats this process thrice more: pull a book from the seemingly endless pile, scan through the pages, find nothing, fling the book across the room out of sheer frustration, retrieve a new book and repeat.

Once he's reached the end of the stack—without coming across anything even halfway useful—he can't help but feel angry. Not only is he failing Cerylia, he's also failing Arden. Arden, who's alone somewhere out there in Aeridon. Arden, who likely has no idea about the Mallum and what it's capable of . . .

It's enough to make him rise and forcefully flip the desk onto its side. Being locked in this room with no social interaction is starting to get to him—coupled with searching line after line of text for information that may not even exist—it's no wonder he's reached his breaking point.

His breaths are uneven and ragged as he leans up against the wall, resting his head against the smooth surface. His eyes close as he attempts to focus solely on his breathing. The texts in this room are a dead-end—he's sure of it. And if the others haven't found anything either, then the library is yet another dead-end. The only other place he can recall seeing Caldari texts is . . .

Arden's chambers.

His eyes shoot open. He's about to make for the door when he realizes that he can't just roam the halls freely.

I'm not even supposed to be here.

Much to his chagrin, his deviating abilities are no good for sneaking across the castle undetected. Estelle is unaware that he's here, so her cloaking abilities, albeit perfect for this scenario, are out of the question. So are

Xerin's shaping abilities—and those wouldn't matter anyway because he's not even here.

Either Braxton can risk being seen and go to Arden's chambers himself, or wait for Delwynn to return and ask him to do it. The latter doesn't do much to remedy his feeling of confinement.

If he's going to do this, he needs to be incognito.

With the sun making its final descent, it's an opportune time to change his clothes. He checks Delwynn's armoire for a black tunic and trousers, which, surprisingly, he finds neatly folded in the first drawer. He removes his beige trousers and white tunic, replacing them with the darker ones. He looks for something to cover his white-blonde head of hair, but comes up short, so he grabs another black tunic and wraps it around his head.

Clad in black, he can't help but feel like one of the Cruex—ready to take on anything and anyone. It makes him wonder if this is how Arden felt as an assassin for his father. Cold, ruthless, and prepared for anything. Not that he's going to kill anyone who might get in his way— that would be outrageous in and of itself. He simply wants to blend into the shadows and remain as hidden and discreet as possible on his way to Arden's chambers.

In his head, he does his best to recall a rough map of Sardoria's layout. If he's not mistaken, there's one corridor that's remained abandoned—one that Cerylia had accidentally mentioned when they'd first arrived. It would mean taking the long way, but it seems to be the best—and only—option, given his current predicament.

Quietly, Braxton slips out the door, making sure to check both directions before heading right. Delwynn's chambers are on the floor just below the queen's, so while a run-in with Cerylia isn't likely, it's not implausible.

Even through the fabric of his shirt, the wall is like ice on his back. He presses against it, peering around each corner before advancing further. Right, right, left, right—until he finally reaches a hallway that isn't lit. The wall sconces remain empty—untouched. It's completely dark, save for the slivers of moonlight penetrating the overhead windows.

Braxton waits for his eyes to adjust before continuing down the abandoned corridor. Thankfully, he hasn't crossed paths with anyone yet. The chance it'll happen here? Highly unlikely. There's no need to stay pressed up against the wall, what with him blending into the darkness and all, so he continues to walk right down the middle of the hallway—at least, what he *thinks* is the middle.

The corridor stretches on for what feels like an eternity. He almost trips over a pile of something soft— *were those linens?*—but it's too dark to tell what it is. He kicks whatever the object is from his feet and keeps moving forward. A small archway of light appears in the distance. Smiling to himself, he quickens his pace. If he's not mistaken, this corridor should dump him right into Arden's hall, which also happens to be his own hall—or maybe now it's considered his past hall? He's not sure exactly what his residence status is since he's been covertly hiding out at Delwynn's.

Just as he'd pictured, the hallway takes him a mere two steps away from Arden's door. Fortunately, it doesn't look like anyone's been here since he and Felix last rifled through her belongings. The door is still unlocked. He pushes it open, making sure to shut it securely behind him once inside. He surveys the room—a refreshing reprieve to discover that everything's just as they'd left it.

He makes for the bookcase, his eyes scanning the rows and rows of books. His fingers trace the spines of a few that catch his eye, and he pulls them out as he moves along the shelf. Left to right, down, right to left, down, repeat. By the time he's finished scanning the bookshelf, he's pulled four texts. It's somewhat disappointing, as he'd been hoping for a few more to better his odds. The Mallum certainly hasn't been an easy topic to come by up to this point.

He plops down on the ground and begins reading through the first two books, finding only dark magick references—nothing explicitly about the Mallum. It's not until he opens a text about the Crostan Islands that he comes across something directly linked to this enigmatic force.

Thought to have originated in the Crostan Islands, the Mallum was birthed from the inherent nature of evil. Drawn to those who have an urge for darkness, the Mallum exploits illusié by drawing it in and absorbing the abilities, but only if those abilities are used in defense or in attack on the Mallum. The only known way to . . .

Braxton turns the page to find . . . a chapter on something completely unrelated. "The only known way to *what?*" he says flipping through the rest of the book, but there's nothing more. He opens up the fourth and final text, his eyes flitting across the pages, but there isn't another word written on the Mallum. He opens *Legends of the Crostan Islands* up once again, turning past the page about the Mallum. From the looks of the tear, there are at least three or four pages missing . . . three or four pages that would likely tell him everything he needs to know.

Lords be damned.

He pushes himself up from the ground, replacing the three useless texts back in their designated spaces on the bookshelf, but intentionally tucks *Legends of the Crostan Islands* underneath his arm. At least Delwynn will have something to show Cerylia in the morning . . . even if no one will ever know that *he's* the one who found it.

ARDEN ELIRI

ORIHIA IS EXACTLY how I remember it. Even in the winter months, the brush is colorful and the animals are spritely, dashing to and fro, as if hibernation is a thing of the past. I suppose in a place like this, it is. I pass by a familiar set of oversized mushrooms—the same ones I'd landed on when I'd seen . . . well, the Mallum. It's strange to think there's a name for what's been haunting me.

I shake off the shiver that's making its way down my spine before continuing onward toward my dwelling. I'm happy to see that everything is just as pristine and beautiful as I'd left it—although, it would have been nice if I'd actually had the time to properly decorate. Perhaps that's a task I'll take on while I'm here, but only if I stay long enough.

Juniper trots beside me as I walk down the pebble-and-wildflower-lined road, until I reach Estelle's place, and then not much further away . . . Felix's place. I know I shouldn't expect him to be here, seeing as I'd left him behind in Sardoria, but I have the urge to check anyway.

As soon as I enter, I immediately wish I hadn't. I try to suppress the overwhelming sense of longing, but it's no use. Although not physically here, Felix is indeed *here*—in every corner, in the wood detailing in the decor, in the lingering scent of pine and mint. It only grows stronger as I move closer to his bed, and I can't help but wrap one of the wool blankets tightly around me. I take a deep inhale and fall into a nearby chair before closing my eyes.

In that moment, I'm in a state of pure bliss—that is, until I open my eyes and realize I'm alone, save for Juniper. I grip the blanket, pulling it snug as I scan the room. I hadn't spent much time in Felix's dwelling when the Caldari first introduced me to Orihia. I'd been too busy talking with Estelle—learning from her; forming a friendship. Little had I known Felix's true feelings for me.

And mine for him.

I scan the room slowly, not looking for anything in particular, but more so to get a better sense of Felix himself. No matter what my eyes land on, I find it to be neat, organized, and overly tidy. I suppose we have that in common.

My eyes flick to the bookcase. It's empty. Looks like the Queen's Guard didn't just stop at the hidden library at Estelle's—they'd searched every dwelling until every last book had been seized and taken to Sardoria.

My eyes continue to move across the room, landing on something familiar on the nightstand. The blanket drops to the floor as I rise from the chair and walk around the bed. When I reach the nightstand, I can't help but smile as I carefully pick up a miniature wooden carving . . . although this one's not of a ship, but of a bird. As I examine it closer—the tapered wings, the sharp, triangular-shaped beak—it dawns on me that it's a carving of a falcon.

The moment I process this, I whirl toward the window, half expecting to see Xerin, in falcon form, perched on the windowsill, but the window is closed. I keep my eyes glued to it, just in case something soars by, but there's only stillness.

I come back to the carving. Suddenly feeling uneasy, I return it to its proper place on the nightstand. To my knowledge, Xerin still hasn't returned with any news of Rydan and Elvira's whereabouts—at least, not before I'd left. *I'm sure he's been back to Sardoria by now,* I tell myself, but the voice inside my head isn't exactly reassuring.

My thoughts scatter as Juniper circles my feet, pawing at my boots. She rolls onto her side and attempts to bite into the leather. I sigh as I pick her up. "I know, I know. I'm hungry, too."

I decide to take a closer look around Orihia, not only in search of food, but also to explore a little more. Last time, we'd been in such a rush to leave that I'd only ventured into the main dwellings. There's so much more to see. I take a path I've never been down before, and when I look up, my jaw goes slack—as it should. Above me, hundreds of walkways shimmer in the setting sun. It seems their sole purpose is to connect the trees to one another. Upon closer inspection, it appears even more dwellings are built *into* the branches—into the actual trees themselves.

I set Juniper down and tell her to stay put before clambering across two oversized mushrooms that lead to granite steps. I climb them, two at a time, until I reach one of the walkways. It glows indigo and silver in the expanding moonlight, the twinkling giving it an almost transparent look, like I could fall right through. Carefully, I touch a toe to it to make sure it's stable, which, surprisingly enough, it is.

Before stepping onto the slick walkway, I notice that there aren't any more stairs to get to the upper tree levels. *How do I get up there?* My question is quickly answered as I raise my right arm to catch my balance, because, in doing so, I'm immediately transported up *through* to the next walkway, to the next level.

"Neat," I say as I glance back down at the ground. I begin to stroll along the treeline, Juniper mimicking my movements from below. There are so many houses tucked away up here, more than I had originally thought, and it makes me wonder if anyone is lucky enough to call them home. There *must* be more Caldari out there in Aeridon— *it'd be foolish to think that we're the only ones*—but if they're not here, then where are they?

I raise my right arm again, palm open, fingers pointed to the sky, and ascend another level to find even more dwellings. On a whim, I decide to enter one, just to feed my curiosity as to whether or not it's being lived in. To my surprise, it appears this one has residents—or *had*. Women's clothing hangs in the armoire and there are small boots stationed by the door. Hope flickers within me until I notice an alchemy set sitting on the desk. The flowers and herbs sitting right next to it are dried to a crisp . . . not fresh. From the looks of it, it's been quite some time since anyone's been here.

I shut the door behind me, then step back onto the walkway. I go up a few more levels, checking random dwellings on each floor only to find more of the same— empty, but previously lived in. The sound of rushing water catches my attention, and as I climb higher, I can clearly make out the sounds of a waterfall. How a waterfall can exist this high up in the treeline baffles me—but I can't seem to pin down its location.

I ascend even higher, repeating the process, until I grow tired of seeing the same thing over and over— abandoned dwellings and no people. With a grunt, I shut the last door, deciding that I'm finished with my pointless quest for the day. As I gaze at the sky, it dawns on me that I have *no idea* how to get back down to the ground.

My heart flutters in my chest as panic begins to set in. I remind myself to be rational—if I got up here, then surely I'll find a way to get back down. If I had to guess, it probably has something to do with my arm motions—but one wrong move and I could either fall flat on my face or go soaring through the treetops with nothing to break my inevitable fall.

50/50 shot. What fantastic odds.

I take a deep inhale through my nose before trying the first motion I can think of—extending my right arm straight out in front of me. As soon as I do so, I find myself moving at an incredible speed across the walkway to the other side. When I put my arm down, the movement ceases. I lift my left arm in front of me and it backtracks at the same speed, returning me to where I'd just been. When I raise my right arm out to the side, it takes me right, my left arm takes me left.

I stop, keeping my arms pinned at my sides, trying to discern some sort of pattern. If arms down keeps you where you are, and right arm up is up, right arm out is forward, and left arm out is backward . . . then it would stand to reason that left arm up would take me down.

Once I have my wits about me, I raise my left arm straight into the air. As I'd hoped, it takes me back down, but only one level—and by this point, I'm at least twelve levels up.

"Okay, *think*," I say to myself, knowing that if it's something designed by illusié, there must be a more efficient way. I do the next thing that feels natural to me and lift both arms into the air. Immediately, I catapult downward through all of the shimmering walkways, like sliding through some sort of tunnel, until I land safely on the ground.

Feeling energized by my recent discovery, I reason that if I can get down that quickly, then there must be a way to get all the way to the top in a flash—and not just one level at a time. I try out a few different arm motions, like arms up palms together, as if I'm about to swan dive into a body of water, but nothing happens. I try sticking both arms out on either side of me—even going so far as to flap them like a bird—but still, nothing happens.

I realize how idiotic I must look, and for the first time in a while, I'm thankful no one's here to witness this. The last motion I try is similar to arms down, except I bring my arms into a downward V-shape and point my wrists outward, as if I'm pushing off from something.

It does the trick.

In mere seconds, I find myself soaring through the glimmering walkways, and at this speed, they're all different colors. Reds, blues, pinks, and purples—a twinkling rainbow of epic proportions. Coupled with the multi-colored leaves on the trees and the flowers blossoming on the branches, the sight is beyond breathtaking. I repeat this travel pattern a few more times, mostly to marvel at my surroundings and take it all in. Each time feels like the first time—like I'm seeing it all with a fresh pair of eyes.

Eventually, I let my arms fall to my side. I stop moving, then take another look around. I try to stop them, but my thoughts run away with me. With a place like this, how can darkness and evil even *exist*? I sigh, trying to push the Mallum and its raspy whispers far from my mind. Although I'd never admit it out loud, I've felt myself steadily unravelling ever since leaving Trendalath—and I don't know why.

The fact that I'd let Elias go free makes me wonder if I'm growing soft. The old me—ruthless Cruex assassin—would have had his head in mere seconds, no questions asked . . . especially when my safety, and the safety of the Caldari, is in jeopardy. Elias works for Tymond, after all, and if there's anything I've learned about Trendalath's king, it's that he's tainted, merciless, and dishonest—a perfect target for the Cruex.

How ironic.

Is it possible I'd spared Elias's life *because* of this darker aspect, the nature of his work—work that I once took part in? Or had I spared his life simply because he had the means to get something I needed in return? I'm not sure which is worse. I also don't know which one rings true. The only thing I'm coming to realize—right now, in this very moment—is that the more time I spend away from being an assassin . . . the more I miss it.

These thoughts have so consumed me that I don't even realize when I've made it to the end of the uppermost walkway. My gaze travels skyward to an utterly perfect stargazing spot. Seeing as there's no walkway to help me, all I have to do is climb a few branches to get to the very top of this tree.

I begin my ascent, swinging back and forth between branches, my boots digging into the bark, twigs and leaves coating my hair. When I reach the highest point, I see there's a shimmering platform—not a walkway. I test its stability by placing my hand on it and pressing down. It's stable. I push off from the tree and hop onto it, tumbling onto my back with my mouth agape as I look out into the ever-expanding iridescent sky. I'm so high up that it feels like I'm actually floating on a cloud, in the midst of all of these twinkling stars. Any lingering remnants of cloaked figures and King Tymond and Elias Kent fade into the background—into the seamless beauty before me. It's one of those moments I don't think I've ever had the chance to experience—where you're so engrossed in where you are and what you're witnessing that you never want to leave.

It doesn't take much to convince myself that I could fall asleep up here. So I do.

RYDAN HELSTROM

RYDAN STUDIES ELVIRA from afar as she clangs around in the kitchen, pulling pots and pans from the cabinet, to ready their next meal. He hasn't known her for too long, but from what he's witnessed thus far, she seems to cook when she's feeling anxious or worried. Not that he's complaining—her cooking is impressive—but they *had* shared their last meal about an hour or so ago.

The mounting tension between them is palpable—ever since discovering that her childhood friend, Avery, had dropped Arden off in Lonia. What exactly Arden's doing there, he hasn't a clue, but her unpredictable nature as of late doesn't do much to put his mind at ease. There's no telling what she's thinking or what she might do next, especially after the way he'd left things. Not exactly his proudest moment, but discovering that he's the *one thing* he's spent his whole life despising? That does a lot of damage to a person. Frankly, he hadn't known how to handle it.

And so he'd fled.

His thoughts disperse as a pan clatters to the floor. He's about to ask Vira if she needs a hand, but one look at her tells him she's managing just fine. A crisp breeze sweeps across the room, causing the skin on his neck to prickle. He eyes some nearby kindling and decides to light a fire. Although it's warmer in Chialka than it is up north, the permanent openings in the cottage aren't very forgiving—and, seeing as it borders the ocean, the temperature indoors always seems to match the temperature outdoors.

He gathers a few of the logs before kneeling by the hearth and attempts to light it the old-fashioned way— knowing full well that he could use his illusié abilities to do so—but the thought alone is sickening. He'd never asked for these abilities—these *powers*—but he hadn't been given a choice. He briefly wonders what this means of his parents, his grandparents, his whole family . . .

Anger roils inside of him. When he looks down, the tips of his fingers are sparking. He tries to calm himself, hoping the sparks will cease as well, but they refuse to let up. Another cool breeze sweeps through the room. It's pointless to deny the inevitable. He thrusts his hands near the firewood, scowling as it lights almost instantly.

The racket in the kitchen stops. He glances over his shoulder, but as soon as he does, the clanging resumes.

Elvira seems to have made herself busy, yet again.

Using the side of the wall to push himself upright, Rydan turns and walks into the kitchen. He knows he's going to have to broach this subject soon—might as well get it over with. It's not like the tension will lessen anyway. He decides to go for a direct approach. "Vira, you and I both know we can't stay here."

Even though her back is to him, he can clearly see that she's stopped moving. She doesn't say anything, and, after a moment, resumes peeling the potatoes.

"You father isn't here and neither is your mother. I doubt Xerin's just going to pop in at any moment." He eyes one of the windows, prepared to eat his words. Xerin does have a way of suddenly just appearing out of nowhere. Much to his surprise, no falcon or other animal lands on the windowsill. "This is likely the first place Tymond would come looking for you—it *is* your childhood home, after all."

She turns to face him before finally breaking her silence. "There are so many cottages in Chialka, I doubt he'd even remember which one is mine."

"That may be so, but with his Savant," Rydan treads lightly, "you really can't be sure. We have no idea what types of abilities they possess. We don't know how powerful they are."

He seems to have struck a chord because she drops the potatoes onto the table and rakes a hand through her wavy hair. "And where *exactly* do you suggest we go,

Rydan? Trendalath and Sardoria are out of the question, seeing as we've fled from both. You're saying we can't stay here, and I'm certainly not going back to Lirath Cave to live with Haskell like some rogue scallywag."

That last one almost has him sputtering with laughter. He tries to compose himself, but she's just so damn charming when she's upset—and she doesn't even realize it. She seems to sense his lighter mood because a hint of a smile touches her lips. "What's so funny?"

"You just called Arden's brother a scallywag."

Her face falls but mere seconds later, she lets out a small giggle. "I suppose I did. But it's the truth!"

His heart feels as though it's about to burst. It's the first time in days they've been amicable toward one another. "Listen, I understand how you're feeling. I know we don't have many options—but you know Avery, and Avery has a ship that can take us to Lonia," he proposes.

Vira seems to consider this as she regroups the potatoes and drops them into a pot of boiling water. "I've never been to Lonia before."

"I've only been once, but it's a magnificent town. Not only is the scenery beautiful, but the food is fresh and the fruit is ripe season-round . . . " He stops himself, realizing it's the first time he's talked about Lonia in a positive light.

"Oh . . . I don't know, Rydan."

He's so close. "We can try it out for a little while and if you don't like it, we can go somewhere else," he offers, hoping he doesn't sound too desperate. "How does that sound?"

Her jaw moves from side to side as she weighs her options. "Fine, I'll go. As long as you promise me one thing."

He tries to mask his delight. "What's that?"

"That first and foremost, we find Arden and tell her about her brother."

His joy fades. *That's the stipulation? Really?*

Even so, he's well aware that if he *doesn't* agree now, they'll likely revert to hardly speaking, weeks going by where they'd stay in Chialka, becoming even more prone to Tymond's Savant discovering them and taking them captive. He refuses to be locked up a second time—once was more than enough.

With a reluctant nod of his head, he says, "Okay. We can find Arden and tell her about her brother. But after that, we'll find a nice place to settle in Lonia. We can start over." The thought brings a genuine smile to his face. "No more of this illusié or Caldari business."

She smirks. "Except to light fires."

So she had seen him! He glances down at the floor and shakes his head. "Only in emergency situations."

When he looks up, she's stone-faced. "You're not going to like this, but there's one more thing we need to tell Arden."

His stomach drops.

She rubs her hands on the front of her apron before reaching into the back of her trousers. From it, she produces a small scroll. He recognizes it as the same scroll she'd taken—actually, *stolen* is the more appropriate term—from Haskell's cave. She grabs his hand and places it in his palm. "Read it."

Rydan unfurls the parchment, knowing that whatever he's about to find won't be good. He scans over the document, then looks back up at her.

"This can't be . . ." He rereads it just to be sure. When he looks up, the sadness in Vira's eyes is reflected in his own. Turns out the King's Savant was responsible for the death of Lavinia Eliri . . .

Arden and Haskell's mother.

DARIUS TYMOND

DARIUS WALKS THE castle grounds, hoping to enjoy the cooler weather while it lasts. Living in the southwest region of Aeridon certainly has its perks, namely in the colder months—breezy autumn months and mild winters. On the other hand, the summers in Trendalath are brutally unforgiving. He's always preferred winter, Aldreda summer—just another thing they've always held opposing views on.

With each passing day, his wife grows steadily weaker. Frailer. What's worsening her condition is beyond his comprehension, but the handmaiden is quick to remind him that the longer they wait, the less likely it is she'll fully recover. Knowing all that's currently at stake, he's seriously considering seeking out a Healer. His unborn child needs to survive.

He's on his daily stroll in the courtyard when the scent of a nearby lavender bush stops him in his tracks. He admires it before plucking one of the magenta-hued thistles from the plant, then presses it to his nose. Lavender has always had a calming effect on him. He inhales deeply, immediately feeling its effects. Sadly, they're short-lived, even more so with the sudden commotion that's approaching him.

Thistle in hand, he ducks behind the overgrown bush, only poking his head out upon hearing two familiar voices—ones that belong to Cruex members Cyrus and Elias. The two men are at the far end of the castle grounds, and by their mannerisms alone, he can tell that the conversation is intended to stay between them. He briefly wonders what Elias is doing back, seeing as he'd *just* sent him to Lonia.

His hearing isn't what it used to be, so he can't gather much from their hushed voices. Neck craned, he attempts to make out the conversation, but the effort is futile. He can't hear a damn thing. The thistle falls from his fingertips as he rises from behind the bushes and marches directly at them, choosing to ignore the trace of purple dust lingering on his robes.

At first, Cyrus and Elias are so engrossed in their conversation that they don't even sense his arrival. It's only when he's standing about ten steps away that they finally turn to face him. Upon recognition of their ill manners, they each bend into a low bow.

"Sir Kent, I didn't expect you to be back so soon," Darius says, keeping his hands concealed beneath his robes as he fidgets with the amethyst ring. "Have you any news for me?"

Elias looks to Cyrus before saying, "Unfortunately, Your Majesty, I do not."

When he doesn't expand further, Darius takes a deliberate step forward. "If that's so, might I ask *why* you are here?"

Elias doesn't flinch. "Actually, I'm quite glad you've happened upon our conversation. You see, Lonia is quite large—it's a lot of ground to cover—and I thought it'd be a better use of resources to bring Cyrus along with me."

"You mean to say that you came all the way back here just to ask permission in bringing Cyrus back to the place you've just returned from?"

A mere blink and Elias has the gall to answer, "Yes."

What a preposterous request.

Darius tries to control his rising temper. "And what of your cousin, Sir Darby?" The name spews from his tongue. "Could he not be of assistance?"

Elias glances at Cyrus, throat bobbing, before replying, "Hugh's taken on the Crostan Islands, which, if you don't mind my saying, is a feat in and of itself."

"So let me get this straight," Darius says, his mouth tightening in disapproval. "Of all the Cruex and all the Savant, you are the *only one* who needs a companion to fully cover your region?"

Elias catches onto his meaning. He looks down at his feet before muttering a pathetic, "Yes."

Darius angles his head so that Elias has no choice but to meet his gaze. "I would have expected this from Sir Garrick, but not from you, Elias." He shakes his head.

Elias remains silent, but, as if a wordless exchange has passed between them, Cyrus interrupts, "If you'll allow it, Your Majesty, I would very much like to assist Sir Kent in Lonia. I believe I can be a great asset to him."

Darius can hardly believe his ears. As the most senior member of the Cruex, Cyrus brings knowledge and experience to the table—which a lot can be said for, especially in times like these—but what Darius needs now is to ensure that his current assets are guarded and protected . . . and that duty falls on Cyrus. Even through his cloud of irritation, an idea emerges. "Sir Kent, leave us for a moment."

Elias shoots the king a confused look, but gives a quick nod of his head before scurrying toward the stables located clear across the grounds. Once Darius is certain he's out of earshot, he focuses his undivided attention on Cyrus. "Sir Alston, I need to ask a favor of you."

"I'm at your service, Your Majesty." The shadows flickering across the old man's eyes have Darius thinking twice, but if there's one person who won't thwart his wishes, it's Cyrus.

"On your way back from Lonia," Darius says, lowering his voice with each word, "I'd like for you to locate a Healer and discreetly bring them back to Trendalath."

"A Healer as in . . . illusié?"

Darius nods.

A muscle feathers in the old man's cheek as he considers this unusual request. "Forgive my meddling, Your Majesty, but is everything all right? Need I be concerned?"

Darius sighs before patting him gently on the shoulder. "I'm afraid Aldreda has fallen very ill—"

"But she's with child—"

"Yes, and she still is," Darius snaps at the unwarranted interruption, "however traditional medicine has only been successful for the short-term. The handmaidens are convinced that only a Healer can aid her into full recovery."

"How much time do I have?"

"We can't be certain," Darius says as he glances up at the healing ward, "so best to make it a quick trip."

Cyrus seems to catch onto his meaning because he says, " Of course, Your Majesty. I shall return with the finest Healer before a fortnight."

As he makes for the stables, Darius grabs him firmly by his forearm. Suddenly feeling sentimental, he whispers, "Cyrus, my old friend?"

He stops to look at the king. "Yes, Your Majesty?"

For a moment, Darius wants to tell him of his plans, to not be alone in this. Instead, he goes for a subtle, yet unusual kindness. "Thank you."

Cyrus places his hand atop the king's. "I won't stop until I've found one. You have my word."

Conflicted, Darius releases his grip, watching as Cyrus retreats to the stables. He casts his eyes downward, pretending not to watch as the old man meets up with Elias. He can't quite put his finger on why, but that last interaction was unsettling. Something tells him to change his mind—to keep Cyrus here . . . but that opportunity slips right through his fingers. When he looks up, they're gone.

BRAXTON HORNSBY

IT'S STILL DARK when Braxton braves the hallways to leave Arden's chambers. With the book tucked securely underneath his arm, he slips through the doorway, tiptoeing along the abandoned corridor. When faint voices echo from down the hall, he immediately halts in his tracks before pressing his body flat against the wall. For a moment, he's almost certain the voice belongs to Felix, but as quickly as it'd come, it begins to fade away.

He exhales, releasing the breath he'd been holding in, and then carries on down the corridor, looking behind his shoulder every few seconds to ensure he's not being followed. His paranoia only grows worse when he hears what sounds like wings flapping a short distance away.

He's about to scold himself for not grabbing the bracketed torch just outside Arden's chambers, but quickly reminds himself that he's *supposed* to blend in with his surroundings—to remain hidden. Illuminating the abandoned hallway would do just the opposite, although it *would* help him see what in lords' name is making that noise. With each step he takes, the fluttering grows louder and louder. The answer presents itself in the form of a familiar golden shimmer.

He'd know that glow from anywhere.

"Xerin?" he whispers into the darkness. A whooshing sound bounces off the walls and Braxton realizes that what he'd almost tripped over earlier was a knapsack—Xerin's knapsack. "Hello?"

"Braxton." The voice is gruff and *could* be Xerin, but it's hard to know for sure. The figure draws closer, but that doesn't make who it is any clearer.

"Who's there?" Braxton angles his head as if it'll help him see better, his heart picking up pace. He braces himself against one of the walls, ready to attack if needed.

The golden glow reappears, illuminating the distinct features of Xerin's face. "Lords, Braxton! You startled me," he says, sounding more like himself this time. "What are you doing roaming about this corridor? How do you even know about it?"

"I could ask you the same thing," he counters.

A palpable silence ensues, giving Xerin plenty of time to craft his answer. "I suppose you could say that there are some things I just *know*. I've been around for a long time, and as a Shaper, I probably know a lot more than I ought to. So again, I'll ask—what are *you* doing here?"

His answer is vague to the point of being cryptic, which infuriates Braxton even more. In that moment, he's not sure just how much he should disclose to Xerin—if anything at all. He makes a swift decision to err on the side of caution. "Queen Jareth has all of the Caldari busy with a fact-finding mission. I remembered seeing a book in Arden's room that would be of help, so I went to retrieve it." He gestures at his surroundings. "I stumbled upon a shortcut, so I took it."

"Why didn't Arden just bring it to Cerylia's attention?" Xerin pries.

Braxton looks at him curiously. *He doesn't know she's fled.* "Because Arden isn't here."

Xerin's mouth rigs to the side. "Where did she go? Did Cerylia send her somewhere?"

"No. It seems she's . . . fled."

Xerin runs a hand down his face. "If I'm being completely honest, I'm not surprised. It was only a matter of time." Braxton's about to ask him what he means when he unabashedly changes the subject. "So what exactly is this fact-finding mission you're on?"

For some reason, Braxton hesitates. Does the queen even know Xerin's here, that he's back? From the way he'd swooped into the *abandoned* corridor, he guesses not. Once she *does* find out, though, she'll likely assign him to fact-duty, just like the rest of the Caldari. "We're looking for information on," he lowers his voice to a whisper, "something called the Mallum. Do you know anything about it?"

Suddenly, Xerin's entire body stiffens. He takes one step backward, followed by another, and another. Instead of answering the question, he simply says, "Run."

Even though there's hardly any light in the corridor, it somehow grows darker. Braxton's blood chills as a cool sensation wraps around his shoulders, moving to his neck, and then his head. It's enough to make him shiver, but it's not like a draft that comes and goes—it lingers. He freezes in place, doing the exact opposite of Xerin's command. His mind screams at him to run, but his legs won't move. Slowly, he raises his head. He can't make out what it is, but there's *something* hovering over him.

Watching him.

Observing him.

His mind finally catches up. His first instinct is to turn and run back toward Arden's chambers—seeing as it's closer than Delwynn's—but before he can move his feet, he's met with an indescribable force, greater than anything he's ever felt. He's thrown backward with such intensity that he lands flat on his back, sliding along the marble floor, the book flying from his grip. With the wind completely knocked out of him, he struggles to catch his breath, let alone rise to his feet. His inability to see certainly isn't helping any.

"I told you to run!" Xerin shouts again, but this time, he sounds much farther away.

Braxton knows he should listen—that he should get up and run like hell—but something stops him. Arden's book. Through ragged breaths, he crawls on his hands and knees, frantically searching left and right for it. His hands shake each time they make contact with the icy marble floor—that is, until his fingers finally brush the spine of the book. With trembling hands, he grabs it and tucks it into the back of his trousers. He manages to find the strength to pull himself upright—but instead of running, he presses himself up against the wall.

His panting is so shallow that he almost chokes on his own breath as he attempts to take a deep inhale. He implores his pulse to slow, but the steady decline in the corridor's temperature continues to work against him. It's then terror ripples through his mind as he recalls his last encounter with Cerylia—specifically her answer regarding what the amethyst ring protects from . . . *Even if I were to explain it to you, you wouldn't understand. Not until you* **feel** *it.*

Never in his life has he experienced a feeling so fully—yearning, angst, darkness. It's like there's something hidden deep within his very core that must be exposed, right here, this instant. It's a simultaneous longing and aching—a thirst for something intangible and otherworldly.

Shift the focus. He closes his eyes, recalling his many training sessions with Delwynn. "Know what your enemy wants, sense the attack, and *deviate.*" It'd sounded so simple at the time—and yet, in this very moment, it feels wholly impossible. How can he focus on what he can't see?

Not until you feel it.

The phrase rings in his head. He focuses on each word, each syllable, until suddenly, it's as though he's somehow transformed into the darkness itself. Its every thought, desire, and movement becomes his own. An irrevocable and undeniable bond.

Another attack hurtles his way—another stone-cold blast that's sure to knock him from his feet. But this time, he's ready. This time, he'll deviate.

The tethers binding him hiss and shriek as he whips back and forth, desperately pulling from their grasp. They squeeze tighter and tighter, refusing to let go—but his determination is unparalleled. With each calculated movement, the bond begins to loosen, weakening more and more as it unravels at an astonishingly rapid rate. A final overpowering heave is what finally does it, allowing him to fully detach from the arcane force surrounding him.

Upon regaining his footing, he immediately braces his body to deflect the next attack. As expected, it comes in full fury, aimed directly at him. He focuses, homing in on it, as it approaches—closer, closer, closer. Until . . .

As if another force has claimed its stake in the fight, the attack shifts *away* from him, and instead barrels toward some unseen target. There's a horrific screech as it comes into contact with whatever the *thing* is, and a cacophony of deafening shrills follows suit. His hands fly to his head, palms pressing against his ears to block out the dreadful sound.

Without warning, a blur of shadows charge straight for him. Before he knows it, he's been scooped up in a mad dash toward the end of the corridor. It all happens so fast that only when they've arrived at the end of the hall, and Xerin releases him from over his shoulder, does Braxton realize what's just transpired. Blood-red eyes meet his own. "Have you completely," Xerin huffs through uneven breaths, "lost your mind? What in lords' name were you thinking?"

"Was that . . . ?"

Xerin presses an icy hand to Braxton's mouth before shoving him against the wall. "Don't even think of speaking it."

Braxton looks at him wide-eyed, then nods as Xerin lowers his hand and releases him.

"No one can know I was here. Understood?"

Before Braxton can get another word in edgewise, a golden glow blinds him. He gawks as he watches Xerin, in falcon-form, take flight through one of the open windows.

And just like that, he's alone once again.

Wanting to get as far away from the corridor as possible, Braxton hurries down the next few halls, back to Delwynn's chambers. He slips inside, undetected, and makes a beeline for the nearest chair. As he goes to sit, he lands on something uncomfortable, remembering that, in his trousers, he'd tucked away the book he'd almost lost to . . .

He pats himself down before rushing over to a gold-plated mirror. No cuts. No scratches. No bruises. No open wounds of any kind. This should make him happy, but instead, anger consumes him. He removes the book from the waistband of his trousers and flings it across the room. It lands on the floor with a loud thud. That damn book had almost cost him his life.

Braxton hadn't known the Mallum was anywhere *near* Sardoria—hell, he'd just learned about it from Delwynn earlier that week. There's no way this is his fault, but he can't help but wonder . . . how had it gotten in? And why had it targeted him in its attack?

He tears himself away from the mirror, his gaze settling back on the book. He doesn't bother to retrieve it. Who needs research anyway, especially when he has something better, something more valuable? Who else can say that they've successfully deviated an attack from the Mallum?

CERYLIA JARETH

CERYLIA CAN'T REMEMBER the last time she'd dreamt so heavily—or so vividly. Her late husband, Dane, sits next to her on his throne in Trendalath, looking as regal as ever. His midnight hair and cerulean eyes stand out against his silver and navy robes. He turns to face her, giving her the perfect view of his pronounced jawline—those thin, but soft lips. His eyes twinkle as he reaches for her hand. She obliges him, smiling as his fingers interlace with her own.

The dream takes her forward a few years—where she gives birth to a beautiful baby boy, his eyes the same bright blue as his father's. She watches as Dane teaches him everything he needs to know about Aeridon, and instills in him the importance of illusié and how it can—

and should—coexist amongst the regular townspeople. She watches their son grow, play, eat, walk, and befriend others. His first words, steps, and laughs are all moments she and Dane will cherish for eternity. He grows up to be kind, compassionate, and strong—everything she could ever want in a son . . .

And in Aeridon's future leader.

Once he is of age, he participates in his first coronation. Cerylia proudly stands by as her son is crowned prince. As the crowd cheers, he turns over his shoulder to look at her. The look in his eyes gives her more validation than she ever could have asked for—that she did *exactly* what she was supposed to do: birth and raise a remarkable leader who would ensure that the Jareth legacy carries on long after her and Dane are gone.

And then, as if a dark cloud has been cast over her seemingly flawless life, the Tymonds emerge from the shadows, despicable intentions in tow. Not only do they slay illusié, but also the townspeople of Aeridon . . . as well as her son. She watches in vain as her boy is murdered in cold blood—the Jareth legacy crumbling before her very eyes. She should be thrilled that her husband's life was spared, but not at the cost of her son—their heir.

As the years pass, she and Dane only grow to resent each other. She blames him for not saving their son, and he blames her for having one in the first place. For without their son, they'd know no pain. Without their son, everything had been perfect . . .

Suddenly, the dream stops and begins to tick backward. Cerylia watches as everything happens in reverse, erasing everything she'd worked so hard to build. And everything she'd lost along the way. There's nothing she can do except watch—as an outsider—as the life she's always desired, save the Tymonds' intrusion, slips away from her, one fragment at a time.

An electrifying screech of nonhuman-like proportions causes the dream to fully escape her. Stuck between reality and fantasy, she jolts upright in bed. Her ears ringing, she surveys her surroundings. She's safe, in her chambers, in Sardoria. But . . . *that sound.*

A chill snakes down her spine. Had she merely imagined it? Or had it actually happened? Slowly, she slides across the bed, shimmying out from under the sheets before setting her feet on the floor. She rises, then swiftly grabs her cloak from the door of the armoire and throws it around her shoulders. Its warmth provides a welcome reprieve from the icy cold currently settling in her veins. She tiptoes to the door and gently presses her ear to it.

The sound had been so eerily familiar—something she hadn't heard in a long while. She remains at the door for some time, expecting to hear it again, but only silence greets her. It briefly crosses her mind to wake Delwynn, but something tells her not to go venturing the halls. Not right now.

She removes her cloak and flings it back over the wrought-iron doors of the armoire before climbing into bed for the second—and hopefully final—time that evening. With her eyes glued to the door, she tries to calm her racing heart. Between the unnerving shriek and her dream-turned-nightmare, she's not sure she wants to fall back asleep. She gets precisely what she asks for because not even a wink of sleep is had.

ARDEN ELIRI

WHEN THERE'S NO sign of Elias or Cyrus after a few days, I start to worry. The journey from Lonia to Trendalath is a long one, but I'm almost certain they would have shown by this morning. I was wrong.

I fix myself a bowl of porridge from the cauldron resting over the fire, then transfer some into a separate bowl for Juniper. I set hers aside to allow it to cool down, but don't bother waiting to dive into my own. The oats nearly burn the roof of my mouth, but I'm so famished that I devour it in its entirety.

Juniper paws at my chair as I hastily grab the canteen of water I'd filled up at a nearby spring earlier that morning, guzzling the majority of it within seconds. I manage to ignore her until her paws end up landing on my leg, just below my knee.

"Your persistence knows no bounds," I say to her before gently nudging her off. Her bowl of oats is no longer steaming, so I place it in front of her, smiling as she rubs her face against the back of my hand. Her face disappears into the bowl, and, before I know it, she's looking back up at me, clearly still hungry.

I rummage in my bag for some berries, dishing a handful into her now-empty bowl. She licks the remnants of porridge from her lips before starting on those—her second breakfast. When she's finished, I can tell she's finally satiated because she curls up into a ball at my feet for her afternoon snooze.

With Juniper down for the count, I look around my dwelling, wondering what I'm going to do with myself if Elias and Cyrus don't show soon. I could go for yet *another* walk around Orihia or take a visit to the treetops—there's still plenty I haven't explored—but I feel like doing so somehow takes the intrigue and wonder out of the place. I *could* search through more of the dwellings, but I already know I'll find them empty. It dawns on me that I might be . . . bored. Which is certainly a first.

My initial intent in coming back to Orihia was to discover more about the cloaked figure who routinely pays me visits—but so far, the only thing I've found is seclusion. As an ex-assassin, I suppose I should be used to feeling isolated and alone—but that was before I'd met Estelle and Opal, Xerin and Braxton.

And Felix.

I suck in a sharp breath at the thought of Felix in Sardoria, the days passing by without so much as a hint as to where I've gone. I left Sardoria because I couldn't keep hurting people, like I'd hurt Delwynn and Braxton—Felix, too. I'd lied to the queen over and over; it was only a matter of time before she'd catch on. I'm sure, by now, she already has.

My thoughts flit from Cerylia back to Felix. I'm afraid that if I don't recall our memories—our indescribable connection—that I'll forget . . . Forget what he looks like. Forget the way he makes me feel. Forget the way he looks at me, like he can make me whole again.

Like he *wants* to.

As much as I want to stay rooted in these pleasant memories, a more recent one shoves its way to the forefront of my mind—the wooden carving of the falcon I'd found in his dwelling. Why had he carved both a wooden ship *and* a falcon? Does Xerin have something to do with it? And speaking of, where *is* Xerin?

War wages within me. Not only do I wish to see him, if just to be in his presence again—I also wish I could ask him the many questions that have plagued my mind as of late. To be able to look deep into those russet eyes and *know* that I can trust him.

But, like everything else, assurance is fleeting.

I shake the thought away before reaching into the right pocket of my trousers. I pull out my timepiece, and from the other pocket, I retrieve the photo of the King's Savant. Now that I look at it more closely, I suppose I can see the resemblance of the younger Cyrus to the older, wiser Cyrus I've come to know. His eyes are what give him away—full of kindness with a tinge of sadness.

What will Cyrus think once Elias brings him the news that I've asked to see him? It dawns on me that perhaps neither of them will come. There's always the possibility that Elias could go back on his word and send both the Cruex and the Savant to Orihia.

How Tymond would love that.

A rustling in the distance grabs my attention. I return both of the items to my pockets, drawing the curtains up from the window. I can see movement in the brush, but it's too far away to determine exactly what it is—could be Elias, could be an animal, could be the Mallum . . . it could be anything, really.

I ready my chakrams and slip out the back door, pressing my back against the wooden structure. I peek around the side of the dwelling so that the forest is directly in my line of vision. Something emerges, slowly, and a graying head of hair comes into view.

Cyrus.

I smile as I return my chakrams to their holsters and step out from the side of the dwelling. "Cyrus!" I call out, briefly wondering where Elias is, then remembering that, given his non-illusié status, he can't see Orihia.

Cyrus gives a small wave as he makes his way over. I take his amicable demeanor as a good sign. When he finally reaches me, he stands back for a moment and looks me up and down. "You look well, Arden. I must say, I was surprised when Elias delivered the news."

"Is he just"—I angle my head at the forest—"waiting out there? By himself?"

"Yes." The old man's eyes crinkle at the sides as he smiles. "I told him I'd be back soon and not to worry."

I give him a playful nudge on the shoulder.

"So," he says as he looks around, "is this where you live now?"

I stifle a laugh. "Truth be told, I'm not even sure how to answer that."

"Is this one yours?" he asks, pointing to the dwelling behind me.

"I suppose you could say that," I respond with a shrug. "Follow me." I walk over to the deck and open the door to let him inside.

"It's . . ."

"Quaint?" I finish for him. "Most of them are. Believe it or not, some are even smaller than this one. But what I *can* tell you, with the utmost certainty, is that it feels more like home here than Trendalath ever did."

Cyrus shoots a sidelong glance my way as he scans the items on the kitchen table. He doesn't waste any time cutting to the chase. "Elias tells me you've found something that belongs to me?"

I nod as I empty my pockets. Cyrus shakes his head at the watch, but his breathing nearly stops at the sight of the photograph. He slides it across the table, gingerly lifting it by the corners. He turns it over in his hands, brows furrowed, but remains silent.

I give him a few moments to sort through his thoughts. "Something wrong?"

The photograph slides from his fingertips back onto the table as he takes a seat. "May I bother you for a glass of water?"

Something's clearly shaken him and I'm desperate to know what it is. "Sure," I say as I retrieve the canteen of water and a glass from the cupboard. I can sense his nerves as I pour the water into the cup. He takes it in both hands before taking a long, steady drink. Not wanting to seem overly curious, I wait for him to finish before asking, "Is there something I should know about that photo?"

His shoulders stiffen as he sets the glass back on the table. "Forgive me, Arden, for I am ill-prepared. I—I wasn't aware I'd be delivering this news."

Every cell in my body feels like it's about to burst.

He seems to weigh the information he wants to share before saying, "The men in the photo are the King's Savant."

Not all that shocking, but it's nice to get confirmation. I want to ask him if he's still in the Savant, seeing as he's in the photo, but I wait for him to continue.

"I'm sure you noticed some similarities between yourself and this man," he says, pointing to my near look-alike—the angled nose, the wide eyes.

"I suppose I can see some similarities." I look to Cyrus, realizing his face has paled completely. "Oh . . ."

He nods, as if to confirm my suspicions. I almost fall from my chair as he says, "That's because he's your father."

RYDAN HELSTROM

NOW MORE THAN ever, Rydan's happy he was smart enough to let Vira do all the talking. After the way he'd treated her childhood friend, he'd rightly expected that Avery would be less than pleased to have to deal with him . . . again. Vira, in her charming and delicate way, had struck up a great bargain, offering some of her family's infamous homemade potato and leek stew, and after five minutes or so of expert persuasion, Avery had agreed to take both her *and* Rydan on his next trip to Lonia—which just so happens to be in half an hour.

Although she tries to hide it, Vira seems to be having a difficult time saying good-bye to her childhood home. It wasn't long ago she'd openly expressed her deepest desires in coming back to Chialka—that she might finally have the chance to reunite with her family, namely her mother—after years of being apart. But he can tell, through her forced laughs and the smiles that don't reach her eyes, that she's utterly disappointed. Honestly, she has every right to be. Her expectations, however far-fetched they may have seemed, weren't met—not even in the slightest.

The thought leaves a hollow feeling in his stomach.

"Almost ready?" he calls out to her from the main entrance. Vira emerges from one of the bedrooms, carrying two knapsacks *and* a satchel. "Here, let me help you with those," he offers, taking one of the bags from her. For a moment, he thinks about condensing all of the items into one, but it's much heavier than it looks. The sheer weight would likely rip right through the fabric, so he throws it over his free shoulder and opens the door.

"After you."

Another artificial smile as she turns around and takes one last look at her childhood home. He can tell by the way she says *good-bye* that she fully understands she won't be coming back here any time soon—if ever. She hikes both of her bags up onto her shoulders before following Rydan out the door.

It's a short journey to the harbor. Rydan can't help but stare at the vibrant Yoshino cherry tree hovering over them as they make their way to where *The Corsair* is docked. As they draw closer, Rydan can clearly see Avery's auburn head bobbing up and down from behind the rails of the main deck.

"Right on schedule!" he yells, flinging a rope ladder over the side. "Hope you don't mind the climb. Since this trip wasn't scheduled, I wasn't able to dock at my usual port." He angles his head in the other direction. "Drawbridge entry's on the other side."

Rydan helps Vira toss her bags up to Avery, which he swiftly catches, and as she's climbing the ladder, he figures he may as well toss his up, too. He watches as Avery pulls her safely aboard before ascending the ladder. The rope is on its last leg and feels like it could snap at any moment—and under Rydan's brute weight, it very well might.

Avery doesn't bother to help him finish boarding, which leaves Rydan lugging himself over the rails. He swings his legs a little too aggressively and winds up tumbling over the side. From the far end of the ship, Vira drops the bags she's carrying to rush over to help him.

"I'm fine, I'm fine," Rydan murmurs, rubbing the bump that's rapidly forming on the back of his head. "Go make sure your friend is happy. Lords know my presence already irks him enough."

Vira checks one more time to make sure he's really okay before gathering her belongings and heading to the helm. Rydan remains seated, watching the two of them converse from afar. While he doesn't fully trust Avery's intentions, it seems that this is their *only* option in getting where they need to go. Part of him wishes they could have met a nice fisherman at the wharf, but perhaps this is for the best. After all, Avery can take them exactly where he'd left Arden . . .

A knot swells in his throat as he thinks about the reason they're even *going* to Lonia—to inform Arden that she has a brother . . . *and* that the King's Savant murdered her mother.

Heavy news followed by even heavier news.

He tries to dismiss the thought, already feeling the burden of what they're about to do, but it lingers. Sitting still certainly isn't helping any, so he pushes himself upright, grabs his bags, and marches across the main deck. Just as he's about to join Vira and Avery at the helm, a staircase catches his eye. A quick glance tells him that they're not paying attention—they're still deep in conversation.

He makes a sharp left turn, ducking underneath the low overhang, and plods down the steps. He finds himself in what appears to be the galley, which must be divine intervention because he's *starving*. He searches the pantry, tossing aside cans of vegetables and beans he's never even heard of. He comes across some fruit—apples, bananas, and other berries—and that's when he notices something familiar on the lower shelf: juniper berries . . . wrapped in a torn piece of what he *knows* to be a Cruex uniform. That confirms it. Avery definitely took Arden to Lonia—and on this very ship.

"Rydan!" Vira's voice echoes down the stairwell, interrupting his thoughts. "Are you down there?"

"I'll be up in a minute," he shouts back.

Carefully, he rewraps the berries and places them in one of the outer pockets of his knapsack. He closes the pantry doors, but not before grabbing an apple. He takes his time going up the steps, full well knowing that a very long trip awaits him.

ARDEN ELIRI

FOR THE PAST couple of days, it's just been Cyrus and me in Orihia. I'm not ashamed to admit that I've actually enjoyed having the company of someone who's known me practically my whole life. It's like a piece of home came to find me and is choosing to stay. It's nice.

After he'd brought Cyrus here, Elias had left to meet up with his cousin, Hugh, in the Crostan Islands. I don't blame him—knowing that I'm here, in the region he's supposed to be keeping an eye on, could get him into serious trouble with Tymond. If I were him, I would have left, too.

Since Cyrus arrived, I've learned some really important things about my past. The first being that my father is the most powerful illusié in the King's Savant;

and the second being that he's been "missing" from said Savant for years. I've tried to pull even more information from him, but he won't budge. He says I know everything I need to—for now.

Dinner is quiet that night, almost to the point of being uncomfortable. I reach for his plate, about to clear the table, when his hand lands on mine. "Arden, there's something else I need to discuss with you. Something unrelated to your family."

I keep my hand in place before meeting his gaze. I'm not sure what I expect him to say, or what it could even be about, but regardless, I want to know. "Okay. What is it?"

He reaches for the two goblets at the end of the table, filling them each halfway with verdot. I stifle a yawn, looking at my pocket watch to check the time. I'm already exhausted and this wine will really do me in, but his tone tells me that I need to hear him out—even if it *is* unrelated to my family.

I look up when the sound of something heavy lands in front of me. He lifts his goblet, angling his head at me. A silent proposal that I do the same. I oblige him and we clink our glasses together before each taking a long, steady drink.

"I have a proposition for you, but to be honest, I'm not sure you're going to like it."

My heart sinks. I take another swig of verdot.

"Here it is." He sets his glass down. "Queen Aldreda is with child and has fallen severely ill. King Tymond has tasked me with"—he pauses, shadows dancing across his eyes—"finding a Healer."

My head spins at the request. "*Me*? You honestly aren't proposing to bring *me* back to *Trendalath*?"

Cyrus scrunches his face, as if in pain, then nods.

I almost laugh, but disbelief overpowers every one of my emotions. "That's preposterous and you know it. Tymond would have my head the minute I set foot on castle grounds."

His voice is quiet. "Not if you can save his wife."

I look at him with wide eyes, unable—no, *unwilling*—to believe what I'm hearing. "Cyrus, I'm sure there are other Healers out there—ones that Tymond doesn't currently have on his most-wanted list."

He doesn't hesitate. "It has to be you, Arden."

The way he says it, the expression of absolute certainty on his face—it's enough to make me want to retreat to Sardoria and never leave again. He doesn't give further explanation. Just sits there and stares at me, waiting for my decision.

"I can't go back there, nor do I want to. I'm sorry Cyrus, but the answer is no."

"He can offer you complete freedom," Cyrus tries again. "He'll leave you be. You can go on to live your new life—as a Caldari."

I scoff and roll my eyes, but strangely, for someone whose adrenaline *should* be pumping, I also feel a yawn coming on. "King Tymond, keep his word? King Tymond, let illusié go free?" I shake my head adamantly. "My answer is still no."

"I was afraid you would say that." His expression is contrite—almost shameful. "I hope you can forgive me, Arden."

My heart skips a beat as I look down at the goblet, my eyes growing heavy with each word. "Cyrus, what did you . . . ?"

My words trail off as my surroundings fade from view.

DARIUS TYMOND

A FAMILIAR CARRIAGE draws up to the gates surrounding Trendalath castle. Has Cyrus truly returned so soon? And with a Healer? For the first time in months, Darius feels a glimmer of hope. "Allow them to pass!" he shouts down to the guards. He waits until the drawbridge begins to lower before rushing to the Great Room.

"Escort them inside immediately," he commands the guards standing just outside the double doors. They mutter a quick acknowledgement before hurrying off. He closes the doors behind him, the sound echoing in the chamber. He turns to face his empty throne, shadows lurking in every crook, every corner. They call to him, beckoning for him to take action. Much to his chagrin, things have been less than eventful around here.

When he reaches his throne, he whirls his robes around him in one swift movement, straightens his dragon brooch, and then takes a seat. The familiar texture of the jewel-encrusted armrests brings a small smile to his lips as he slides his palms along them. He glues his eyes to the entrance, his ears strained for any sign of footsteps just outside the doors.

He's met with silence. And more silence. And . . .

His patience is wearing thin when he finally hears a flurry of footsteps. His back stiffens as he sets his shoulders back, counting down in his head until the doors open. As if on cue, the guards enter first, followed by Cyrus, followed by another guard who's carrying none other than . . .

Arden Eliri.

CERYLIA JARETH

A LOUD BANGING on the door startles Cerylia from her half-asleep state. She jolts out of bed, grabs her robes from the armoire, and throws them around her shoulders. When she arrives at the door, a wave of hesitation washes over her—which isn't all that surprising, given the unsettling shriek she'd heard just a few short hours ago. Pulling the door slowly, she presses her face to the opening, so that only her nose and right eye can see through it. She almost slams the door shut because standing on just the other side is the last person she'd expected to see.

Braxton.

A moment of clarity follows before she decides to swing the door open and face him with her usual regal demeanor.

Braxton, who's clearly flustered, given the color of his cheeks, seems to realize his faux pas—being that he isn't even supposed to *be* here. "Your Greatness, please forgive my"—he pauses as he searches for the right words—"sudden and unexpected appearance."

Knowing that he couldn't possibly have left for Trendalath and returned with the amethyst ring so quickly, Cerylia yanks him inside her chambers and shuts the door. "What are you doing here?" she hisses. And then, as if she's had the wind knocked out of her, "Did you lie to me?"

Braxton looks down at his feet. "Unfortunately, yes, Your Greatness. I did deceive you, but you must know how terribly sorry I am. I've come here tonight to report what I've discovered about . . . the Mallum."

She studies him with lethal calm, noticing that he's not carrying a book or a scroll. His tone indicates that there's something more—something *heavier* behind his words. It takes her no time at all to put two and two together—his disgruntled appearance and the unsettling shriek she'd heard earlier. She stumbles backward, hands searching for a chair, until she finds one and falls right into it. Guilt coils in her stomach. "It was here."

His expression is pained as he nods, slowly, as if allowing adequate time for her to process the information. She hardly even notices as he takes the seat across from her. "The Mallum attacked me tonight."

"On castle grounds?"

He grimaces as he confirms her suspicions. "Yes, on castle grounds."

"Where?" she croaks.

His eyes go frank and cold, a stubborn refusal to reveal the rest of the story.

There's a slight edge to her voice as she presses again. "*Where* did the attack take place, Braxton?"

He levels a steely look back at her before saying, "In the abandoned corridor."

Silence falls between them. He stares at her with such intensity—so desperate for her next words—that she feels as though she might retch on the spot. "Were you alone?" she manages to ask. "Do any of the other Caldari know?"

A flicker of uncertainty flashes across his eyes. "No, it was just me. I was alone."

Cerylia tenses. She pushes herself up from the chair and makes for the foot of the bed. "Honestly, I'm shocked you're alive and well to tell the tale. Most aren't so lucky," she says, starting to pace. "Before I ask why you lied to me and never left for Trendalath, I want to know one thing."

With his eyes locked on hers, he straightens in his seat. He looks almost . . . hopeful. "Yes, Your Greatness?"

"How did you get away from the Mallum?" she asks quietly. And then, even softer, "How are you still here?"

Much to her surprise, a crooked smile crosses his face. "I deviated."

Perhaps she hadn't heard him correctly. "You mean to say that you . . . deviated the Mallum's attack *back* onto itself?"

He gives an affirming nod. "Yes."

Cerylia stops in her tracks, falling onto her knees before him. She looks at him with great sorrow as she takes his hands in hers. "And what of your abilities?"

Braxton's face falls. He looks down at his hands before deliberately pulling away from her grip.

Suddenly, she rises, swiping a metal tankard from the table. "Stand," she orders.

Braxton does as she says.

"Deviate." With her right hand in play, she chucks the tankard straight at his chest, watching in angst as the realization dawns on him—what she already knows.

The tankard knocks into him before falling to his feet. The look on his face says it all.

Braxton is no longer illusié.

BRAXTON HORNSBY

WITHOUT A WORD, Braxton flees from Cerylia's quarters in the direction of Delwynn's chambers. Like a rabid animal, he bursts into the room completely unannounced, half expecting to startle the old man from his dreams, but the bed is empty and untouched.

Braxton scans the room to see if perhaps Delwynn had fallen asleep in the chair by the hearth, but there's no sign of him. Panic rises in his chest as he considers his limited number of options. *Stay here. Or flee.*

He decides to stay, which means going to search for the old man—paying no mind that, less than an hour prior, the Mallum had attacked him and somehow taken his abilities. He'd been almost certain he'd successfully deviated. *How did I let this happen?*

He searches the castle far and wide, tempted to check the courtyard *and* his fellow Caldaris' rooms, but knows that it's highly unlikely for Delwynn to be training—let alone visiting—anyone at such a late hour.

After checking many of the rooms—the dining hall, the courtyard, the White Room—only to find them empty, he has a sudden urge to check the bell tower. He makes a swift left turn, his bare feet hardly making a sound as he ascends the spiral staircase. Hushed voices come into earshot the higher he goes. As he reaches the top, he slows, steadying his breath. He pokes his head around the corner, somewhat surprised to see Opal and Delwynn whispering forcefully back and forth.

Opal senses him immediately and, for a moment, Braxton considers ducking and running the other way, but there's no point. "Show yourself." Her voice is sharper than broken glass.

Remembering he's clad completely in black, he *could* still run and they'd probably never know it was him—but the urgency to talk to Delwynn straight away convinces him to emerge from his hiding place.

"Delwynn," he says with both hands upraised, "if I may speak with you . . ."

It's then he notices Opal's bleak expression.

They already know.

ARDEN ELIRI

WHEN I WAKE, I find myself in an unpleasant, yet familiar setting—my old room in Trendalath castle. Although my mind is foggy, I'm still able to partly recall how I ended up here. I'd been in Orihia with Cyrus drinking wine when, suddenly, I'd blacked out. I'd been absolutely fine, and completely coherent, up until the wine. There's no question about it.

Cyrus had drugged me.

I'd probably feel more panicked if it weren't for the groggy aftereffects of . . . whatever he'd used. I take my time sitting upright, trying to calm the pounding in my head. I attempt to swallow, but my mouth is so dry that it makes me cough instead. In my periphery, I notice a canteen sitting next to the bed. Fortunately, it's filled to the brim with water, so I guzzle it down.

Once I feel steady enough to stand, I drag myself toward the door. I try to open it, tugging on the handle a few times, but it's locked. *Figures.* My only other option seems to be the window—but, in my current state, scaling down the castle wall would be a death wish.

I slowly scan the room for Juniper, my chest tightening when I realize that she isn't here. I try to remember the last place I'd seen her—if she'd been in the room with Cyrus and me—but my memory escapes me. I can only hope she's safely curled up somewhere in Orihia. Tears prick my eyes, but I blink them away.

I heave a jagged breath as I scan the room for my knapsack, but, much like Juniper, it's nowhere in sight. My heart stalls as I realize that Felix's gift was in that knapsack. *What else was in there?* Frantically, I check the pockets of my pants, breathing a small sigh of relief as I pull out my pocket watch, but it's short-lived as my hands swipe by my holsters. They're empty. My chakrams are gone. Meaning I'm unarmed and locked in my old room in Tymond's castle.

Great.

There's a knock on my door. It's difficult to think like my normal self in this groggy state, so it doesn't come as much of a shock when I verbally welcome the visitor inside without even checking to see who it is—as if I *haven't* been taken captive and held on enemy grounds. I feel both relieved and slightly irked when I see Cyrus poke his head into the room.

"Good. You're awake," he says, closing the door behind him.

Whatever he'd used to sedate me must carry a tranquil aftereffect because I've never felt calmer than I do at this very moment. "You brought me here against my will." The words don't come out angry or harsh—just neutral, like stating a fact.

Cyrus frowns. "I do hope you'll forgive me, but it was the only way. You wouldn't have come otherwise."

"Where's Juniper?" I ask. After receiving a confused look, I clarify, "My fox."

"She's safe in Orihia."

"Thank the lords." My tone turns serious. "Cyrus, I demand that you release me. I need to get back—back to my life."

"You can, and you will, as soon as you do what is asked of you." His expression is unyielding. "Arden, you must heal Aldreda."

My normal, *un-drugged* response would be that I mustn't do *anything*, but that's not the person I am right now. I'm indifferent. Neutral. Void of emotion.

Instead, I ask, "Why?"

"He will let you go free. You'll be able to live on your own terms without having to look over your shoulder every minute of every day. Isn't that what you want?"

His attempt to instill a sense of hope almost works. It does sound quite nice—until I remember that we're talking about *King Darius Tymond*. If there's anything I've learned from my time in the Cruex, it's to not trust *anyone* in the Tymond family, save for Braxton, of course.

The resurgence of my failed Soames mission is enough to yank me from my haze and get me thinking more like myself again.

Right . . . Or I could . . . The cogs turn in my head.

I realize that, if I'm going to pull off the plan I've just devised in my head, I'm going to have to be as difficult as possible—nearly intolerable to work with. I level a steely gaze at my captor. "Well, Cyrus, you may as well just kill me now."

He just stares at me, not a flicker of emotion on his face. "And why would I do that?"

"Because," I say with lethal calm, "I refuse, today or any day, to heal any member of the Tymond family."

RYDAN HELSTROM

THE TRIP TO Lonia feels even longer than Rydan remembers. He'd assumed that departing from Chialka instead of Trendalath would mean a shorter ride, but the waves seem to carry on endlessly with no plot of land in sight. At least Avery is a decent captain—the ride has been bearable and mostly smooth. He'd even offered to stop exactly where he'd dropped "Opal" off, which was exactly what Rydan had wanted—but Vira's insistence they go into town instead had won over. Seeing as she's never been to Lonia before, Rydan couldn't deprive her of having the best first experience possible, so he'd agreed.

Rydan exits the ship first, watching as Vira waves farewell to Avery. He gives the captain a full salute back, paired with a toothy grin, and they wait until he's departed the docks before entering the stunning town of Lonia. It's exactly how he remembers it, except for one thing. This time, there are . . . people. Lots of them.

Vira's eyes light up at the many wooden carts and wide array of items for sale—fruit, jewelry, grains, silks, spices. Rydan can't help but match her smile as she weaves in and out of the stands, striking up friendly conversations with each merchant as she goes.

He keeps his attention entirely focused on Vira until something catches his eye—a girl, one with chestnut hair that falls in loose waves just past her shoulders. He stops mid-step. She's tall and slender from the back—almost identical to Arden. His breath hitches as the girl turns, but as soon as he catches a glimpse of her side profile, he sees that it isn't her.

His heart begins to slow, resuming its normal pace— that is, until he realizes he's lost Vira in the sea of people. With wide eyes, he scans the crowd, searching for her head of blonde hair, until someone approaches him from behind and grabs him by the arm. He jumps, feeling foolish once he hears her familiar voice.

"There you are. Come on!"

He looses a breath, relieved that he hadn't actually lost her. He follows closely behind her as they journey down one of the backroads, quickly discovering that it leads to row after row of colorful residences. As if she wasn't already, Vira seems to be even more excited at the prospect of potentially living here. It appears Chialka is now a distant memory.

"These homes are beautiful," she says, taking in the difference in architecture, color, and style. "I've never seen anything like them. My hometown is so *bland* compared to this place. I can't believe I've never been here before."

After taking her away from Chialka—a place she'd clearly wanted to stay—he'd been afraid she'd be more or less upset upon arriving in Lonia. This shift in her perspective, coupled with her open-mindedness, is not only a relief, but also a welcome surprise. "You . . . like it here?"

She spins around in a circle, her arms making a wide sweeping gesture. "Well, we've only just arrived, but so far, yes. What isn't there to like? It's charming and quaint, yet somehow vibrant and full of life at the same time."

"And that's a good thing?" Rydan asks, half-jokingly.

She rolls her eyes, then smiles. "A very good thing."

For a brief moment, he lets his thoughts run away with the possibilities. He imagines what it would be like to live here with her—away from Trendalath, away from Sardoria . . . away from the Caldari and illusié. They would go to the market every morning and pick only the finest fruits, vegetables, and grains. Rydan would finally take up woodworking, something he's always been interested in, but never had the chance to try. Vira could grow her own garden, if she so pleased, and they'd enjoy the beautiful weather season after season. It sure beats being locked up in a stone castle as a prisoner, assassin, or handmaiden with no real chance of escape or survival.

Although unlikely, a small part of him hopes that she'll forget about their agreement to tell Arden about her brother and mother. Frankly, it's none of their business—not if they're going to start a life in Lonia, away from their unwanted pasts. Why complicate something so seemingly simple? Why not just start over . . . and build a new life together?

An earsplitting shriek jars Rydan from his daydream.

"Would you take a look at this nest?" Vira coos, jumping up every couple of seconds so she can see over one of the branches. "It's so intricate and detailed. I wonder what kind of bird built it." She stops jumping before throwing him an ear-to-ear smile. "Perhaps it can build one for us."

Before Rydan can respond, she's taken off even farther down the path to explore, dare he say, what *could* be their new home.

There's not a question about it.

He could get used to this.

DARIUS TYMOND

"SIR ALSTON, A WORD," Darius demands without even the slightest inflection in his voice. He excuses himself from his throne, pulling on the sleeve of Cyrus's uniform, and heads for the doors. Once in the hallway, he raises his voice just enough to emphasize his anger, but not so much where passersby can hear. "Your assignment was to bring me a Healer, and while I'm thrilled you've brought me Arden, that was not the directive I gave you."

Cyrus stills, rattled by the king's harsh tone. "Forgive me, Your Majesty. I thought you'd be pleased, seeing as it's the best of both worlds."

Darius arches a brow. "In what way? I asked you to bring me . . ." His words trail off as he realizes what Cyrus has done. "No—"

"You know who her father is," Cyrus whispers, cutting him off. "Which means she possesses a level of power that is unmatched. She's a Healer, probably the most powerful in all of Aeridon. If Aldreda's truly in the shape you say she's in, you don't have much choice."

A knot of anger swells in his throat. How could this be? Moreover, how had he not come to this realization on his own? His thoughts flick to his Savant, to the empty chair at the table, to the mess they'd made—one he certainly hadn't asked for. And Aldreda . . . for taking from him the only thing that had actually mattered. For deceiving him for so many years, light and unencumbered by her actions. For forcing him into this predicament— one that shouldn't even exist in the first place.

He fights against the bristling rage, the perfectly rational urge, to object to Cyrus's proposal. To forego the use of Arden's abilities. But he can't.

Too much is at stake.

After she saves his wife . . . what then?

Is he to let the girl go free?

Allow her to roam the lands of Aeridon?

Are Aldreda and his unborn child worth that risk?

Cyrus interrupts his internal dispute. "The longer we stand here, the worse Queen Tymond gets."

Darius sighs, for once wishing that someone else could make this choice for him—that he could walk away and pretend this conversation never happened. That he could continue on with his reign, alone and unbothered.

"So, Your Majesty, what'll it be?"

Darius closes his eyes as what he must do becomes painstakingly clear. "Wake the girl up."

CERYLIA JARETH

CERYLIA DOESN'T DELAY in asking Delwynn to gather the remaining Caldari and escort them to the White Room. She waits until his footsteps are far enough down the hall before checking her reflection in a silver-plated mirror. Sleep hasn't come easy to her, which is evident from the deepening dark circles underneath her eyes. One more nightmare of Dane and their "son" and she's utterly convinced she'll lose her sanity entirely . . .

There's always a chance that the news she's about to deliver could inherently speed up the process.

The soothing scent of rosewater is a welcome distraction as she dips a cloth into a nearby dish, gingerly dabbing the liquid onto her face. It does little to help her physical appearance, but internally, she feels more at ease. She stares at her reflection for a few moments before flinging her robes around her shoulders and heading for the White Room.

When she walks through the doors, Felix, Estelle, Opal, and Braxton are waiting patiently before her throne. She doesn't bother sitting—just positions herself in front of them, directly in the center. As expected, Delwynn joins her, standing just off to the side.

Cerylia looks each of them in the eyes before saying, "I'm afraid I've called you here this evening with heavy news—"

Opal steps forward immediately and says, "Forgive us, Your Greatness, but . . . we already know." She looks to Felix and Estelle who nod in confirmation. "I've already told them about the incident between the Mallum and Braxton."

Cerylia stiffens, trying not to appear rattled. "Seems you talk amongst yourselves rather quickly," she mutters under her breath, but not quietly enough. "Very well, then. Now that you know what the Mallum is capable of, I'm sure you can understand my reasoning behind recent decisions."

Silence follows.

"Until I can retrieve what I seek"—she gives Braxton a harsh look—"the castle will remain on lock-down." She begins to pace back and forth, readying her next statement, when she realizes that everyone's attention has turned to something else.

Something behind her.

She freezes in place, thinking the worst, but when she turns around, it's just a falcon, perched in the far west window.

"Open it," Cerylia commands.

Delwynn rushes over to it and does exactly as she's instructed. They watch as the falcon glides into the castle and lands behind a marble pillar. A golden glow follows.

Unbelievable. For Xerin to finally show up after weeks—*months*—have gone by? Knowing his fickle nature, she should have expected it, but to *this* degree? This will take more than simply swallowing her pride—it will take wearing a mask of cold indifference for all the Caldari to see, even though she feels anything but.

The level of disrespect doesn't seem to go unnoticed amongst his peers. A wordless exchange passes between the Caldari before they lean in to one another and begin whispering. Cerylia can hardly make out what they're saying, but she's certain they're all thinking the exact same thing she is. The shift in the room is palpable as Xerin emerges from behind the pillar, a solemn look on his face. The murmurings cease completely.

Cerylia waits to speak until Delwynn secures the window's lock in place. She levels a steely gaze on Xerin, but his attention is elsewhere. "How thoughtful of you to finally grace us with your presence," she says coolly. "Your timing could not be worse, so I hope you have news we actually *want* to hear."

The words seem to fall on deaf ears as Xerin marches to the center of the room, right in front of Cerylia. The menacing look he gives each one of the Caldari is enough to stop an enemy dead in its tracks. He turns, his gaze settling on the queen.

"Arden has been taken to Trendalath castle."

ARDEN ELIRI

THE TOXINS MUST still be in my system because I dream heavily that evening, but it doesn't feel like a dream. It feels more like a memory, similar to the ones I've encountered with the Mallum—like I can reach out and touch everything in my surroundings, but when I do, there's no sensation in my fingertips. The wind blows around me and the waves crash violently against the rocky shore, but I feel nothing.

I turn away from the water, my eyes settling on a familiar structure. Trendalath castle. Panic doesn't seize me like it normally would. With lethal calm, I trek up the hillside until the sound of the ocean is merely an afterthought.

Small voices grab my attention. I continue to walk toward them, stopping only when I'm a short distance away. Two young boys play in a field, running in circles as they chase each other with wooden swords. A messy white-blond head of hair flops in the breeze. As soon as I get a glimpse of his face, I immediately recognize the younger one as Braxton.

With sheer determination, he yells, "On guard!"

My gaze shifts to his opponent. The back of his head doesn't give me much to go by, but as he dances around Braxton, sword at the ready, I finally get a look at his face. My breath hitches as I take in his features. Thick russet hair, bright jade-colored eyes . . . I've seen him before. But *where*?

Lost in my thoughts, I don't so much as flinch when both boys turn their attention my way. I notice that they look right *through* me, instead of *at* me. *They can't see me.*

"Promise you won't tell anyone," I hear Braxton say, pointing the sword at the other child's neck.

"I promise."

Braxton shoos him away. The other boy runs across the meadow, to the side opposite me. I survey the area around me, looking for the king, the queen, or a handmaiden—finding it somewhat unsettling that these two children are out here, alone and unsupervised. Then again, it *is* the Tymonds.

I draw closer to where Braxton stands, watching as the other boy raises his weapon from across the field. It dawns on me that he's going to throw it. The sword flies through the air at an astonishing speed, heading straight for Braxton. My first instinct is to jump in front of him, so that's exactly what I do. I raise my arms, crossing them in front of my face. I grimace as the pointed edge of the wooden sword sails toward my face . . . until it stops. In mid-air.

I lower my arms, watching in awe as the sword rotates in the air so that the hilt now faces me. I turn over my shoulder to look at Braxton, whose focus, especially for a child, is unlike anything I've ever seen before. *Of course. He's a Deviator.*

Even though he can't see me, I step out of the way, watching as he prepares to deviate the attack. I suddenly feel very nervous for the other boy—the one I don't even know. I try, once again, to place where I've seen him before . . .

From his pocket, he produces a small toy.

Of a gold dragon.

The realization hits me right between the eyes—the boy in the field; the woman in the cottage; the knock on the door . . . It's the same boy the Mallum had shown me.

I hardly have time to process this as the sword suddenly blasts through the air in the other direction, back toward the other boy. "Look out!" I yell, knowing that neither of them can hear nor see me.

The other boy remains still.

Panicked, I begin to run toward him. "Duck!" I scream. I pump my legs and arms as fast as I possibly can, but it isn't fast enough. The sword draws closer and closer, that piercing spear barreling straight at his face.

I'm about to watch this young boy die at the hands of Braxton—at the hands of yet another Tymond. The thought is crippling.

"Move!" I yell once more, hoping that he'll hear me, but he doesn't. It's then a blinding flash of green stops me in my tracks.

The boy vanishes right before my very eyes.

DARIUS TYMOND

"IS SHE AWAKE?"

Darius watches impatiently as Cyrus enters his chambers. The old man begins pacing back and forth in front of the door, stroking the stubble on his chin as he goes. "Cyrus?"

He stops pacing. "Yes, Your Majesty. She's awake."

"And?"

He lets out an exasperated sigh. "*And* she still seems to be a bit rattled, which might have something to do with the fact that I brought her here against her will."

His response triggers a question—one Darius can't believe he hadn't thought of before. "How *did* you manage to find her so quickly, Sir Alston?"

Cyrus stares at him blankly, as if he's suddenly forgotten how to speak, but Darius doesn't repeat the question—just waits for him to answer.

"Fortune of the lords and stars, I suppose."

Even from where he's standing, Darius can clearly see the sweat forming along his brow. "And the truth?" he presses. "What would that be?"

More hesitation. "I'd rather not say, Your Majesty."

Darius takes a step forward, raising his chin ever so slightly so that he's looking down on his old friend. "As your king, I demand to know how you found Arden Eliri so quickly after my Savant has spent countless weeks searching for the Caldari."

Cyrus clamps his mouth shut before casting his gaze downward.

"Very well," Darius huffs. "I hoped it wouldn't have to come to this . . ."

The old man lifts his gaze, eyes widening as the king retreats to one of the bedside drawers. It creaks open on rusty hinges. But before Darius can reveal his chosen device, Cyrus folds. "Wait. I—I had inside knowledge."

Darius slams the drawer shut. "From whom?"

The words come out strained. "Sir Kent."

Ah. He fists his hands at his sides. So Elias hadn't truly wanted Cyrus's assistance in searching for Arden because he'd *already found her.*

"Allow me to explain," Cyrus continues, fumbling over his words. "You see, Arden *saved* Sir Kent—she healed him in the woods. Without her help, he wouldn't have been able to go on." His voice grows quiet. "That's why I brought her to you."

Darius takes a moment to consider the severity of the situation. There's no doubt that Elias will need to be punished—for not following a direct order to return Arden to Trendalath upon his first encounter—but now is not the appropriate time. There are larger things at stake.

Something shatters just outside the window, disrupting him from his thoughts. He observes the turmoil below—much like what's happening *inside* the castle—watching as the guards seize the perpetrator. It seems that even the peasants have joined the merchants' rallying cries of disapproval. Although he refuses to believe it, he has failed them—all of them.

Despite his best efforts to keep things quiet, every last person in Trendalath seems to have caught onto his ill-conceived façade. He's covertly been housing the Savant—his own group of illusié—for years. He's lost the respect of the Cruex. His marriage is a sham. His wife loathes him. And now, the one foolish girl he *should* make an example of is the one he can't kill.

How utterly ironic.

A deep inhale. The air is so crisp that it rattles his bones. They threaten to splinter under the weight of his breath. Slowly, he turns to face his old friend. "Fetch the girl and bring her to the Great Room."

"Your Majesty—"

"Not another word, Cyrus" Darius interrupts. "I don't care if you have to drug her again—just get her there."

A muscle feathers in his cheek, but Cyrus doesn't fight back. Instead, he turns to the door with his head held high. "For the record, I advised against this." Before Darius can yell at him to leave, the chamber door slams shut.

Rage coils in every one of his muscles as he kicks the toe of his boot against the leg of the armoire. It shakes violently—which is surprising given its size—and he has to press his palm against the embossed surface to still the movement. He eyes the door again before straightening his robes, resecuring the dragon brooch that has since come loose, then strides across the smooth stone floor.

He doesn't bother checking the hall for Cyrus, or anyone else, before heading to the eastern corridor. Up, up, up he climbs until he reaches what most would assume is a bell tower—but its purpose is not to tell time.

No, it's far more useful than that.

Sitting in the middle of the tower is a giant well with no water or liquid of any kind, and in the center sits a curved bronzed plate that extends just slightly past the border. Darius unclasps his dragon brooch and sets it on the edge of the plate. It's been some time since he's performed this ritual. His full attention is directed at the brooch as it begins to shake. He watches as it slowly glides to the center of the plate, as if being pulled by an invisible force. The well rumbles, its low gurgling reminiscent of boiling water.

He steps back at just the right time. The brooch is catapulted upward from the plate before disappearing altogether. Wisps of red and orange flicker in its place. The two vibrant colors dance, joining together to create a faux sunset brighter than even the finest rubies.

It is time.

Darius raises his arms. "*Reditus*," he whispers.

Ribbons of color explode out the window, each one diverging onto its own path. They travel so fast that the night wholly consumes them, leaving nothing but darkness in their wake. The dragon brooch reemerges from within the plate and slides back to its original place, teetering on the edge. Before it falls to the ground, Darius catches it and gently clasps it back onto his robes.

Mere moments from now, the Savant will receive his signal, requesting that they return to Trendalath castle immediately. Until then, he only has one place to be—one place to ready.

The Daegrum Chambers.

RYDAN HELSTROM

RYDAN SLIPS OUT into the bleak morning, a heavy fog rolling over the bank. It's a completely different sight from yesterday's jaunt through town. No visibility, no people, no chatter. It almost reminds him of his mission with Arden when they'd first arrived in Lonia, sans the fog. His final Cruex mission.

A lot has changed since then.

He sighs, shaking the thought as he treads to the merchants' alley. It's early, but one of the vendors is bound to have opened up shop, especially in the current economic climate. Although Lonia stakes its reputation on commerce, Tymond's reign hasn't been easy on any of Aeridon's towns, Lonia included. In fact, Tymond has restricted many of the island's export trading—Lonia brings items in, but hardly ships anything out. It's a shame, really, seeing as the town is known for producing the finest silks, spices, ales, and ceramics Aeridon has ever seen. And speaking of ale . . .

Ever since Avery had dropped both him and Vira off a mere three days ago, Rydan's been sneaking out in the mornings to explore the little island town. Of course, he tells Vira a different story each day he returns—that he'd ventured off into the Thering Forest in an effort to "find" Arden, when all he's *really* been finding are some exceptionally delightful ales and wines.

Deep down, he knows he should feel guilty for lying to Vira and running off to do whatever his heart so desires, but *he* wasn't the one who wanted to go on this little escapade. That was all Vira. If she's not making the effort to find Arden, why should he?

The rising sun almost blinds him as he steps out of an alleyway onto another cobblestone street. He's not sure exactly where he's headed today, so he decides to follow the intoxicating sounds of laughter and chatter—because where there's fun, there's likely to be a tavern or pub. A mug of ale first thing in the morning is just what he needs.

Although he can't physically see the merchants' tents, he's certain he must be getting close. The deep laughter grows louder and louder until he reaches a navy and gold tarp. There's a woman sitting out front, wearing an indigo pashmina, her back facing him. A small wooden bowl filled with riyals, the amber-colored currency of Lonia, stares him in the face.

He searches his pockets frantically, the clinking of mugs and deep-belly laughter taunting him, but he comes up empty-handed.

Charm it is, then.

He straightens his tunic and rakes a hand through his unkempt hair before clearing his throat. "Excuse me, miss?"

The woman tenses, but does not speak. She doesn't stand, nor does she turn around.

Rydan tries again. "How much to enter this fine establishment?"

With her back still facing him, she rises. Slowly, she unwraps the pashmina from around her head. Loose golden curls spill out from underneath the silky fabric as she tosses it to the ground. His stomach sinks as he immediately recognizes who she is.

"This certainly doesn't look like the Thering Forest to me," Vira says, eyes blazing like hot coals. "It seems to me like you have a lot of explaining to do."

CERYLIA JARETH

"WHEN?" CERYLIA DEMANDS, her tone steady and unwavering. "When was Arden taken to Trendalath?" She notices Xerin exchange a glance with Braxton, and before he can answer, she figuratively digs her claws into his counterpart. "Is there anything you'd like to admit to?"

Dumbfounded, they both just stand there.

"Well?"

Xerin speaks first. "Braxton knows nothing of Arden's capture, so please refrain from questioning him."

Cerylia bristles at the hostility in his voice. If there's one thing she's learned as queen, some battles are worth fighting, others aren't. This one falls into the latter category.

"When?" she repeats.

"Not but two days ago."

"The King's Guard?"

Xerin shakes his head. "The Cruex."

She raises a brow. "Who exactly?" Her question seems to catch him by surprise, as if her keeping tabs on her enemy's armed forces is ill-advised. *Please.*

"Cyrus Alston."

The name slices right through her. She reaches behind her, fumbling until her hand grazes the back of a chair. Estelle and Opal run to her side, but she swats them away. Heaving her body over her knees, she stares at the floor. Dots float in and out of her vision. Her breath is even harder to come by as her chest constricts, like a coiling serpent has lodged itself inside. A part of her wishes it would wrap around her heart and squeeze the life out of her, like it would any other prey.

Cyrus wouldn't betray her like this.

Wouldn't? No—*couldn't.*

After what had happened with Dane . . .

After everything they had discussed . . .

He wouldn't dare take such a risk—would he?

These thoughts wholly consume her for what feels like an eternity. She can't be certain how long she stays crumpled over her knees, but eventually, the constricting in her chest ceases. Her breathing returns to a normal pace. The clarity in her vision resumes, her mind mere steps behind. With a renewed sense of self, she finds the strength to push herself upright.

She stands tall.

No one makes a mockery of the Jareth legacy—not even an old friend like Cyrus Alston.

Her gaze settles on Braxton as the rest of the Caldari fade into the background. "I think it's time you and I had a chat."

BRAXTON HORNSBY

KEEPING STRIDE WITH the queen, who has clearly made up her mind about *something*, is no easy task. Braxton attempts to keep his calm as they wind through the corridors. They arrive at a wing of the castle he hasn't yet had the opportunity to explore. But instead of taking him to a nice, open room, as she usually would, she shoves him into a nearby closet-sized pantry.

"Your Greatness," Braxton starts, but he's instantly silenced by her hand covering his mouth.

"Listen to me because I am only going to ask you this once." Her tone hardens. "Have you been conspiring against me with Cyrus and your father?"

Even in the dim lighting, he can tell that this is not a joke. The audacity of the question brings his blood to a

KRISTEN MARTIN

boil. How could she possibly think this? He rips his head away from her hand before saying, "Of course not! Before I found the Caldari, I was just a hand to an innkeeper, living in Athia. If you're looking for someone to blame, you couldn't be further off."

A shadow falls across her face. "He wouldn't betray me like this." It comes out as a murmur, but given their close proximity, Braxton is able to hear every word. The queen seems to sense her faux pas. She tenses, then pulls away.

Before either of them can say anything else, the door flies open. Delwynn raises an eyebrow at the sight of them crammed into such a small space. "Your Greatness," he says as he briskly pulls her out, "is everything all right?"

Braxton watches with apprehension as her thoughts play out on her face. Her expression shifts from calm to stormy. *She doesn't believe me.* He can sense exactly what she's about to do—but if she's the type of queen she *claims* to be, she wouldn't dare . . .

"The dungeons," Cerylia says, her steely gaze set on his own.

His eyes flick to Delwynn.

"Take him to the dungeons this instant!" the queen orders. "We have a traitor in our midst."

"Your Greatness—"

"Do it now, Delwynn."

Braxton doesn't flinch. Much to his surprise, his pulse remains steady as he waits for Delwynn to call the Queen's Guard. The clanking of metal on the marble steps is all too familiar—except this time, *he's* the prisoner.

Delwynn is shoved out of the way as the guards approach Braxton. He extends his arms, keeping his eyes locked on the old man. Delwynn stares at him, mouth agape—clearly wondering what had just happened between the two of them in that small broom closet.

Funny really, because Braxton just so happens to be wondering the exact same thing.

ARDEN ELIRI

MY EYES OPEN to an unfamiliar sight. The lighting is dim, and as far as I can tell, I'm in a circular shaped room, not much larger than my old chambers. It's dank and musty and somehow I'm . . . upright. I try to take a step forward but my feet don't budge. I turn my head to the left, noticing the iron chains securing me to either a wall or table—I'm not exactly sure which. My neck also seems to be restrained as I can't look down or up, just side to side.

As I'm contemplating the situation I'm in, my gaze lands on the heavy metal door before me. It's cracked open slightly, and I can hear, albeit barely, muffled voices on the other side. They draw closer and it dawns on me that perhaps I should pretend to be asleep, but what good would that do? I've never cowered in the face of danger—I've always looked it straight in the eye. And that's exactly what I plan to do right now.

The door swings open with tremendous force. In walks a group of men I've never seen before, each wearing an intricately designed mask in varying colors—maroon, gold, forest green, slate gray—but with one striking similarity: a rectangular crest with thick red and black stripes, and a coiled serpent—sitting, waiting—in the lower right-hand corner.

A chill lodges in my chest. Although I can't see their faces, I look pointedly at each of the masks—four, to be exact. When Tymond enters, he's not wearing a mask—just the usual smug look that's always on his face. His hands are clasped at his waist, and even in the dim lighting, I notice the glint of a violet-colored ring. My attention shifts as he clears his throat, a signal of some sort. I get the uncanny sense that these men must be illusié—his Savant. Slowly, they form a circle around me so that I can barely see the last two members out of my periphery.

I keep my eyes on Tymond, fully aware that it's me against them. Restoration versus destruction. Light versus dark. Or perhaps it's dark against darker? Given my recent encounters with the Mallum, the latter seems more appropriate. No matter—I'm severely outnumbered.

Each of the masked men takes a single step toward me and I can't help but briefly squeeze my eyes shut. It feels like a bad dream—one I should wake up from at any moment—but it's not. It's real.

"I remember you," one of the men says. His voice is jarringly familiar, one I know I've heard before, but for the life of me, I can't place where. His hair is tightly coiled to his head in ringlets and, if I had to guess, it appears to be a shade of auburn, although the dim lighting makes it overly difficult to ascertain. "You've been giving everyone a lot of trouble as of late."

"Renegade Cruex," another says, this voice much surlier than the one before. "I never thought I'd see the day."

Snickers fill the room until King Tymond slams the door shut. He glides to the center of the circle and stands two steps in front of his Savant. His gaze lands directly on me, his eyes nearly black—a stark contrast to the icy blue I'd become so accustomed to. I recall the days when all I wanted was to hear him call my name for the next mission—to impress him, to be his right-hand. But now, knowing what he's done and what he's capable of . . . even the slightest indication of approval makes my stomach turn.

It will rain crimson with Tymond blood.

He addresses the room in a language I've never heard before, then turns his attention back to me. I keep my eyes locked on his. "Arden Eliri." His tone is certain; his words are unwavering. "You will heal Queen Tymond."

I nearly laugh out loud. It takes everything in me to keep from spitting in that smug, pompous face of his.

When I don't respond, he presses, "I presume Sir Alston has presented you with the agreement?"

I remain silent. Lords help him if he thinks I'm actually going to heal Aldreda.

"Answer me."

Again, I don't say a word.

He moves closer and takes my chin in his hand, pressing his thumb deep into the tender skin. "Now."

My eyes burn the longer I stare into his traitorous eyes, and my teeth grind together as my mouth forms the only word I'm fated to say. "No."

His eyes go frank and cold as he rips his hand from my chin. "Conjurer!" he huffs. He whirls away from me and retreats to the door.

I watch as the deep-voiced man takes center stage, readying himself as he puts on golden gloves—to match his mask—and gets into position. The room is silent as his arms open outward beside him, palms rotating upward. He raises his head and, even though I can't follow his gaze, a shaded light appears around him, growing larger and larger. I can hear something opening, and even though my neck is restrained, I sense the room must have a skylight or an opening of some sort.

The man lowers his gaze, staring at me through his mask, until suddenly, he draws his elbows in and closes his palms into fists, the word *Accudo* leaving his lips.

Not even a second has passed when I suddenly feel a jolt of electricity reverberate within me, from my skull all the way down to my heels. I begin to shake uncontrollably as sparks ignite in my chest, my heart entering into what feels like cardiac arrest. The space around me heats up like that of a brick oven, and I'm convinced that the sleeves of my tunic have been singed off.

I scream out in pain as the chains securing my wrists reach a scorching temperature. I writhe back and forth in protest, trying to escape the hell on either side of me. I can feel the rusted metal burning into my skin, eating away at my flesh, my veins throbbing from the rising temperature. Every inch of me begs for mercy, my body bare and stricken against the heat. I plead for it to stop, but I'm trapped in my own nightmarish hellscape.

My eyes roll into the back of my head as my body convulses over and over—thrashing violently—and I want to scream again, but the death bolt has obliterated my lungs. Not even a croak is able to escape. An inner voice tells me that this is *not* how I'll die—that it's not my time yet, but I don't believe it. The only way out of this—to eradicate this immense pain—*has* to be death.

And then, as if confirming that inner voice, I hear the word *Perfluo*, and my convulsing begins to cease, albeit slowly. My eyes roll forward to their proper place. The scorching heat around me fades to a bearable temperature. My heart slows and my breathing returns to its normal rhythm. Drool dribbles down my chin as my mind floats back into consciousness—back to reality. My vision is blurred and the corners of my eyes twitch, as do my hands—but these subtle movements are more than welcome compared to what I've just experienced.

From what I can tell through the fuzzy lenses that are now my eyes, the figure in front of me steps back in line with the circle and another figure takes his place. My ears are ringing as King Tymond's voice floats through the air once more. "Arden Eliri. You will heal the queen."

Never, in my seventeen years of living, did I ever think I'd feel this torn. Going through another—well, whatever *that* was—is intolerable. Unbearable. And yet, so is the thought of healing the woman this monster loves.

An impossible decision.

In my mind, I'm making a face of pure and utter disgust at King Tymond, but I'm almost certain it's not coming off that way. The synapses in my brain and my muscle memory aren't connecting at the moment. I briefly close my eyes, trying to focus my energy—to find my light and bring it forth—but after being zapped with that kind of voltage, my mind and my body are of two different planes. No longer are they united.

"You will heal Queen Tymond."

Even in my semi-obliterated state, I can tell that he's losing patience. How does he expect me to answer in a state like this? I open my mouth, only to feel more drool slide over the corner of my lips and onto my chin.

I do the only thing I *can* do. Gingerly, I shake my head back and forth, as if to say . . . *No. No. No.*

I must have a death wish.

Internally, I cringe as I wait for him to call the next member of his Savant forward, unable to fathom what the "next level" of punishment could possibly be. Surely, it has to be death. But, much to my surprise, Tymond doesn't say anything, doesn't call anyone forward. Instead, he retreats to the door and disappears behind it.

I blink a few times, still feeling jolted and fuzzy, but I notice a slight improvement in both my eyesight and my breathing. It doesn't last long, though, because my heart drops into my stomach when I see whom Tymond brings into the room by the scruff of his neck.

Elias Kent.

He's bruised up pretty badly already, what with his swollen lip, a dark ring around his right eye, and numerous scrapes and cuts along his jawline and forehead. Even though I'm no longer a part of the Cruex—and even though I'd almost killed him myself—I can't help but feel empathetic toward Elias, especially in a situation as twisted as this one. True, he and his cousin, Hugh, are obnoxious and immature, and I can hardly stand either of them . . . but seeing him here now, so broken, so damaged—and knowing who is fully responsible for it—is enough to get my adrenaline pumping. I attempt, once again, to open my mouth, but still, no words come out.

Elias yelps as Tymond kicks him in the back of his legs, bringing him to his knees on the cold stone floor. "It appears I should reassess our induction standards for the Cruex, seeing as the majority of you have betrayed me."

Elias looks me straight in the eye. It's the first time I've actually seen fear on an assassin's face. The image sends my mind spiralling, but my outward expression remains indifferent.

"Arden Eliri, you *will* heal Queen Aldreda Tymond or your fellow conspirator will die." The king gives me a sickening grin, one that makes my stomach turn in on itself. "And it will be at your own two hands."

His words are already hard to comprehend, and in my impaired state, they're even more so. Silently, I repeat what he's just said until the meaning becomes clear. How could I possibly kill someone when my mind and my body—and therefore my actions—aren't connecting?

It hits me then. Adrenaline is replaced with panic.

His Savant.

Without even realizing it, the word *no* escapes my lips. It's more of a gasp and it's barely audible, but the king hears it. And what's worse is he hears it in the wrong context.

"Curser," Tymond says between gritted teeth.

I begin shaking my head uncontrollably, which only adds to the confusion—and to the king's anger. I try to speak the words, to tell him that I *will* heal the queen, and to let Elias go, but they won't come.

The chains securing my wrists and ankles fall to the ground as another masked man, this one in maroon, approaches the center of the room. I begin to panic as my mind tells me to find a way out, but my body remains still. I am not in control. I am not in control.

I am not in control.

Elias is going to die.

Without my consent, I feel my body go rigid, my arm reaching out next to me to grab the hilt of a longsword. Somehow, without telling my feet to move, I take one step forward, then another. The maroon-masked man steps to the side to let me pass. I unintentionally raise the sword as I approach my target. Elias stares back at me with a quivering chin and fear-stained eyes.

My mind screams at me, louder and louder. *Holy lords, you're about to assassinate him! Stop!* But I can't stop. It's as if I've been hypnotized—cursed somehow.

The Curser. His title becomes clear as day.

I reach Elias sooner than I'd hoped and lower the sword to his neck. I place the edge of the blade right underneath his chin, making my mark. I press the blade into his neck, just enough so that a streak of crimson trickles from the fresh wound. The sight immediately brings me back to a similar moment in the Thering Forest, when I'd almost done what I'm about to do now— except this time, it's entirely against my will.

Elias is shaking now, convulsing just as badly as I had been moments earlier. His eyes plead with me not to do this. I don't want to, but it's not my choice.

I am not in control.

I take a step back, the sword coming with me as it slides outward, now parallel to his neck. A cry of desperation escapes his lips.

Do something!

I've killed dozens of people before.

And I've lived with it.

I've assassinated innocents.

And I've lived with it.

But I cannot live with what I'm about to do.

I attempt to push against the curse in my mind, but it's like pressing against a wall of sand. It delivers me straight through to the other side so that I'm only pressing against myself. Ribbons of maroon surround me, looping in and out of my mind, suffocating me with the

Curser's relentless demands. I reach for then, grasping at each wisp of air, but it's no use. They sail right through my fingers.

He's going to win. Tymond is going to win.

With all of my strength, I focus on the face in front of me, on those big russet eyes—eyes the same color as Felix's. Suddenly, I imagine it's his face before mine and not Elias's—his wide shoulders, angled jaw, the shadowed glimmer that always seems to line his eyes.

Keep going.

His nightly visits—the way he'd stood at the foot of my bed as Estelle left the room; the way he'd knelt before me, grazing his cheek against mine; the way my heart had exploded in my chest when he'd turned to leave when all I'd wanted was for him to stay. *Why didn't I ask him to stay?*

His words play over in my head. *You're a good person, Arden. I never should have doubted that.*

Felix is right. Against my greater instincts, I hadn't killed Elias—I'd spared his life. There may be darkness in me, but I *am* a good person. I have to be.

Using this as momentum, I dig and dig and dig, trying to find it—my light. I roam through the darkest fragments of my mind, the fissures expanding only to contract further, each movement more unyielding than the last, until I . . . feel it.

It's here.

The sword lingers in the air, Elias's life at the edge of my fingertips—for the second time. I break through the

Curser's barrier as I hear a voice that sounds hazy and unlike my own say, "I'll heal her!"

Instantly, the sword clatters to the ground. I collapse along with it. My shoulder takes the brunt of the impact, but my head still takes a hit. Sturdy hands grab me, raising me up by each arm. Out of the corner of my eye, I can see that Elias is still alive. I didn't kill him.

I didn't kill him.

"Take her to the healing ward," Tymond says curtly.

Relief washes over me as I realize it's over.

I'm alive. Elias is alive. The Savant's torture is over.

For now, we are safe.

But then, as I'm dragged out of the circular room, I hear a sickening crack as a body hits the ground.

DARIUS TYMOND

SEETHING, DARIUS WATCHES as Arden disappears from the room. "Clean this up," he orders one of the nearby guards, kicking the underside of Elias's boot. "Now."

He doesn't give the fallen Cruex another thought as he straightens his robes and strides through the open door, in the direction of the healing ward. His mind roils with images of Arden's hostile expressions, her brows furrowing and her eyes narrowing as she spat the one word he hates hearing most.

No. No. No.

Knowing she's wounded and hurting, he shouldn't expect her to be in a state to properly heal Aldreda—but, he barges into the healing ward anyway, eyes wide, each breath more ragged than the last. Cyrus regards him with a bewildered expression as he blunders over to where Arden is propped up. One of the medics is lifting a cup of water to her mouth when Darius bats it away, the cool liquid splashing across the stone floor.

"You will heal her this instant," he huffs, pulling her up by her scorched wrists. The delicate, freshly singed flesh feels strange against his own. He expects Arden to whimper, to scream, to make *some* sort of sound, but she is completely silent. Only when he looks into her dulled eyes—her lifeless, pale face—does he realize that perhaps he's taken things a little too far.

Her head begins to roll backward, as if she has no spine, and the medic immediately interjects, pushing Darius out of the way. He places her gently back on the bed, propping her head up with a pillow. Her eyes remain closed.

"Leave!" the medic orders. "Now."

Taken aback by the sudden commotion, Darius just stands there. He considers charging at the medic when Cyrus steps right in front of him. He places his hand on the king's chest, shaking his head in what can only be disapproval. "She must rest, Your Majesty. She is not fit to use her abilities in her current state."

Too prideful to admit his cohort is right, Darius shifts his gaze from Cyrus to the medic before asking one simple question. "How long?"

"At the very least, three or four days," the medic responds.

"She needs to be ready by tomorrow."

The medic sighs and shakes his head. "I cannot guarantee that, Your Majesty."

"I don't care," Darius hisses. "Make it happen."

He turns on his heel, but not before stopping by his wife's bedside. His eyes land on her lower abdomen. Her slow, shallow breathing is the only indication that she's still alive. "Soon," he says, lowering his voice to a whisper so that no one else can hear him. "Soon we will all get exactly what we deserve."

ARDEN ELIRI

I FADE IN and out of darkness. My mind spirals as my subconscious explores the depths of my psyche.

Where am I?

How did I end up here?

Have I finally joined them like they'd always wanted?

As I come back to, a bout of nausea rushes over me, and I find myself floating back into unconsciousness again—at least, I think it's unconsciousness.

Is this a dream?

Will I wake soon?

The space around me is void of color, absent of light and existence. I float in the ever-expanding abyss, a speck of dust in my subconscious mind.

I can't feel.

I can't speak.

I just am.

I continue to float through the darkness, waiting for something to bring me back. To wake me up.

A flash of light.

The marching of hooves.

The slicing of a blade.

But nothing comes. It's just me and the darkness.

Quiet. Still. Lifeless.

And yet, I find that I feel refreshed.

Renewed.

Recharged.

Strangely enough, I feel right at home.

RYDAN HELSTROM

VIRA'S DISAPPOINTMENT IN Rydan lingers every time they cross paths, which is often, seeing as they're occupying a space smaller than their residence in Chialka. She hasn't spoken to him in two days and the silence—once something he yearned for during his Cruex days—is enough to make him want to journey back to Trendalath and turn himself over to Tymond. Perhaps that's a *slight* exaggeration, but nonetheless, he's growing quite irritable.

He sits at the kitchen table, unintentionally carving the Cruex symbol into a scrap of wood, when Vira bolts through the front door carrying a bag of fruits, vegetables, and . . .

A bottle of ale.

She slams it down in front of him, nearly causing it to shatter into hundreds of tiny pieces, before carrying onward to the pantry.

So *this* is what he gets for staying out of trouble and minding his own business. Rydan stops fiddling with his knife and flings the partially carved piece of wood to the side. "What's this?"

Vira doesn't respond. She continues to unpack the bag—the apples, onions, and beets rolling around on the countertop.

Rydan pushes himself up from the chair, grabs the bottle of ale, and sets it down in front of her. She pretends not to notice it and busies herself with some other meaningless task.

"Vira." His tone is like ice and immediately makes her stop what she's doing. "What is this?"

She grabs a cloth and begins polishing one of the apples. Her eyes lock on his. "I figured you'd want a drink, seeing as you haven't had your *fix* in a couple of days."

Rydan had heard the phrase *don't poke the bear* when he was younger, but only now does he fully understand its meaning. "What are you trying to say?"

She stops polishing the apple and with the straightest face says, "I'm just trying to make your time here—with *me*—a little more bearable."

Her response hits him right in the gut. Contrary to what she may believe, he actually *enjoys* spending time with her. It's the thought of facing *Arden* again that's causing his old habits to resurface. Something a bit like guilt coils in his stomach.

He moseys around the counter until he's standing directly in front of her. Erring on the side of caution, he takes the apple from her hands and returns it to its rightful place amongst the others. He gingerly sets his hands atop her shoulders, trying to judge whether or not she's going to pull away, or worse, slap him. When she doesn't do either, he pulls her in closer, until her cheek is resting on his chest. He strokes the back of her head before whispering, "Forgive me."

He can feel her small body release a heavy sigh against his own. The tension between them dissipates. After a few moments in each other's embrace, she slowly pulls away. Her expression is calm, but like her eyes, her words are guarded. "No more lies, Rydan."

He nods in understanding. "No more lies."

His response seems to satisfy her because she bops him on the shoulder before saying, "Grab a cutting knife."

Not wanting to disrupt the harmonious reconciliation they've just made, Rydan moves to the other side of the kitchen—but as he pulls one from the drawer, his focus settles on something completely unexpected. The knife clatters to the ground. Perched on the windowsill is a black falcon, its blood-red eyes staring right through him.

Nothing like Vira's brother to bring everything crashing down again.

BRAXTON HORNSBY

"WHAT THE HELL did you do?" Delwynn demands, fuming behind Braxton as two burly guards lead him to the dungeons.

Braxton presses his mouth into a firm line before rolling his eyes, even though Delwynn can't see him. His tone doesn't warrant a response and, even if it did, he wouldn't know what to say. He'd gone from Queen Jareth's confidante to deviant traitor within a single week.

The chains around his ankles and wrists clank against the white marble floor, and even though he hadn't been an actual prisoner at Trendalath castle, somehow it all feels the same.

Entrapment. Confusion.

But, most notably, *unjust guilt.*

His thoughts go elsewhere, intentionally drowning out Delwynn's persistent questioning. He can empathize with the queen's point of view—Arden's unexpected capture is definitely cause for concern. And seeing as Cyrus, someone he grew up calling *Uncle,* was the one to take her there is not only perplexing, but extremely out of character.

Even more baffling still is Cerylia's accusation that *he,* Braxton Hornsby, fugitive and ex-prince by choice; *he,* who changed his own last name to rid himself of his royal identity, would ever even consider conspiring with the kingdom he's come to despise.

As they reach the entrance to the dungeons, the smooth marble floor turns to uneven slate-gray stone. His focus *should* be on making sure he doesn't trip and fall, but his thoughts are elsewhere. Although it's been a decade since he's lived with his mother and father, that doesn't mean they've changed. If anything, they're likely still the horrible, rotten people he'd grown to hate during his childhood years. But, if there is *one* ounce of good in either of his parents, it's certainly in Aldreda. Her love for Darius knows no bounds. She'd do anything for him— humiliate, torture, even murder anyone who got in the way of their reign.

The guards pull him forward as they reach the bottom of the staircase, Delwynn still whining incessantly behind him. He watches as one of the guards removes a gigantic key ring from his belt. They jangle as he flips through them, one by one, his other hand tightening around Braxton's bicep, as if he's suddenly going to head off somewhere. The thought alone almost makes him laugh. *Right, as if I could go anywhere. Perhaps if I could still deviate . . .*

The guard opens the door, not bothering to free Braxton's wrists and ankles, before shoving him inside the dank, musty cell. Sardoria is *much* nicer than Trendalath, and yet the quality of the cell—and the dungeon itself—isn't much different. Although he'd never been locked up in Trendalath, he'd frequently gone to visit some of the prisoners without either Darius or Aldreda knowing. He'd brought them scraps of bread and canteens of water—whatever he could find to help make their stay less miserable. When he'd found out that many of them were illusié awaiting their trials, he'd tripled his number of visits. It makes him wonder if any of the Caldari would do the same for him—if any of them even know he's down here.

The metal door clangs shut. The guard inserts the key and twists the lock in place, sealing his fate. Braxton grabs hold of the bars, gazing out through the small square openings at Delwynn. He studies the old man's face. His soft features and subtle expressions actually remind him a lot of Cyrus.

He hadn't known it at the time—seeing as he'd only been a child—but he'd played many a convincing role when it came to getting what he wanted, particularly with Cyrus. As his "uncle", Braxton had really learned how to pull on his heartstrings. And while he may not be able to do this with Delwynn, there *is* one other way he can think of . . .

Opal.

Opal must know he's innocent. All he needs her to do is take Cerylia back in time, to show her that he'd never conspired with Cyrus or Darius or any of the Tymonds. But . . .

The letter.

The letter from his mother could certainly pose some issues. Had it already? Could *that* be the reason he's locked in here? If so, Opal could help with that, too. She could invert time, take them back to before he'd been locked in this cell—give him more time to think and come up with a plan.

I must find a way to speak with Opal. But how?

Delwynn's voice breaks his train of thought. "The Queen's Guard will deliver your meals at dawn, noon, and dusk. As soon as the queen has decided how to proceed, I'll deliver the news. Until then . . ."

He begins to retreat toward the dungeon doors, but Braxton stops him. "Wait."

The old man turns around.

"I know I'm not in any position to ask a favor, but of all the people in this castle, you're the one who knows me best, Delwynn. You've worked with me, trained me, and warned me of the Mallum when Cerylia was hell bent on me leaving." He presses his face against the bars. "I hope you know that you can trust me. And I have a way to prove that I did not do what I've been accused of—but I need a little help."

Delwynn remains by the doors, half of his face shadowed. "I've already gone against Cerylia's will by hiding you in my chambers—"

"I didn't tell her it was you," Braxton pleads.

"I know," Delwynn says softly. "I did."

"What? Why?"

Delwynn sighs. "I am her most loyal advisor for a reason. I never should have gone against her wishes. It's a mistake I will not repeat again."

He turns to leave. Braxton knows it's now or never. "I understand your loyalty to Queen Jareth. It's quite admirable, in my opinion." He hesitates, hoping the words don't come out brash. "Would it be possible to have the Caldari bring my meals instead of the Queen's Guard?"

Delwynn seems to consider this for a moment, but then shakes his head. "I'm sorry. It's just not my place to decide. I hope you can understand."

"Could you just . . . present it as an option?"

"I can't promise anything one way or another." He reaches for the door handle. "I'm sorry, Braxton. I wish there was more I could do."

Braxton doesn't say anything else. He pushes away from the bars, hanging his head so that he doesn't have to watch as his only hope vanishes before his eyes.

CERYLIA JARETH

CERYLIA'S JUST SEATED herself in the dining hall when Delwynn bursts in unannounced. Before he can utter a word, she lifts a brow and simultaneously raises her index finger into the air. She gives it a quick wag before saying, "Not now, Delwynn. It's already been a long morning."

She can feel his gaze searing into her as she lifts her steaming cup of tea to her lips. Much to her surprise, he remains silent and allows her to finish at least half of her beverage. The teacup clinks against the saucer, the remaining liquid on the verge of spilling over the edge. She gestures for him to take a seat across from her. Realizing that she's finally paying him some attention, he obliges her and scurries over to the chair. Cerylia pinches the bridge of her nose before asking, "What is so urgent that you felt the need to interrupt the only time of day I have to myself?"

Her loyal servant bows his head, clearly disappointed in himself. "Your Greatness, I hope you know that I would never question your actions, but I feel it's important to reconsider—"

"He is a prisoner," Cerylia interrupts, her tone flat.

Delwynn appears to be taken aback as he redirects his train of thought. "And you must have good reason for locking him in the dungeons."

"Conspiring with the enemy."

"Is there proof?"

Cerylia averts her gaze in annoyance. Why is he wasting her time with this? She doesn't have concrete proof per se, but Braxton *is* a Tymond. Enemy blood runs through his veins. She'd been skeptical the very first night he'd shown up on her doorstep with Xerin, but she'd taken a chance on him—it was only a matter of time until he'd turn on her. Better to rein it in and do things on *her* terms instead of his. And that's precisely what she'd done.

She breathes a long, intentional sigh before turning to face her advisor. It's more than obvious that she needs a break from the Caldari—from everything, really. She's about to dismiss him when he says, rather bluntly, "He's requested the Caldaris' presence."

She angles her head at him. "Did he say why?"

Delwynn shakes his head. "I mentioned that his meals would be served by the Queen's Guard and he asked for the Caldari to serve them instead."

Her grip tightens on the handle of her teacup, causing it to shatter into dozens of tiny ceramic pieces. Delwynn flies across the room to take care of the mess, but she bats him away. She takes a moment to compose herself, eyes glued to the glass shards just below her bosom. After grasping at fleeting thoughts, she finally whispers, "Can I trust no one?"

His eyes grow wide. "You can trust me, Your Greatness."

"The Caldari—do you think they're all in on it?"

"Absolutely not."

Her paranoia gets the better of her. "Then why would he request such a thing?

Delwynn lets out a long sigh. "I don't know, Your Greatness. Perhaps after living a life of isolation, he just wants to be around people who care about him."

Cerylia studies him carefully, allowing each word to sink in—but even so, her response escapes her. She turns her head to gaze longingly out the window. Ever since the Caldaris' arrival in Sardoria, her life has been nothing short of chaotic. The truth is becoming harder and harder to come by. Even Delwynn—someone she's innately trusted for years—has deceived her. Sure, he'd admitted his wrongdoing and resworn his oath, but Cerylia knows better than to place her complete trust in him again. It would seem the only person she can trust is herself.

There's an edge to her voice as she says, "Given the current circumstances, I refuse to grant his request."

Delwynn opens his mouth, probably to counter, but she raises her hand to silence him.

"I need a few days," she says sharply, "away from everyone and everything. I can't think straight with everything that's happened." She holds his gaze. "You are dismissed, Delwynn."

His face falls. "Your Gr—"

"And that," Cerylia interjects with a surly wave of her hand, "is an order."

BRAXTON HORNSBY

HOURS, DAYS, EVEN weeks could have passed, and Braxton wouldn't know the difference. The dungeons in Sardoria are much darker than the ones in Trendalath—or perhaps it's the unrelenting winter weather and its subsequent stretches of darkness that seem to go on for hours and hours on end. The Queen's Guard does bring him food somewhat regularly, although he wishes it were the Caldari—but even before he'd made the request to Delwynn, he'd sensed it'd be a long shot. Thankfully, along with the meals, he's also been provided a pillow, extra clothes, and some wool blankets to layer for warmth. The northern winters haven't been kind to Sardoria or the neighboring towns.

Just as he's settling in for the evening, the sound of footsteps steals his attention. They're light and gentle, and he knows exactly to whom they belong. Perhaps Delwynn's still looking out for him after all.

A figure in a sage-colored cloak emerges from around the corner. Silver hair spills out in loose waves from underneath the hood. Once its removed, eyes the color of the cloak meet his own. "I didn't think it was true, but I had to see for myself," Opal says. Her tone is callous, but her expression is soft, angelic even.

"I didn't—"

She raises her hand to silence him. "I already know you're not guilty of what Cerylia has accused you of." She shakes her head. "It's a shame, really."

Braxton throws the blankets to the side and marches over to the cell door. "What is? That I didn't live up to her accusations, or that I'm innocent and stuck in here?"

A hint of a smile tugs at her lips and a faint chuckle follows. "Both, I suppose."

"So you came here to gloat, is that it?"

Her face falls. "That's not why I'm here."

"Then enlighten me." His eyes fall to her hands as she removes them from the pockets of her cloak. No key ring. *Damn it.*

She seems to catch onto his train of thought because in mere seconds, her eyes narrow. "I'm loyal to Queen Jareth, so if you think I came here to break you out, you've got the wrong idea."

"Actually, as an Inverter, I was hoping you'd take us both back in time and keep this from happening in the first place."

"That would not be in my best interest nor would it be in yours." She says this with such certainty that he immediately feels like a fool for even proposing such an idea. "I can, however, help you in another way. But I need something from you first."

"Anything. I will do anything to get out of here, to win Cerylia's trust again."

"Thing is," Opal says quietly, "before you gain her trust back, I need you to betray it."

He clicks his tongue in mock disapproval, then smirks. "What happened to being loyal?"

Opal rolls her eyes. "Asking this of you will not make *me* disloyal—just informed. But you . . . seeing as you're already in a state of distrust with her, I need you to tell me something. It's about a conversation the two of you had."

A chill lodges in his chest. He knows exactly to what conversation she's referring. "But I thought you—"

"—could go back and see it for myself?" Opal finishes. "I thought I could, too. Somehow, I've been . . . *blocked* from that moment in time. I can see the conversation and who it's between, but when your mouths open to speak, it's completely silent. Everything grows foggy—as if a filter has been placed over my mind's eye."

Intrigued, Braxton runs his index finger along the smooth iron bars, leaning into the door. "If I tell you what you want to know, what's in it for me?"

"Braxton, this is serious. I will not be toyed with."

He matches her grave demeanor, the words slipping coolly from his lips. "Neither will I."

She studies him, her eyes roaming his face for answers. After an extended silence, she folds. "Fine. You have my word that I will speak with Queen Jareth and *show* her what I know to be true—that you did not betray her, nor did you side with Cyrus Alston or King Tymond."

He's tempted to ask her to omit the discovery of his mother's letter, but something tells him she doesn't actually know about it. If she does, he wouldn't be the wiser. "And you will do so immediately after our conversation?"

"Yes," she confirms.

"Here it is then." He steps to the side, glancing around her shoulder to ensure they're alone, then whispers, "Cerylia wanted to use my relationship with my father to have me return to Trendalath."

Opal narrows her eyes. "Why?"

His breath hitches as he realizes what she's really after. She wants to know the one thing he swore to Cerylia he'd keep secret. If he chooses to reveal that information to Opal, he actually *would* be a traitor—but who knows how long Cerylia plans to keep him locked up in here? Not to mention, she hasn't even come to visit him herself after locking him up. She'd sent Delwynn to do her dirty work, and the Queen's Guard to do the rest.

The thought makes his blood boil.

Opal stands impatiently before him as he goes back and forth between what to do. *Cerylia already sees me as a traitor. Opal likely won't even know what the ring represents anyway. What do I really have to lose?*

"Cerylia requested that"—he hesitates, but follows through—"that I retrieve a ring from my father." Knots form in his stomach as recognition flashes across her face.

"An amethyst ring?"

He has, perhaps, just made a mistake there is no coming back from.

RYDAN HELSTROM

RYDAN WATCHES IN silence as Vira rushes to give her brother a hug. It's a warm embrace, but he notices that the entire time, Xerin's eyes are fixed on him. Reading him. Analyzing him.

"I can't stay long," Xerin declares, his tone unnerving. "Please, have a seat."

The shift in the room is palpable. Vira's face falls as she glances at Rydan, as if seeking his approval. He gives a firm nod before pulling three wooden chairs out from under the kitchen table.

"What is it? What's happened?"

The alarm written all over her face is enough to make him want to pull the leg of her chair closer to him and console her, but with Xerin here, he thinks better of it.

"Two of our own have been compromised."

Our own. Rydan can't ignore the pointed stare Xerin throws at him as he speaks the words. That, coupled with the news, is enough to make him cringe. He is *not* one of them.

He never wanted to be.

Vira takes a strand of her blonde hair, twirling it around her finger. "Arden and Braxton?"

"Yes." Xerin regards her for a minute, curiosity sparking in his eyes. "Wait—how do you know that?"

"Lucky guess."

Rydan's eyes flick back and forth between the siblings. The uncomfortable silence that follows is far longer than it should be. He clears his throat before asking, "What happened with Braxton?" to which Vira immediately elbows him square in the ribs.

"We came here to find Arden, and you're asking about Braxton?" She shakes her head in disapproval before turning her attention to her brother. "Don't listen to him. Tell us about Arden first."

A trace of conflict darts across Xerin's eyes. "No—Rydan's right."

Although a short respite from his roiling thoughts, it's a welcome one. He nods at Xerin to continue.

His intake of breath is heavier this time, as if the weight of a thousand secrets rests on his shoulders. "Braxton is . . . well, he's no longer illusié. Just the other night, he had an encounter with the Mallum. Although brief, the damage has been done. His powers have been absorbed entirely."

Rydan glances at a disconcerted Vira. Her hand covers her mouth in complete and utter shock. He should probably have the same reaction, but he has no idea what Xerin is even talking about.

"The Mallum?"

His eyes lined with intrigue, Xerin shifts his gaze to Vira, but directs his question at Rydan. "How long were you an assassin for King Tymond?"

Rydan tries to swallow the lump that's formed in his throat. It's like a boulder going down and falls straight to his stomach. "Long enough."

Before he can reply, Vira whispers, "The Mallum is the origin of darkness itself—the one true source of evil and immorality." She chokes down a breath, her eyes vacant as she turns to look at him. "It is worse than any depraved king or queen Aeridon's ever seen."

Feeling ill-equipped to respond, Rydan clasps his hands over his knees before pushing himself to stand. "And this 'source of darkness' somehow absorbed Braxton's abilities?" The question isn't directed at anyone in particular, so they both nod. "And there's no way for him to retrieve them?"

"According to our mother, no." Xerin's expression is eerily calm, as if he's discussed this before—almost as if he'd *expected* it.

"There's even a legend she used to tell us . . . " A single wordless exchange with her brother causes Vira's words to taper off. She doesn't expand any further.

A knot forms in Rydan's chest as another thought occurs to him. "And what about Arden? Did the same thing happen to her?"

"It's hard to know for sure," Xerin says, "seeing as she's no longer where we can get to her."

The knot swells, nearly suffocating him. "Where is she?"

The look on Xerin's face tells him what he already suspects. "Trendalath."

Heat rises to his temples. "He's going to kill her."

"On the contrary," Xerin tisks, wagging a finger in the air, "the king actually *needs* her abilities."

"To heal?" Rydan nearly laughs out loud. "Tymond doesn't heal anything. He only destroys and wreaks havoc—"

"Aldreda," Vira whispers, her palms now pressed flat against her cheeks. "She's with child. He'd never do anything to jeopardize the heir to the throne, especially after his only son vanished and relinquished the Tymond name." She shakes her head. "Knowing what we know, we cannot allow Arden to heal Aldreda. She'll never forgive herself."

It's a lot to take in, but he understands exactly what Vira is getting at. The King's Savant killed Arden's mother and she doesn't know. She also has a brother that she doesn't know about. Making an impulse decision, Rydan turns his attention to Xerin. "How quickly can you fly to Trendalath?"

"From here?" He glances at the ceiling, doing a quick calculation in his head. "In a day or two, depending on the weather. Impending snowstorms make things a little more complicated this time of year." He looks between the two of them, brows raised. "Why?"

"Make it a day," Rydan orders, even though he has no authority to do so. "We need you to deliver Arden a message that could change everything."

ARDEN ELIRI

MY EYELIDS FLUTTER open at the sound of someone bustling nearby. My head feels fuzzy and flickering dots fill most of my vision. It takes a moment to fully focus on the white-robed figure in front of me, but it doesn't take long for me to realize that I'm in the healing ward.

Still in Trendalath castle.

Still in my own nightmarish hellscape.

I groan at the thought, but as I turn over onto my side, the noise turns into a full-fledged howl. Millions of tiny needles jab every inch of my skin—at least, that's what it feels like—and my fingertips buzz with the residual electric current that's still coursing through my body. To top it all off, there's a persistent hum in my eardrums, which is completely throwing off my sense of stability. When I attempt to sit up, the white-robed man neighs and rushes to my side.

"Take it easy," he says, gently placing one hand at the small of my back, the other in my palm. At first, the contact startles me, but he doesn't push or force the upward movement. For the first time in a while, I feel in control—which is exactly what I need after my latest traumatic encounter with the dark side of illusié.

"Thank you," I manage to say as I sit fully upright, coughing between the words. We're closer in proximity now and I notice his eyes are compassionate and calming, gray like a rainy winter day. Soft amber waves frame his porcelain complexion. The hand he'd laid on my palm leads me to believe that he hasn't seen a hard day's work in his life—not all that surprising since he works in the healing ward of Trendalath—but his frame suggests otherwise. His muscles ripple underneath the white of his garb, and if it weren't for the allure of his eyes, I'd certainly be staring elsewhere. Strangely enough, I feel an energetic pull to him. "What's your name?" I ask, the words coming out as a croak.

He smiles and holds up a hand as if silently directing me not to overexert myself, then turns to fetch a glass of water. I can't help but watch him, admiring the tactful way he carries himself, gliding across the room with ease. His movements are deft, like an assassin's, but his touch—as I'd just witnessed—is far too gentle. Upon his return, I maintain eye contact with him from the moment he hands me the glass to the moment I finish my drink.

"The name's Harrod Oakes, but you can just call me Harrod. None of that Sir Oakes, Lord Oakes nonsense." A wide grin stretches across his face. "No need for me to ask who you are. That I already know."

I can't help but laugh a little. "Is that a good thing or a bad thing?"

He winks at me. "Depends on who you ask."

I'm about to laugh again, enjoying this bit of normalcy, when sparks suddenly fly across my vision. My hands shoot to my temples as my mind figuratively catches fire. I make yet another noise between a groan and a howl before he's coaxing me to lie back down. He disappears for a moment, then returns with a concoction of liquid and herbs in a small bowl. He mixes it together before pouring the golden substance into a vial.

"This will rid your body of any illusié toxins," he says as he lifts my head. I open my mouth, not even questioning what it is before consuming it in its entirety.

"I'll come check on you in a little while," he assures.

His docile face is the last thing I see as I return to the darkness that awaits my subconscious mind.

When I come back to, Harrod is standing at one of the healing stations with his back to me. I stir when I hear a familiar voice call for him, then quickly close my eyes, stilling my movements and my breathing just as Harrod turns to check on me. I hear his robes swish back and forth as he leaves the room, the door shutting softly behind him.

I remain still with my eyes closed until I'm certain I'm alone—well, except for Aldreda. Her breathing is so shallow that, from my current vantage point, I'd assume she's passed onto the next life. Just as I attempt to bring myself upright, the handle on the door jiggles. I ease back down and turn my head slightly before closing my eyes, keeping them cracked just enough to where I can still see.

The door opens slowly, cautiously—and in walks a familiar face, although I can't quite place where I've seen him before. Wiry copper curls bounce with each step he takes. He's one of the Savant, no doubt, and I'm almost certain he was a part of the . . . *incident* in the Daegrum Chambers earlier. And possibly in the Thering Forest when I was with Estelle . . .

He breezes by my bed without so much as a glance and waltzes straight over to Aldreda. He falls at her bedside, taking her pale, nearly lifeless, hand in his own, and presses it to his forehead. I'm so intrigued by this interaction that I almost sit straight up, as if watching a scene in a play, but I quickly remember my place. I needn't give myself away.

Something tells me to remain a bystander.

I open my eyes a little wider, but even so, I have to rely heavily on my auditory senses.

"My Queen," he says through ragged breaths. "My love."

At this, my eyes can't help but shoot open. I watch with intrigue as he gently lays his other hand on her lower abdomen. I have to stifle a gasp as the pieces fall into place.

Darius is not the father.

ARDEN ELIRI

KNOWLEDGE OF AN affair isn't an easy thing to sit on, especially when it's one that can destroy my enemies—and the Tymond reign. After just two days, my wrists have almost fully healed, thanks to my illusié abilities—and Harrod. Every time he comes to check on me, I behave as though I'm still in mountains of pain—mostly because I enjoy the company. He brews up his herb concoction, telling me stories as I slowly ingest it, and then, an hour or so later, he leaves.

But this evening will be different. There will be no stories, no witty banter. Hell, there may not even be an herb concoction. I may feign sleeping to ensure he just walks in and leaves. Because I need answers—and tonight is the night I'm going to get them.

My plan seems to work because Harrod enters and exits the room within minutes after arriving—just enough time to administer another healing potion. The room is dead silent, save for my shallow breathing as I pass by Aldreda's bed. She's still as stone as I carefully open the door. I poke my head out to find an empty hallway. If my memory serves me right, I'll end up exactly where I need to be.

I round a couple of corridors and climb a few staircases, using caution with every turn I take. Finally, I reach a door with an iron B on it. During my days in the Cruex, I'd wandered the castle halls late at night—I'd come across this door multiple times. Knowing what I know now about the Tymonds' long lost son, I realize that this had been Braxton's childhood room before he'd fled to Athia.

The door creaks open. I slide through the narrow opening, scanning the room to ensure I'm alone. Cobwebs line the corners of the walls and layers of dust sit idly atop the furniture. I run my hand along a wooden crib that's been stashed in the corner, then along the frame of a child-sized bed. The room is mostly bare, save for a sheepskin rug, an armoire, and a bookcase. An enormous window overlooks the ocean—a sight a young boy likely wouldn't appreciate—but something tells me Braxton had.

A full moon glimmers in the distance, putting the vast number of once twinkling stars to shame. Although brief, something glints in the moonlight, catching my eye. My toes graze the plush sheepskin rug as I move toward it. I remove the rectangular object from the second shelf of the bookcase, running my finger over the corner of a picture frame. With a light breath, I blow onto the glass, watching as a film of dust particles float into the air. I rub my index finger over the glass in an attempt to remove some of the smudges, but it doesn't work. I slide the portrait out of the frame, my heart skipping a beat as I examine it.

An elegant woman with white-blonde hair smiles proudly while a young boy, no older than three—and with the same shade of hair—holds her hand. Next to them is another woman, who's also smiling, with wavy brown hair that cascades around her shoulders. A young boy with brown hair, around the same age as the other, stands tall by her side. I recognize him as the boy from my dream— the one who suddenly disappeared right before my very eyes.

I examine the photo further. The woman is holding something—a bundle of blankets. I turn the portrait over to reveal a date scrawled across the back in beautiful calligraphy. *Janus XXVII.* My breath hitches.

It's my birthdate.

ARDEN ELIRI

I HAVE NEVER moved as quickly as I do in this moment. Not in my training to become an assassin. Not during a Cruex mission. Not ever.

My feet fly across the stone floor like seagulls foraging the water for fish. I must be making an excessive amount of noise, but I don't care. The edge of the portrait flaps in the breeze under my watertight grip until I finally arrive back at the healing ward. Without hesitation, I fling the door open and kneel by Aldreda's bedside. I look between her and the photo, even though I know it to be true. Her and Braxton stand on the left. A mother, her son, and her newly born daughter stand on the right. With *my* birthdate scrawled on the back.

My mother. My brother.

I can feel my chest constricting as the meaning dawns on me. I don't have all the answers yet, but what I do know is that *I* am the baby in that bundle of blankets—and that Aldreda knew *my mother*.

I tuck the portrait into the side of my trousers. With a deep breath, I gently put my hand on Aldreda's shoulder. I press lightly, giving her a little nudge, but she doesn't flinch. I press a little harder, desperate for her to wake. Questions swirl throughout my mind like a ship lost at sea. I whisper her name once, twice—and then a third time, a little louder, just for good measure.

Nothing.

I sit back on my heels and let out an exasperated sigh. My head falls into my hands, my fingers traipsing along the undersides of my eyes. The key to unlock my past—everything I've ever wanted to know—is sitting right before me, unconscious and unaware. It's enough to make me want to pull every hair from my own head.

I roll forward onto my knees and gently place two fingers on her wrist, checking for a pulse. Though faint, it's there. Just as I'm removing pressure from her wrist, Aldreda's eyes shoot open. Startled, I lose my balance, scurrying backward until I'm at a far enough distance to bring myself safely to my feet. I shake away my nerves as I approach her bedside. Her gaze doesn't shift to me when I arrive—she continues to stare blankly ahead.

"Aldreda?" I whisper, suddenly feeling foolish for calling her by her first name—but I'm sure as hell not going to call her *My Queen.*

She remains silent, then blinks once. Twice.

What happens next is the most startling thing I've ever seen or heard. A pool of blood begins to flow at an alarming rate around her midsection. Crimson stains her gown, the blankets. She screams, the sound quickly transforming into full-fledged shrieks.

Panicked, I run toward the door and yell for help at the top of my lungs. I call for Harrod, Darius, Cyrus, Elias—although I'm pretty sure he died at the king's hands—I call every name I can think of until my screams whir together with Aldreda's. Shouts ring out from multiple corridors, but I don't visibly *see* anyone.

With everything I have in me, I rush back over to Aldreda and place my hands on her lower abdomen. I close my eyes to focus, doing the best I can to block out the incessant shrieking. I search for that white light—that beautiful glowing orb—desperately reaching for it, but every corner of my mind is darker than the last. I curl into myself, calling the light forth, coaxing it to make itself known.

A high-pitched wail breaks my focus.

My eyes pop open and I realize there are multiple people standing around me, gawking. Darius, Harrod, Cyrus, the handmaidens. I look down at my crimson-stained hands.

Hands covered in the queen's blood.

Cyrus is the first to speak. "My lords, what have you done?"

"I didn't . . ." I sputter, realizing how bad this must look. "It wasn't . . ."

I slowly back away from the scene, the image of Aldreda's blood-ridden body seared into my mind. I catch Darius's eye and, I must be hallucinating, because I'm almost certain I see a sinister smile touch the corners of his lips.

Harrod impedes my view, dashing toward me, pulling me back to the scene of the crime I did not commit. "Heal her," he whispers. "Show them what you can do."

Out of the corner of my eye, I notice a familiar figure enter the room. Curly hair and hazel eyes sweep by me, then fall to Aldreda's bedside.

Clive.

How do I know his name?

From that point forward, everything seems to happen in slow motion: The handmaiden announcing that Aldreda is no longer with child. Tears falling from Clive's eyes while a pained moan escapes his lips. The stark realization that falls over Darius's face. I feel Harrod's arms go limp beside me—they were the only things keeping me upright and stable.

With rage burning in his eyes, Darius lunges for Clive. Even in my shocked state, I'm somehow still able to register what's going on. I leap out of the way and roll toward the river of blood that is now gushing over the sides of the table. Two strong hands reach over the edge and grab me by my forearms. I'm forced upright on shaking legs, Harrod's gray eyes locking with mine. He places my hands on Aldreda's chest cavity and presses down. "Focus." His determination and his tone remind me so much of my first healing encounter with Estelle. How I wish she were here to guide me through this.

How I wish I weren't here at all.

I do as he says and focus on my hands before taking a deep inhale. I close my eyes and search for my white light, desperate to call it home.

It seems I'm not a place it wants to come back to.

DARIUS TYMOND

THE GUARDS INTERVENE to try and drag Clive away from the king's death grip, but his hold is rock solid. "You traitorous, backstabbing snake," Darius seethes, almost spitting in Clive's face. "I should have banished you at first sign of your treachery."

Even through the king's hold on his throat, Clive manages a smile. "You've always been a fool for love, Darius. You're no less of a fool than the day your beloved—"

"How dare you," Darius cautions, his grip tightening with each word. "After what you did . . . " He looks to his fading wife. "After what you *both* did."

Clive swallows, but remains silent.

The amethyst ring glints in the light, catching Darius's full attention. He could end this, right here, right now. All of the pain, suffering, doubts, and worry this vile man has caused—it could all go away. He could make it right. Yes, he could end Clive's miserable, worthless existence with one single decision.

Just like it's called to him so many times before, the darkness reaches for him, begging him to make use of its existential power. Pleading with him to release it from years of unjust confinement—to take from those who have taken, and will continue to take, from him.

His grip loosens on Clive's throat as he turns over his shoulder to witness a peculiar exchange between Harrod and Arden. Before giving it another thought, he readjusts his grip and throws Clive's body backward, into the arms of his waiting guards.

Clive becomes a mere afterthought.

It's Aldreda who requires his full attention.

Darius watches as a glowing white light appears around Arden's hands, hovering over his wife's body. He takes a step forward as the light grows, absorbing all darkness in its wake. He twists the amethyst ring around his finger, readying himself.

It is time.

ARDEN ELIRI

MY PANIC CEASES as a sincere smile graces my face. After searching and failing and searching some more, I feel *it*—the good, the pure.

It's finally arrived.

A blinding white light radiates from my hands, erasing the crimson stains from my prior failed attempt. Although I don't look up for fear I'll somehow break my concentration, I can feel Harrod smiling at me. The goodness seeps into my pores, traveling through my veins at a steady rate. Clarity flows into every inch of my body, every crevice, every open space.

It's found me and, subsequently, I've found it.

It dawns on me that I can do this. I can heal Aldreda.

I *will* heal Aldreda.

And I will get the answers I seek.

Murmurs of encouragement escape Harrod's lips, but my focus is too great to hear what they are. I can feel Aldreda's body rising and falling, her breaths becoming less shallow, her eyes fluttering with movement. I restore the parts of her that are broken and unbound. I renew her energy, her life force—her slow but beating heart. I can *feel* the healing, as if it is my own.

In this moment, we are one.

The answers are just within my reach. She's going to pull through with me as her Healer—her savior. As expected, the queen's eyes fly open. She inhales a long-awaited breath. Her gaze lands directly on me, but it isn't comforting—it's filled with something else entirely.

Fear.

Doubts swirl around my mind as I break eye contact with her and look down at my own two hands. Where there was once pure, white light now hovers an obsidian mist. I try to remove my hands from her chest, but an invisible and unrelenting force keeps them there. I cry out in angst as I attempt to pull away from it, but my hands won't budge. I am stuck—trapped—in a sea of black. It's so thick, so dense, that I can barely see through it. It's then that my senses alert me to the fact that Harrod is no longer in front of me.

Something much, *much* darker is.

I suck in a sharp breath as the vapor begins to fade, revealing an all-too-familiar crimson cloak. I blink again and again, shaking my head, trying to do anything and everything I can to bring the light back to the surface. I can feel it lingering, waiting—like the final autumn leaf on a tree branch—but when I reach for it, it's ripped away by the inevitable winter winds.

Slick whispers cascade from the Mallum's hood with steadfast conviction. *You've missed this, Arden. Don't deny it.*

I cast my eyes downward, vigorously shaking my head. I tell myself that it isn't real. That it's all in my mind. That it's just a poorly executed, deranged vision.

But it hears my thoughts.

It hears everything.

It *knows* me.

You are ready. Will you join us now?

As I look up, my gaze collides with the dark expanse underneath the hood. I realize that this moment will define me. I refuse to cower in fear. I refuse to let the darkness win.

"Show yourself," I say.

A sinister laugh fills the space between us. It moves closer to me, forcing my hands to remain planted, pushing harder on Aldreda's chest.

You already know what I am.

I can see Aldreda growing pale again, her eyes rolling into the back of her head, as the black tethers seeping from my hands pull the life force out of her—taking the life I'd just given back to her.

Think of all the innocent lives she's made you take.

Think of the man she's sworn her loyalty to.

She doesn't deserve to live.

She doesn't deserve your mercy.

Seeds of persuasion are planted in the depths of my mind and I suddenly can't discern which thoughts, if any, are my own. Memories of my first assassinations flood over me, drowning me, not in regret and sorrow, but in yearning and desire.

This is who I am. This is what I know.

I raise my head to the cloaked figure. Perhaps the Mallum is right. Perhaps I *am* ready.

DARIUS TYMOND

THE MALLUM HAS almost completely pulled her under. Darius circles them like a predator, knowing full well that Arden can only see Aldreda and the cloaked figure. Everything else is nonexistent. He watches in anticipation as the darkness swarms her from every angle. She doesn't have it in her to resist it. Just like those who came before her—she will succumb. She will falter. And everything he's ever wanted, everything he's ever worked for, will finally be his.

The amethyst ring grows heavier on his finger as the Mallum hums its toxic melody. As Arden fades into darkness, Aldreda withers into death. It's really quite poetic—something he's waited to witness for far too long.

He stops at the crown of his wife's head, looking into her dull, lifeless eyes.

It is almost complete.

"I told you," he whispers. "You sealed your fate. We'll all get exactly what we deserve."

Just as Aldreda's about to take her final breath, a flash of green light appears. It mingles with the black fog, dangerous and uninviting. Darius jumps back as two pairs of emerald eyes land on him before vanishing from the room altogether—as if they were never here to begin with.

It can't be . . .

Darius cries out in defeat, throwing the amethyst ring onto the ground. He flings himself into the middle of the chaos, trying to grasp whatever he can—to regain control of the situation. But she is gone. And so is he.

"Eliri!" he yells in vain.

The mist closes in on itself, forming a single speck of midnight-colored dust before catapulting straight into the air. His eyes flick to Aldreda's lifeless body as he falls to his knees to reclaim, what seems to be, his only source of power.

CERYLIA JARETH

REMORSE HAS FOLLOWED Cerylia around for days and while she appreciates the Caldaris' attempts—namely Felix and Estelle—in cheering her up, it seems nothing is able to do the trick. She hasn't utilized the Sardoria dungeons in years. Indeed, imprisoning a Tymond, amongst other things, was exactly what she'd had in mind, but it's the wrong Tymond.

It should have been Aldreda. Cyrus failed me.

She pushes herself up from her throne before walking in a circle around the White Room. Heavy streaks of sunlight shine through an open window, illuminating her white robes in such a way that she nearly becomes one with the floor and the walls. She goes to the window, smiling as a soft breeze ruffles her hair. It's the first time she's seen the sun in weeks. Its sharp rays melt the layers of snow, albeit slowly, revealing cracks of greenery around the castle walls. It's quiet and calm—unlike the days since the Caldari arrived. She leans on the ledge, gazing out the window for some time, not a single thought clouding her mind.

❧ ❧ ❧

The peaceful silence is interrupted far too soon. She shudders at the sound of the White Room doors slamming shut. She assumes it's just Delwynn, but as she turns to face the intruder, she's surprised to find Opal rushing toward her instead.

"Your Greatness." The girl's bow is rushed and, from her ragged breaths and widening eyes, it's clear that something has caused her great distress.

"What is it?" The queen asks, gently setting her hands on Opal's shoulders. "What's happened?"

"It's about Arden." Even under the weight of the queen's hands, she's shaking, so Cerylia pushes down harder. "I need to sit."

Cerylia nods and leads her to a table across the room, feeling both concerned and intrigued by the impending news. She fills a goblet with water and places it in Opal's hands, watching intently as she downs it in one gulp. She doesn't even bother to set the glass upright on the table and it falls over with a loud clank. "Cyrus did not betray you. And neither did Braxton."

"You've spoken with them?" Her tone is sharp, but when Opal shakes her head, Cerylia softens. "You've seen something."

The girl nods. She inches her hand closer to the queen's. "I will show you under two conditions. You must release Braxton."

Cerylia doesn't hesitate. "You have my word."

"I said two."

The queen stiffens at the sudden change in her demeanor.

"Whenever you do retrieve the amethyst ring, you will not request to go back in time. You will not so much as even use it." Her expression darkens. "On the contrary, I must have your word that you will destroy it."

"But that would mean—"

"I know," Opal says sadly. "But you and I both know that it's the only way."

ARDEN ELIRI

WHEN I COME back to, I'm looking at an uneven surface of jagged rocks and . . . dirt? My cheek is pressed against what I'm now certain is the ground, and the smell of damp leaves and musty wood infiltrate my senses. As I push myself to my feet, my eyes catch the tender scar tissue around my wrists.

It all comes back to me in flashes.

The Savant.

The lightning.

The blood.

Aldreda.

Frantically, I search my pockets for the photograph, but come up empty-handed. I rake a hand through my tangled hair as I take in my surroundings.

Am I in a . . . cave?

Before another thought can enter my mind, a gruff voice asks, "Looking for this?"

Startled, I whirl around in a defensive stance, feeling even more jumbled as my gaze lands on the man standing before me. Clasped between his stout fingers is the photograph I'd discovered in Braxton's room.

"That's mine," I say, daring to approach him. He doesn't budge, so I take my chances and snatch the print from his hands. Again, he doesn't even flinch.

"Where am I?" I demand. "And who are you?"

When he doesn't answer, I take a step closer, then another. My breath hitches as I gaze deeper and deeper into a sea of emerald. "Holy lords," I say as I stumble backward. "You're not . . . You can't be . . ."

He doesn't respond. Instead, he gives me a warm smile that can only be drawn from a familial tie. He's the boy from my dream. I look down at the photo again, just to be sure. I hadn't seen the resemblance before, but now I do.

He's my brother.

I'm stunned. Speechless. Before I can fully process the information, I'm suddenly enveloped in the scent of pine and sap as I'm wrapped into a giant bear hug.

"You are welcome to stay as long as you'd like," he says before releasing me.

I take a slow step back. "How did I get here?"

"Like you, I'm illusié. A Transporter." When I give him a bewildered look, he goes on to say, "I can transport people and things to and from anywhere in Aeridon, so long as I've been there before."

That would explain how I'd arrived here. But . . .

"How did you know about me? How did you know where I was?"

He smiles. "Let's just say a little bird told me."

Xerin. Xerin's known this entire time that I have a brother? Just the thought of him knowing something about my past and *choosing* not to tell me makes my blood boil. A drape of crimson falls over my thoughts as my mind takes me back to Trendalath, to the healing ward. Aldreda's lifeless face stares up at me. Her blood is on my hands, blooming through her dress, spilling onto the table, pooling across the floor. My white light had been there. I'd harnessed it. I'd healed her.

But the Mallum had also been there—watching, waiting—as I'd desperately sought answers. It had grabbed hold of me, and my abilities, and had turned them into something dreadful—but something I'd recognized all too well.

"I have to leave," I say suddenly. "I have unfinished business to take care of."

He studies me for a moment before dropping his gaze to the ground. "To Trendalath?"

"Yes," I affirm, rushing toward what I believe to be the cave's entrance. "I need you to transport me there."

"Arden," he says. "You can't."

When I turn back to look at him, I notice his once bright emerald eyes have fallen a few shades darker. The urge for an explanation emerges, and I'm about to ask him for one, but deep down, I know the answer.

I know what I've done.

I know what I'll be held responsible for.

His response only confirms what I wish weren't true.

"The Queen of Trendalath is dead."

ACKNOWLEDGEMENTS

What a ride it's been writing this sequel. This book went through more rounds of edits and rewrites than I care to admit, but I am so incredibly proud of the story it is today. Weaving multiple subplots together to create a cohesive story is always challenging, but not impossible. Writing this book reminded me that, while plotting is essential in writing a series as long as this one, it's perfectly okay to let go of the reins a little, deviate from the outline from time to time, and *just write.*

First and foremost, I'd like to thank God, the Universe, the Divine Spirit. I had many breakthroughs during the process of writing this book, not only as a writer, but also as a human being. I am so grateful for your eternal guidance and for instilling in me the courage I needed to start this journey as an author in the first place.

To the incredibly talented cartographer, Deven Rue, for bringing The Lands of Aeridon to life, and to the cover designers at Damonza who continuously stun me with their artistry and professionalism. Thank you for being such a pleasure to work with!

To my family—Erin, Mom, Dad, Paul, Rachel, Nana, and Papa— who would have thought by the age of 30 that I would have written six books?! Thank you for reading every single one of them and for supporting me no matter what. I love you all immensely.

To Anna Vera, for our late night wine dates over Skype, for always bringing a genuine smile to my face, for always giving me a proper belly-laugh, and for being an all-around incredible human being. I thank my lucky stars every single day that the Universe brought us together. Your friendship means more to me than you could possibly know and I can't wait to see where your author journey takes you—because with your talent (seriously), it's going to be HUGE!

To Kaila Walker, for being my business bestie, my international travel buddy, and my much-needed sounding board. It's hard to believe we only met each other last year and already, we're flying around the world together, building our empires! I am so grateful to have you in my life and can't wait to float on gold unicorn floaties until we're old and senile.

To Kim Chance, Vivien Reis, Lindsay Cummings, Jessi Elliott, and Mandi Lynn—I am so grateful to be amongst such wonderful AuthorTubers in such a positive and uplifting community. I admire each of you for putting yourself out there because it certainly can be difficult at times. Thank you for shining your light and for being such great friends!

To Edward Gray, Sammi Davidson, and Krista Olsen—First and foremost, will you please adopt me so I can move to Canada? Kidding (but not really). While all of my book tour stops were memorable, the Calgary one holds a very special place in my heart. Not everyone is so lucky in this lifetime to come across a single kindred connection, let alone multiple. I love you guys!

To my furbabies—I know you can't read this, but thank you for letting your momma lock herself in her office and write for hours on end—and for being there to snuggle me when I felt like throwing my computer at the wall (which was often). I love you so much, my sweet, sweet girls.

And finally, to my YouTube fam, readers, and fans—HOLY MOLY. What a journey this has been. I wake up some (most) mornings and still cannot believe that this is my life. That I get to wake up and do what I love. That I get to create content and write books in the hopes that I'll make an impact somewhere out there in the world. It is honestly surreal. So thank you for believing in me. Thank you for being such an instrumental part of my journey. Thank you for taking a chance on an indie author and spending your hard-earned cash on her work. And please know that I do not take these things for granted, not for a single second. I wouldn't be here without your continuous support, encouragement, and love. I appreciate each and every one of you more than words could ever express. I love my #KMCommunity!

Don't miss the third installment in the
Shadow Crown series:

JADED

SPRING

TURN THE PAGE FOR A SNEAK PEEK
OF CHAPTER ONE

COMING FALL 2019

ARDEN ELIRI

I'VE GROWN TO like it here.

The sunlight shines through the canopy of trees above me, warming my face. I lay on my back with my eyes closed, absorbing the peace and quiet, sans the sound of rippling water from a nearby stream.

That I don't mind one bit.

A much earlier spring is approaching, thank the lords, and the signs are all around me—in the minimal snowfall remaining on the ground; the green leaves sprouting from the trees, breaking free from winter's cruel captivity; the warmer, but still chilly temperatures; the birds chirping their cheerful melodies in the mornings.

Winter has almost reached its end.

A cloud rolls over the rays of warmth, casting a cool shadow over my face. As I figured it would, it takes my peace along with it. My eyes shoot open as images of Aldreda's pallid face and lifeless body flood my mind. My hands hovering over her abdomen. The dark mist. The white light . . .

The Mallum had prevailed.

A chill lodges in my chest. I *know* what I'd felt in that room with her. I'd called forth my light—my healing ability. I'd witnessed it take shape with my very own eyes. I'd breathed life back into her. Her lips had parted, her chest had risen, her eyelids had fluttered—so how had this happened? How had the Queen of Trendalath died . . . at my own two hands?

As jarring as the thought is, I find myself distracted by two small paws pressing against my thigh. I raise my head to find Juniper aggressively seeking my attention. She pushes on my thigh again before pouncing directly onto my lap. I sit upright before cradling the sweet fox in my arms.

After Haskell had . . . *rescued* me from the horrors of that day, he'd offered to go to Orihia to look for Juniper and bring her back to Lirath Cave. I'd been going on and on about her and how I hoped she was all right. At the time, I'd been too weak to transport with him, so I'd waited impatiently—like a shell of a parent—until he'd returned safely with my sweet Juni in his arms. It'd only taken him a few hours and he'd even managed to pick some juniper berries before his return—a good call since they're her favorite and don't grow in the northern regions of Aeridon.

After coddling Juniper for a few minutes too long—incessant squirming is her "tell"—I finally release her from my arms to which she happily prances off into the brush, chasing after a mouse. I watch her in amusement until I notice someone approaching in the distance. I can tell from the burly stature that it's Haskell.

My *brother*.

For seventeen—almost eighteen—years, I'd been an orphan, taken under Tymond's wing and trained to become a merciless assassin for the Cruex. I'd never known what had become of my family, if I'd even had one at all—and if so, I'd been under the impression that they were no longer living. The Cruex had become my family.

I'd never thought to question that.

But seeing that flash of green light in the healing ward in Trendalath castle, those piercing eyes the same shade as mine . . . I'd known. I'd known that whoever had come to save me was family.

My *real* family.

Haskell approaches with a rather cheery grin on his face, which is discomfiting given his usual rigid demeanor. We've only been here together for about a month, but in that short time, I feel as though I've really gotten to know him. I've caught on pretty quickly to a few nuances: to keep my distance whenever he's preparing a meal; to never wake him before the sun comes up; and to avoid asking questions about that day in Trendalath.

That last one has been a challenge. Not surprisingly, it's the only thing I want to talk about.

When he finally reaches where I'm sitting, I notice that his hands are behind his back. In most situations, my instincts would tell me to prepare to defend myself, but not with him—not with my *brother*—and certainly not with the foolhardy grin that's currently plastered on his face. I push myself up from the ground, brushing off the leaves and twigs from the back of my trousers. I give him a coy smile before greeting him. "To what do I owe this pleasure?"

He angles his head, eyes twinkling, but keeps his arms locked behind him. "I've got a little something for you."

"Oh, do you now?" I proceed to whistle to call Juniper back over from whatever adventure she'd taken herself on.

"Hold out your arms."

I narrow my eyes, but do as he says.

"I know it's a day early, but," he says as he brings his arms in front of him, "happy early birthday, Arden."

A burlap-wrapped sack falls into my outstretched arms. My heart flutters at the sight. I can tell immediately what it is by the weight and the shape of the packaging. I carefully lay it on the ground and unroll the gift to reveal exactly what I'd assumed it'd be.

My chakrams.

My hands fly to my mouth as a squeal of delight escapes. I gingerly pick each blade up and secure them back into my holsters—back in their rightful place. My eyes meet my brother's. "How did you . . . ?"

He remains silent, and it's then I realize what he's done for me. What he's *risked* for me. He went *back* there—back to Trendalath—to retrieve my weapons.

"Haskell, I don't even know what to say. Thank you. I know how dangerous that must have been. Just"—I choke on the words—"thank you."

He gives me a reassuring nod. "For family, any risk is worth taking."

A faint warmth blooms in my neck, traveling upward to my cheeks. "How was it? Being back there?" I clamp down on my tongue to keep from asking what I really want to know—how things are in Trendalath, in the castle, after everything that's transpired . . .

Haskell shakes his head. "Perhaps another time. It's not your concern."

Not my concern? How can he say that?

"But I'm the reason—"

"I'm going to stop you right there," he interrupts. He grabs hold of my forearm and tugs me forward. "It's time to head back. You've been out here for hours and you've hardly eaten anything all day." He sneaks a look at Juniper. "Unless you've been sharing berries."

His attempt at humor is admirable, but it falls on deaf ears. I shrug off his grip and start for the cave, making sure to stay a few steps in front of him with Juniper a step or so ahead of me. A bird's shadow sweeps by and, for a moment, I swear my heart stops beating. I stop in my tracks and gaze up into the sky, half expecting to see a black falcon.

Expecting . . . or hoping?

But it's just a hawk.

It's not Xerin.

Haskell lightly knocks into my shoulder before passing me, murmuring something about the cave being close by, but I'm entirely distracted by my thoughts. I look to the sky again, hoping that perhaps, somehow, Xerin will hear my thoughts and come swooping in. But the expanse above me remains empty, save the few pockets of clouds.

My mind flits to the fellow Caldari I've left behind.

Estelle, Felix, Opal . . . Braxton.

After what he'd confided in me—showing me that letter . . . I'd killed his estranged mother. It'd been an accident, but still. I'm to blame.

And Queen Jareth. What would she think of me now? Had she even known I'd been taken to Trendalath? Do any of them know? Do they think I'd conspired against them this entire time? That my loyalty lies with King Tymond?

The thought is almost too much to bear. I can feel my chest tighten as panic settles in. I grow lightheaded, scanning the area around me as quickly as I can to find somewhere to sit. A giant boulder comes into my dwindling view and, even though I'm stumbling, I manage to make it over, taking a seat before my legs decide to give out, too. I struggle to take a few deep breaths as more thoughts plague my mind. I never would have fled Sardoria had I known the outcome, had Cyrus not . . .

Cyrus.

His name feels like a punch to the gut. Why had he brought me there? And against my will? How could he betray me like that, especially after what he'd told me?

About my *father.*

I look ahead to see that Haskell has already disappeared. If I had to guess, he's likely more than a hundred paces in front of me, probably wondering what in the world is taking me so long. Does he know about our father? Does he *want* to know?

Haskell's voice rings in my head. *No questions about family-related issues.*

Another day, then.

Juniper circles my feet, brushing against my calves. I wait until my vision clears before rising from the boulder. I look ahead with steadfast determination. The cave is just around the corner.

I'd only fled Sardoria to keep from hurting anyone even more than I already had—and to learn what the hooded figure *was*, what it wanted from me. What it *still* wants from me. But I'd failed in that endeavor. It's still unknown to me. I'd left looking for answers only to return with even *more* burning questions than I'd had before. My life has become nothing more than a tangled web of deceit, lies, and betrayal.

Who *is* Arden Eliri? I sure as hell don't know.

Not anymore.

Kristen Martin is the International Amazon Bestselling Indie Author of the YA science fiction trilogy, THE ALPHA DRIVE, the YA dark fantasy series, SHADOW CROWN, and personal development book, BE YOUR OWN #GOALS. A writing coach and creative entrepreneur, Kristen is also an avid YouTuber with hundreds of videos offering writing advice and inspiration for aspiring authors everywhere.

STAY CONNECTED:
www.kristenmartinbooks.com
www.youtube.com/authorkristenmartinbooks
www.facebook.com/authorkristenmartin
Instagram @authorkristenmartin
Twitter @authorkristenm

37322718R00250

Printed in Great Britain
by Amazon